WILDFLOWERS AT THE SUMMER HOTEL LOVELY BAY

POLLY BABBINGTON

POLLY

PollyBabbington.com

Want more from Polly's world?

For sneak peeks into new settings, early chapters, downloadable Pretty Beach and Darling Island freebies and bits and bobs from Polly's writing days sign up for Babbington Letters.

© Copyright 2024 Polly Babbington

All rights reserved.

This book is a work of fiction. Names, characters, businesses, places, events and incidents are either the products of the author's imagination or used in a fictitious manner. Any resemblance to actual persons, living or dead, or actual events is purely coincidental.

1

Nina Lavendar watched the trainspotters on the other side of the station. She smiled as they stood stock still to witness the glory of the moveable platform just down from the old station house at Lovely Bay. When Nina had first moved to Lovely Bay the year before, a few different people had told her that Lovely attracted trainspotters by the dozen. Internally, she'd rolled her eyes and had wondered what all the fuss was about. Now, like the Lovelies who had lived in the area their whole life, she could pick out a trainspotter a mile off. And no, it wasn't because they were wearing anoraks and socks with sandals. More that they had a certain air about them that was hard to put your finger on. Once you'd witnessed how they behaved a few times, they stuck out like a sore thumb. If you were actually on the train with one of them, they'd begin to get a teensy bit itchy as the train started to slow down for Lovely Bay. If they'd come the other way from Lovely itself and were chugging down the river on the boat, they would start to crane their necks towards the station to see what was what. Just all around, really, they were very interested in the station and even more in the platforms and trains themselves. Like many things in Lovely Bay, it was an unusual oddity Nina had come to know and very much love. Plus, she liked the feeling of being in the know. That now she was a bona fide full-time resident of Lovely Bay, she could tell a trainspotter from sixty paces. It was one of the many silly little things that made her feel like she belonged. It was worth its weight in gold.

She leaned against a pillar, her eyes following the group of trainspotters, and she smiled again. She loved watching their faces when the old moveable platform started to do its thing. All of them peered with their chins dropped and marvelled at its engineering. Like the lighthouse, the platform was a magnet to Lovely Bay, drawing people into the little town, nudging the economy with their spending money, and keeping the place buoyant. Just how Lovelies, as locals like to call themselves, wanted it to be and were determined it remained.

In front of her, a man clutched a very fancy-looking camera, a young woman with poker-straight hair was jotting things in a notebook, and a teenager held up his phone, taking pictures of just about anything he could. Another man in a baseball cap scribbled vigorously in a large, worn notebook, and an older woman focused her phone lens on the approaching train. Lovely Bay was abuzz with all things trainspotting.

Nina nodded at their passion as she looked from the group to the old station house, where she was waiting for her friend Nancy. The station house, which greeted visitors as they arrived in Lovely Bay, epitomised the charm of the place with its huge old windows, quaint vintage advertising signs, and bunting fluttering from the gutters. The station, with its well-preserved architecture, scalloped tiled roof peculiar to Lovely Bay, and wide old-fashioned doors, was a reminder of the town's connection to the railway and a very nice place to arrive home.

Nina's gaze followed the train as it smoothly glided into the station and aligned with the moveable platform. The mechanical marvel, a unique feature of Lovely Bay, never failed to impress. Nina watched and took in the enthusiasm of the group of spotters. What she saw on their faces reflected what she felt about Lovely Bay – a simple place, always with a little surprise around the corner. She'd found a community where people appreciated the little things, where history was cherished, and people most definitely knew your name. In Lovely Bay, she had come across not just a place to live but a place where she belonged, a community that embraced her with open arms. She absolutely adored how that made her feel.

Nancy bustled out of the stationmaster's house. 'Hello. Right, that's that lot done, I hope. Did you see their faces? Gets me every time. I'll just get my coat. How are you?'

Nina smiled. 'Good. We'll be busy later in the deli with that lot if they stay around all day.'

'You certainly will.'

Nina watched as Nancy made her way over towards the far door to check if it was locked. Her brisk, efficient steps reflected the years she had spent managing the station. Nina raised her eyebrows in question. 'Busy morning?'

'You could say that. When we've finally seen the back of winter, this place turns into a hive of activity, as you now know, seeing as you were with us last summer.' Nancy chuckled, glancing at the trainspotters, who were still animatedly discussing the features of the moving platform.

'I do. Let's hope for lots of lovely sunny days this year. I love it over in the marshes and by the sea when it's warm. There were so many lovely wildflowers last year too.'

Nancy pulled out a set of keys and began locking up the station house, ensuring each door clicked securely. 'Hopefully, the weather will play ball with us, yes.'

Nina peered upwards. 'We've already had it all today, and it's not even midday yet. It was foggy when I got up this morning, then it rained, and now the sun's out.'

'You must be used to our odd weather by now,' Nancy said

with a roll of her eyes. She tugged at the collar of her blue coat with the striped hood. 'Which is why you need one of these.'

'I do. My name is at the top of the waiting list now, so it shouldn't be too long.'

'It's taken long enough!'

'Yep, and it costs enough too.'

'So, how's everything at The Summer Hotel? Have you heard from Jill?'

Nina replied, 'Yeah, I have. Still, no buyers now that the last lot has fallen through. Jill's in Australia – did I tell you that?'

'Yes, you said.'

'I'm holding the fort until she comes back.'

'*If* she comes back.' Nancy commented, checking one of the ticket machines and making sure it was working correctly.

'I thought that, actually. I think she's got the wandering bug.'

'It's a beautiful place. It needs someone who sees its potential and charm and doesn't care about the fact that it's listed.'

'I hope someone sees all that,' Nina replied, her gaze drifting towards the station's old clock. 'I'd hate to see it go to someone who doesn't appreciate what it truly is.'

'Yeah, you and me both. Anyway, how are things in the deli? Still enjoying the hustle and bustle?' Nancy asked, with a twinkle in her eye. 'Birdie said you've been filling in again.'

Nina laughed. 'Yeah, while they're short-staffed again. As if I don't have enough to do with my own job. Ha ha. It's hectic, but in a good way. I've learned a lot of things that I never knew I needed to know in there, though.'

Nancy rolled her eyes. 'What, like the ins and outs of the Shipping Forecast?'

'Ha. Too funny.'

They walked out of the station and down towards the River Lovely and stood on the jetty, waiting for the riverboat to arrive.

Nancy looked up at the sky, where sunshine had just started

to peep through after a rainy early start. 'I wonder if the sun will stay with us for the day.'

'The forecast said wind and possibly a sea mist coming in later.'

Nancy chuckled. 'Ahh, right you are. Got to love all the weather keeping us on our toes.'

'I'm still getting used to it.'

Nancy turned her head to the side. 'Do you feel like Lovely is your home now? It's been a while.'

Nina nodded, her gaze drifting over the water. 'Yeah, I do. It's strange, I never thought I'd feel so at home in a place I hadn't even heard of a year or so ago. Lovely Bay has this way of getting under your skin if you ask me.'

Nancy smiled knowingly. 'It does, doesn't it? I've seen it happen time and time again. People come here for a visit and end up never leaving if their face fits and they're not looking for batch brew coffee and all that malarkey.' Nancy chuckled.

Nina watched as the riverboat approached, its engine puttering. Its arrival made the water slap against the jetty. 'Too funny. I was lucky you let me stay.'

'You were indeed. You slotted right in from day one, though, when you arrived with the kitchen sink.'

Nina chuckled. 'I never would've guessed. Me, a London girl, fitting into this picturesque little town.'

They watched as passengers disembarked from the boat. 'It does that to people. Lovely must like you.'

Nina gestured to the River Lovely and down towards the sea and the bay. 'I have to admit, I've fallen in love with this place. I *really* have.'

'I, for one, am glad you have. I think there's another person who may have fallen in love, too. How are things with our Robby?'

Nina blushed slightly. 'Good, really good. Just pottering along.'

'Right.'

Nina nodded. Everything *was* good in her life. The grief that had kept her so tightly wound for so long had released its grip, she adored living in Lovely Bay, and things were just right with Robby. Long may it last.

community page had become her new best friends. Late one night on Marketplace, she'd found a sweet, puffy, slip-covered sofa which had just about fit opposite the inglenook fireplace. Gorgeous antique striped linen curtains had been found on eBay, along with a Paisley rug. In the kitchen, she'd gathered plates from the hospice shop next to the chocolate shop, collected mugs and bits and bobs from all over the show, and in doing all of it, she'd had a thoroughly nice time. As if she was putting down roots at the same time as fixing up her heart.

In the small kitchen, she'd wedged in a tiny round table and chairs, dotted little vintage lamps wherever she could, and bought as many jugs as she could possibly find and popped them all over the place. As she'd pottered and gathered and moved in, Nina, along with the little cottage, had blossomed. Now, with the rental agreement coming to an end, the next part of her journey was on the horizon. She wondered quite where she would end up next.

Putting her key in the front door, she slipped her boots off, left them on the mat, and stepped straight into the living room. Fresh flowers sat in a pitcher on the coffee table in front of the inglenook fireplace, a double layer of jute rugs lay on the floor alongside the Paisley rug, and a geranium trailed from a prized wicker flower pot that sat on a tray on the coffee table. Nina had gone for cosy vibes good at healing grief-stricken hearts as her decorating goal and nailed it in one.

Walking into the kitchen, she smiled to herself; a gigantic jug of poppies made itself at home on the small scrubbed pine table, an old-fashioned plate rack on the wall displayed pretty finds from the charity shop, and a tall, skinny lamp with a vintage wicker shade was tucked into the corner ready to be turned on.

Nina took her phone out of her jeans pocket, plugged its charger in the socket, stuck the cable in her phone, and flicked on the kettle. Just as she was pouring a cup of tea, her phone

2

The sun dipped in and out of clouds after Nina and Nancy got off the boat, made their way over a small green and strolled along chatting. When Nina had decided to stay in Lovely Bay the year before, she'd rented a tiny house in the same row of cottages that Nancy lived in. Nancy always laughed and referred to her cottage as a really small two-up, two-down, but Nina had trumped its size with the place she'd rented. If Nancy's place was small, the cottage Nina had moved into was miniscule. The cottage she was living in was a one-up, one-down, but the same as Nancy, she loved it and had quickly come to call it home.

The year before, when Nina had decided that she was mad to be going back to London and had made a U-turn and stayed in Lovely Bay, Robby had right away asked her to move in, but something in the back of her mind had told her it wasn't a good idea. There had been a little bit of caution whispering in her ear, telling her to take things slowly and not run before she could walk. A voice saying that she should hold something back. Remain independent. She'd been on her own for a long time, and a small part of her had wanted it to stay that way. Nancy had mentioned the cottage a few doors down from her was up for rent, Nina had been to have a look and had more or less moved in the following week. She'd loved it from day one. She'd got her feet under the table in Lovely Bay and not looked back since.

As they got to the green situated just in front of the cottages, they took the path through the middle, strolled under the gigantic conker tree in the corner, and stopped as they got to the long row of pretty exposed brick cottages snaking along the road. Nancy's cottage was towards the facing end of the row, with a window box full of flowers and a couple of hanging baskets moving back and forth in the breeze. Nina smiled at Nancy's cobbled front garden, white picket fence, wicker heart hanging from the front door, pretty bench, and the name plaque to the right of the door. All of it appeared as if it had just been plucked from a perfect English country garden scene.

'Right, you are then,' Nancy said as she reached her arm over the gate and lifted up the latch. 'What are you up to tomorrow?'

'I'm going to look at that property over on the harbour.'

Nancy shook her head. 'Course you are. Sorry, brain like a sieve sometimes. I hope you like it.'

'Yes, me too.'

'I'll see you tomorrow, then. Pop in and let me know how it goes.' Nancy held up her right hand with her fingers crossed. 'Fingers crossed, it's the one for you. You never know.'

'Yep, will do, see you.'

When Nina got to her cottage at the other end of the row to Nancy's place, she smiled as the old lady who lived next door, who was standing by the front window fussing with a window box, smiled and raised her hand in greeting. Nina said hello, waved, pushed open the gate, and took a few steps up to the entrance door. Like Nancy's place, the rental cottage had a front door with a window in the centre. Just underneath it, Nina had hung a beautiful willow wreath. To the right on the wall, a pretty name plaque and matching post box engraved with flowers took pride of place. Two planters with bay trees sat on either side of a doormat, and a wicker heart swung from a bracket by the window. All of it very nice and so very different from Nina's London flat, where she'd lived on her own for a long time.

When Nina had first walked into the little cottage, it had hardly knocked her for six and made her want to jump right in and live there. In fact, it had been quite bland, consisting of a small sitting room when you stepped in, stripped timber floors, exposed brickwork and a small fireplace leading to a tiny kitchen. Steep stairs ran up the centre of the house with an understairs latched cupboard and not much room to swing a cat or anything really at all. The kitchen was small, plain, neat and tidy, with exposed beams painted white and French doors onto a narrow back garden with a little suntrap right in the corner at the back. The whole place had ticked all her boxes for somewhere to stay; clean, tidy, neutral, and ready to go.

Without too much thought, Nina had signed on the dotted line and rented what was little more than four small rooms and a garden. From there, she hadn't looked back for a solitary second. She'd loved every minute of being in the cottage. Just as Lovely Bay itself had done, it had helped to rid her of the shackles of grief she'd been bound up in for so long. She'd settled into its bricks and mortar as if it had always been meant to be. In the confines of its neutral walls and little garden, she'd sat back and learned how to be Nina again. It had been a long time coming.

She'd adored pottering in the cottage, nesting as she'd established herself and filled it with things found here and ther Facebook Marketplace, the hospice shop, and the Lovely B rang with a call from her best friend, Sophie. Nina watched Sophie's name across the screen and then tapped. As she held the phone to her ear, it crossed her mind how Sophie used to call her every Friday evening at the same time to check in on Nina and make sure she was okay. That had been in the days before Nina had knuckled down and got her life back on track and moved to Lovely Bay. Then Sophie had been concerned about Nina's welfare because Nina's husband, Andrew, had died, Sophie's regular Friday calls had been accompanied by what Nina had come to call the Pity Smile. These days the Pity Smile was toast. It had miraculously disappeared and made a new home somewhere else along with Nina's broken heart. It had left the building at about the same time as Nina had arrived in Lovely Bay. She'd been ecstatic to see the back of it, truth be told.

'Hiya,' Nina said, her tone sprightly. 'How are you? What are you up to?'

'Yeah, not too bad. You?'

'Good. I tried to call you earlier. Did you have your phone off? It went to voicemail.'

'Ahh, yes, sorry. I was up to my eyes in it, what with everyone being poorly, so I turned my phone off and went for a nap for half an hour. It's done wonders. I think I was up most of the night clearing up vomit and changing beds. Not fun.' Sophie sounded tired and semi-stressed.

'Oh dear, doesn't sound pleasant at all. Do you want me to come and give you a hand?'

'No, I'm fine.'

'Is Nick still away? You said he might come back early.'

'Yes, he's still away, and no, he's not coming back early.'

'So, you're on your own again?' Nina clarified, tutted to herself and shook her head.

'I am, but I'm fine. All good. Don't worry about me.'

Nina *did* worry about Sophie. 'Honestly, I don't mind coming over. I can muck in and do anything you want. It might take a bit of the pressure off.'

'No, no, all good. To be honest, I'd rather just muddle through on my own, you know?'

'Right, yeah, okay.'

'What have you been up to? Oh, I almost forgot to mention those property pictures you sent me. What was all that about?' Sophie asked, referring to a set of pictures Nina had been sent by Ella, an estate agent in Lovely Bay, of the property Nina was going to see the next day.

Nina perched on the edge of the kitchen chair, her phone cradled between her shoulder and ear. She gazed out the window at the little garden as she talked. 'The estate agent sent them to me to see if I am interested. I'm going to go and have a look tomorrow. I'm not sure by the looks of it, but you never know.'

'It looks like it might be what you're looking for.'

'It's a gorgeous old building not far from Robby down on the harbour there, but it's not in the best state. I thought I might as well go along as Ella has been a pretty good judge about what I like so far.'

'Looks like it, err, might need quite a bit of work.'

'Yes, it does. I'll be able to tell you *how* much tomorrow. I won't hold my breath, but it's strange because I have a funny feeling about this one. Not that that really means anything. You know how you get that about things sometimes?'

Sophie's voice was enthusiastic. 'Hopefully, it will be the one. You never know.'

Nina chuckled. 'I hope so. The bottom floor is perfect for an office or a little shop or whatever, and the residential space upstairs has these large windows that look right out over the water. That's all I know so far.'

3

Later that day, Nina was outside, sweeping the path. Lost in a world of her own, she was enjoying the sounds of Lovely Bay all around her: the calls of seagulls from way up above, the leaves on the conker tree opposite rustling, and somewhere in the distance, church bells pealed across the air. Just as she was standing on the bench by the front door, peering into a hanging basket and pulling out weeds, she noticed a woman walk over the green and stop outside Nancy's cottage. Nina squinted and tried to see if she recognised the woman. Not many people came up to the rear of the green where the row of cottages stood back from the street. As she watched the woman continue to stand by Nancy's gate, she assumed it must be a friend of Nancy's she hadn't yet met and got on with pulling weeds out of the basket.

A few minutes later, she heard someone's voice. Still standing on the bench, she turned to look over her shoulder across to the pavement and shaded her eyes from the light to see the woman who had been at Nancy's gate walking towards her. Nina couldn't place her, but maybe she'd seen her around town. She wasn't quite sure.

'Sounds like you could wake up to the sea every day,' Sophie mused. 'How nice would that be?'

'Very nice. There's work to be done, though.'

'It's the best way; it means you can put your own mark on it. You won't inherit someone else's naff bathroom and kitchen.'

'That's one way of putting it. Anyway, we'll see. It would be good to, you know, put my heart into something again. It would be a bit of a new chapter.'

'It would. You are definitely in a new chapter. Actually, I think you're on chapter three. After all the tough times, you deserve this fresh start. By the way, what's happened with the flat? It must nearly be done and dusted now.'

Nina nodded. With a view to buying a place in Lovely Bay, she'd sold the investment flat in London that she'd bought with Andrew. It had been a hard decision and another occasion in her journey to being free of grief or at least not as affected by it. The decision itself had been loaded with emotion, but once she'd made it, she'd felt as if she'd let another thing holding her back go. 'Yes, it is. I just need to go and sign a few more papers, and it's officially done.'

'Wow, that was quick!'

'Well, there's no chain, and it sold the day it hit the internet, as you know. Plus, the couple who have bought it are downsizing and have nothing to sell. I think it was unusual for it to go that way, but I'm not complaining.'

'How do you feel about it now?' Sophie asked.

'One word: sad.'

'Still? I bet.'

'But if there is such a thing as happy sad, then that's what it is. It needed to be done for me to move on even though my actual flat is still sitting there, as you know.' Nina didn't add that Andrew's clothes were still in the wardrobe or that she never wanted to part with them. That once when she'd gone back to the flat, she'd climbed into the wardrobe and stood next to his clothes for ages just to sort of be near him again. She'd keep that to herself.

'What will you do about that?'

'Honest answer is I don't know.' Nina wasn't sure if she would *ever* be willing to sell the place she'd lived in with Andrew. It was still full of memories and emotions, none of them, yet, she felt as if she was ready to let go.

'What will be will be. Let's just hope this place you're going to look at is good.'

'I hope so.'

'It will be great for your little business to have a home and for you to be off that kitchen table. How are things with the business?'

Nina let out a happy sigh. 'Can't keep up with it! Who knew so many people needed decluttering and house organisation services?'

'I do! I need you here.'

Nina chuckled. 'You do not.'

'I have stuff coming out of my ears, Neens.'

'I'll put you on my waiting list,' Nina joked.

'Ha, right, I'd better get back to the mayhem. Send me pics later.'

'Will do. Soph, let me know if you want me to come over and help.'

'I'm fine. Keep me updated on how the viewing goes.'

'I will. Bye.' Nina put down her phone and let out a sigh.

Standing up, she picked up her tea, opened the back door, and mused the conversation with Sophie and the fact that the investment flat she'd bought with Andrew, her husband, had now sold. Things were moving on. Memories were now of a different place. Lovely Bay had become more than just a little town to stay in for a bit and see how it went. She was no longer going to be just renting a house to see what happened. She would be either buying somewhere or renewing a longer lease.

She was putting down roots, cementing her new beginr
getting Nina back.

With thoughts of the property Ella had told her
swirling in her mind, Nina felt a little bit of excitement
pit of her stomach at the prospect of buying a place in I
Bay. As Sophie had said, what would be would be.

'Excuse me,' the woman called out, her voice friendly enough but with an undercurrent Nina couldn't quite read or maybe she was imagining things. 'I'm looking for the old bakery building. I love finding out about the history of places. I know it's around here somewhere, but I seem to have gone around in circles. Do you have any idea at all?'

Nina climbed down from the bench, brushing the soil from the hanging basket from her hands. She frowned and wrinkled up her nose. 'The old bakery? I'm not sure. I haven't lived here long myself.'

'Oh, right. Nice cottage by the way.'

'Thanks. I'm renting it.'

'Lucky you. So, you've no idea where the old bakery was?'

'Nope, sorry.'

'No worries.' The woman smiled, her eyes lingering on Nina for a moment. 'I'm Lindsay, by the way.'

Nina wondered why this woman was introducing herself and put it down to the fact that people in Lovely Bay seemed to do that if they'd never met before. 'Nice to meet you.'

The woman beamed sounding overly friendly and gushing. 'I'm a very old acquaintance of Nancy's, actually. As soon as I walked over the green, I remembered she'd just bought the place back then. Years ago, that was. I thought I might...'

'Oh, yes, right.'

'Do you know her? Being a neighbour and everything.' The woman was unduly smiley and happy. Her voice chirped.

Nina didn't know why, but something about the woman was *very* off. It stirred a slight unease somewhere inside. She tried to keep her tone neutral. She knew Nancy had said she was going to one of her other jobs that afternoon but Nina wasn't going to volunteer any information about Nancy's whereabouts. 'Yes, I know her quite well. She's at work at the moment.'

Lindsay's smile widened and there was something in her

gaze that Nina couldn't quite decipher. 'I've been trying to reconnect with old friends on Facebook. It's been a long time.'

Nina nodded, feeling her unease grow. She made light of the situation and smiled. 'Ahh, good old Facebook.' Nina picked up a watering can and made to get on.

Lindsay clearly didn't want to finish the conversation. 'Yes, it's good, isn't it? I love it, though I probably spend way too much time on it. You know how it is.'

'Hmm.'

Lindsay nodded and continued. 'You can find out all sorts on Facebook.'

Nina frowned. 'Like what?'

It was as if Lindsay was quickly backtracking. 'Oh, you know this and that. Sometimes, you just find yourself on there for hours, wasting time. At least I do anyway…'

Nina wasn't really interested. She picked up one of her gardening gloves. 'Well, nice to meet you. I hope you find the old bakery.'

'Likewise, Nina,' Lindsay said, turned and continued along the pavement.

Nina watched her cross the road and take the path under the conker tree and across the green. She squinted and turned her head from left to right. She hadn't mentioned her name, had she? Shaking her head, she thought that she must have done. She picked up a broom and started sweeping the weeds she'd pulled from the basket into a pile and wondered who the woman was. No doubt she'd find out. Lovelies would be all over it.

4

Nina stood at the jetty watching as the riverboat puttered along towards her. The sun glinted off its polished wooden exterior, and the little lanterns that were lit in the evening swayed back and forth in the wind. She could see Colin in the Lovely regulation coat with the striped hood standing near the back and hear the now familiar hum of the engine as it chugged along. The boat's wake created ripples on the water's surface and caused the waves to lap against the shore.

Colin skilfully manoeuvred the boat alongside the jetty, the engine's hum growing quieter as he reduced its speed and threw a rope to the mooring post. As Nina hopped on, wobbled a bit and settled into a seat, her gaze wandered over the river, the greenery lining the banks, and the distant sounds of Lovely Bay going about its day.

Colin turned and smiled. 'Afternoon. How are we today?'

'Good, thanks. You?'

'Can't complain. Where are you off to going this way?' Colin jerked his thumb downriver in the direction of the sea.

'I'm going to see a property down by the harbour.'

'What is this you speak of?' Colin joked. 'I don't know

anything about that and I know everything that goes on in the third smallest town in the country.'

Nina chuckled. 'Ahh, are you telling me I know something about Lovely Bay that you don't? I thought you knew everything before everyone, or is that Birdie? That's how it goes around here, isn't it?'

Colin frowned and continued the banter. 'I think you could be right that I actually don't know about this. I'd better call the council and complain. Where is this property, then?'

'Just along from Robby's place over on the harbour there.'

'What, near the old fishing buildings?'

'Yeah, the old fishing buildings themselves.'

Colin rubbed his chin. 'Interesting. They cost a pretty penny these days.'

'It's not officially up for sale yet. Ella knows what I'm looking for, and because I've been liaising with her on The Summer Hotel, she sent me some pics. It's a bit of a mess, so the price might be right for me. We'll see.'

'That's why I don't know about it then.' Colin nodded thoughtfully as he steered the boat, the purr of the engine filling the space between their conversation. 'Sounds like a prime spot, especially near the harbour. What's the go-to with it?'

Nina leaned back on the seat. 'Well, it's got an office space of sorts on the bottom and a residential area above. It's perfect for what I need – a bit of a project, but I like the idea of that. At least, I think I do.'

'I think I know the one there. Old Johnny's, back in the day, if it's the one I think it is. It's been empty for years. A fair bit of work,' Colin remarked, his eyes scanning the river ahead. 'Those old buildings have character, but they can be a handful. Lots of elements battering them down that way. I think that one is pretty weathered on the outside.'

'I know, but I'm up for it. After sorting out The Summer Hotel, I feel like I can handle anything.'

Nina walked around the harbour wall as boats bobbed around beside her and sails clanged and banged in the wind. She squinted over towards what were known locally as the fishing sheds on the far side to be confronted with rows of tall, narrow buildings brimming with Lovely Bay's maritime and fishing heritage, a stone's throw from the water's edge of the harbour.

As she got closer to the first row of buildings, she peered at the weathered wood cladding, the old sun-bleached and salt-worn double doors on the second stories with huge rusted hinges, and the sloping roofs with the unique Lovely Bay scalloped shingle roofing tiles. Nina nodded at the feel of the place: a mix of unpretentious working buildings and a lovely rustic seaside charm. She could work with that. As she walked past a shed with its doors open, she smiled at the years of maritime activity that seemed to be looking back at her: nets, buoys, ropes, and other fishing paraphernalia hung up on the walls and neatly piled stacks of floats and fenders sat by the door.

She inhaled the distinct briny scent of the harbour, took in a squealing of gulls overhead, and listened to the sound of the sea as it lapped around by the harbour wall. The further she walked along the rows of sheds, the more weathered and more rustic they seemed. Arriving at the second to last shed, she looked around for Ella, and not seeing any sign of her or anyone else at all, she stood and looked up at the old building. A lower floor with wide barn doors looked back at her as a breeze whipped around her hair. The doors must have once been painted a sea green but now showed lines of rust running down towards the floor and peeling paint along their grooves. The second floor housed a huge floor-to-ceiling window in place of what once would have been the same sort of barn door, and the dormer windows on the third floor up in the sloping roof had seen better days. Nina wasn't sure what to think. The timber

Colin chuckled, 'I've no doubt about that. You wonders with the hotel. The whole town's been talking We just need someone to buy it now. I'm surprised no snapped it up yet.'

'I know.'

'So, this place on the harbour could be for you Interesting.'

'Possibly, we'll see. It's got a great view of the bay, and close to Robby's office is a bonus, plus somewhere for m work and live.'

'Good on you. I hope it's the one for you.' Colin nodded remember when I was a tot, those buildings were bustling w fishermen. Times change, but it's good to see them given ne life.'

Nina smiled. 'I can imagine. It would be nice to buy some thing here, but we'll see. Everything I've looked at so far hasn' been right and way too expensive. Not even close, actually.'

'Lovely Bay has a way of making you want to settle down and be part of it. It's got that charm, hasn't it?'

'It really has. I never expected to feel so at home here, but I do.' Nina agreed with a smile.

As the boat continued down the river in the direction of the sea, the conversation went back and forth about this and that. Nina loved just chatting and being in on things. It really made her feel as if she belonged. It had been missing in her life for *such* a long time.

'Here we are, then. Good luck with the viewing. Let me know how it goes,' Colin said with a smile.

'Will do. Thanks for the ride. Fingers crossed, this will be the one.'

cladding was sun-bleached and faded and not in a good way. There was a crack running right down the centre of one of the window panes, and the chimneys, to her uneducated eye, looked a bit on the wonky side.

However, something about the setting, right on the harbour and the rustic charm of the long line of sheds, spoke directly to her heart. With their weathered wood and sloping roofs, it felt like she was stepping back in time as things were whispering to her through the salty air. Nina could almost hear the bustling of Lovelies and their day-to-day fishing activities from days gone by.

As she was standing chin up, looking at the state of the scalloped tiles on the roof and the windows on the third floor, she heard quick footsteps and looked down to see Ella coming towards her in a fluster.

'Sorry, I'm late! I got caught on the phone and then in those lights over on the other side there. There seem to be temporary traffic lights all over the place at the moment. It's doing my head in, to be quite honest. One minute, the road is fine, the next minute, there are traffic lights in the most inconvenient of places.'

'Not a problem at all. Tell me about it with those awful lights.'

Ella shook her head over and over again. 'I hate being late. It's *so* rude. It makes it look as if I don't respect people's time as much as I do my own. Sorry again.'

'Honestly, no worries. It's fine.'

Ella smiled. 'How are you? You look well.'

'Good, thanks.'

Ella looked up at the building. 'Thoughts so far? What is it saying to you?'

Nina raised her eyebrows. 'Work!'

'Oh yes, there's plenty of that. It's a bit on the tatty side, if I'm honest. I've got to say, though, I think you're going to fall in love in the next ten minutes. It is oozing potential, if I say so myself. As soon as I walked in I thought this is the one for you. Blimey, we've looked at enough, right?'

'We have indeed. I feel like I'll never find something that combines an office and a residential bit, too.'

Ella shook her head. 'Until now. You are currently looking at it.'

Nina followed around the back of the building and scanned the details of the old fishing shed's exterior. They reached a small, sturdy door at the back. Ella fumbled with a large keyring as she tried to locate the correct key.

'Here we go,' Ella said, putting the key into the lock, turning it and unlocking the door. It creaked open, revealing a dim interior that smelt of wood, dust and history.

Nina followed Ella as she stepped inside, her eyes adjusted to the change in light and took in an expansive warehouse-feel room with high ceilings and, despite the murky light and dank smell, a sense of openness. Old wooden beams crisscrossed overhead, huge industrial pendant lamps hung through the centre, and the walls were lined with remnants of its past life – rusted hooks, a few nets here and there, old maritime charts, and faded photographs of fishermen with their catch.

Nina wasn't sure what to think. 'Hmm, right. It's got character, that's for sure,' she remarked. Her voice echoed slightly in the large space.

Ella grinned. 'You can say that again. Imagine what you could do with this space. Office, workshop, retail – you name it. Sure, there's a lot to clean up, but if you look closely, most of it is cosmetic, really.' Ella pointed at the dusty walls and beamed ceilings that looked as if they had seen better days. 'For example, look at that there; no mould, no signs of damp, and built to last. These places will go on forever. I sold one years ago down the other end, they're thriving.'

Nina nodded, taking in Ella's words as she walked further in.

Her steps echoed on the wooden floor. Ella wasn't wrong. She attempted to envision the place after one of her mammoth clearouts, much effort and a lot of paint. 'You're right,' Nina said as she turned around to take in the full scope of the room. 'There's so much potential here.'

Ella gestured to the back. 'You could use this for storage for your business and even partition that bit there for a desk and that sort of thing. I know it's a total mess at the moment, but it's there if you look for it.'

Nina thought about how she currently ran her new business from her phone and how it would be life-changing to have somewhere to sit at a desk and keep all her stuff in order. 'Yes, it's made for it.'

Ella led the way to a super narrow, super steep staircase at the far end. Her heels clipped on the floor. 'Let's go upstairs. I think you'll be pleasantly surprised, that's if I don't kill myself in these shoes. I meant to change them when I got in the car. Another reason I hate being late is it always ends up in me being disorganised.'

As Nina followed Ella up the creaky, steep timber stairs to the second floor, she wasn't sure where to look first. The staircase alone was lovely. Each tread felt as if it came with its very own sound and the open woodwork on the clad walls housed shelving as far as the eye could see.

Once they got to the second floor, Ella carefully picked her heels over extremely dusty floorboards and swept her hand around and over towards the large windows that Nina had seen from outside. The windows were filthy, a broken blind obscured the light, and a rolled-up rug leaning beside them looked as if it needed to make its way to the dump. 'This is it. Your name is all over it if you ask me. I thought that right away.'

Nina took a few steps over towards the window and pulled back the horrid old metal blind. Dust flew up into the air, and she coughed as she peered out the window. The sea view was mesmerising and took her breath away for a second. It offered a sweeping panorama of Lovely Bay, the bustling harbour, and the river snaking off in the distance. She could see the Lovely Bay church spires and the lighthouse as she looked the other way. Her stomach fluttered; the view alone was right up her alley. 'Wow.' Nina's heart skipped a beat; the panorama from the window was worth any amount of work the building needed.

Ella raised her eyebrows. 'Yeah, totally. Wow is the word. You just don't realise what these places look over until you get up here.'

'It's amazing. It really is.'

'This could be a great space,' Ella suggested, walking over to the window. 'Open-plan living, you've already got the kitchen area over there. All of it finished off with that view!'

Nina followed Ella to the kitchen area. She started to chuckle as she looked around. 'Are we calling this a kitchen?' A small run of old timber units had been wedged onto the far side of the room. The same pendant lights as the ones downstairs hung from the rafters, horrid black and white chequered flooring was coming away from the floorboards in the kitchen area, and an old cooker had lost a foot and looked as if it had possibly had a few too many.

Nina nodded as she walked around. In light of the state of the place, especially the kitchen, she couldn't quite picture herself living and working in it, but she could get used to waking up to the sight of the sun glittering on the water and the rhythmic sound of the sea and waves just outside the window. That in itself was worth its weight in gold as far as she was concerned.

Ella turned around. 'Okay, follow me up to the next floor. It's, umm, well, I'll let you see for yourself.'

They continued up an even steeper set of stairs, akin really to a ladder, to the third floor. Clean it was not. It stunk of years of neglect. Absolutely packed to the rafters with fishing para-

'I don't know…'

'Okay, look past the junk. Imagine it with nothing in it. I'm asking not a thing. It will be amazing at some point.'

Nina peered at the green mould. 'That's a bit of a tall order.'

'Nancy said how well you've done with the cottage. That was bare bones when you moved in.'

'Yes, but it was clean, bare bones, and it had just been painted.'

'Which is what you can do with this.' Ella nodded. 'The roof is sound, the floorboards are all in good condition, even the electrics.' She screwed her lips up. 'I really don't think there's a lot to spend. I mean, yeah, eventually a new bathroom and kitchen, but even those you could make do with to start off.'

'Hmm.'

'You have your own decluttering and organising company…' Ella trailed off as if that made everything make sense.

'I suppose I do. I am *used* to junk. This seems on another level, though.'

Ella dipped her finger up and down towards the lower floor. 'That down there is perfect for your storage needs for your business, as we said on the phone.'

Nina was silent for a second. 'Mmm. It could even be used for hot desking. I know many people are looking for that nowadays. Every job I've done in the last few months has been clearing out rooms so that people can make the move to working from home.'

'You're right.'

Nina followed Ella back into the room crammed full of junk. 'It's crying out for someone like you. It really is.'

As they descended back to the ground floor, Nina felt butterflies in her stomach. The place needed work, a lot of work, but it was brimming with potential. It was a project that could really become something special for someone with the

phernalia, Ella squeezed under the sloped c
fishing nets, oars, and what looked like part
the dormer windows at the front. It was du:
junk, and with an attic-like feel, but to Nina, i
intimate and secluded. As if as they'd climbed up,
actual world and moved into a quieter one where t,
different, and everything felt a bit muffled.

There was barely enough room for Nina to stand
between the junk, but as the two of them stood by th
windows surrounded by maritime paraphernalia, n
them said anything for a bit as they looked out over th
The sun glistened, a swoop of birds went past the windo
below in the harbour, a fishing boat started on its wa
to sea.

'I thought bed up here...' Ella trailed off almost as if she
talking to herself. 'Imagine this in the morning as the su
coming up. I reckon it's magical.'

'Mmm,' Nina said, turning around and attempting to look
past the junk.

Ella pointed to a rickety old door with a lifebuoy wedged on
the back of it. 'Bathroom in there.' She winced a little bit. 'I feel
slightly apprehensive about calling it a bathroom, but it has a
toilet and a bath, so...'

Nina squeezed past the door and the lifebuoy. An old toilet
was so dirty that green mould grew in the pan. The same thing
was happening with a ring going around the tub. The roof
sloped, and another dormer window looked out over the back.
Nina let out a whoosh of air as Ella tried to sneakily hold her
hand over her mouth at the stench coming from the toilet.

'It needs a lot of work and it stinks. Nice. I'd have zero
budget for anything like that.'

'Yep.' Ella nodded as Nina peered into the bath and nearly
gagged as the smell hit her fully, and an old toilet brush nudged
her foot.

right eye who was prepared to take on a mountain of effort. Or had a huge bank account, which she most definitely did not.

'So, what are your thoughts?' Ella asked as they stepped back into the subdued light of the ground floor.

Nina paused, her gaze drifting over the room. 'I'm intrigued,' she admitted. 'It's a lot to take on, but... there's something about this place. It feels right, somehow, or I'm imagining it.'

'I thought you might feel that way. There's something about these old buildings – they have a soul or something. As soon as I walked in, I thought about you. You could really bring this place back to life.'

Nina suddenly felt quite vulnerable and alone. She'd never done anything like it before. Deep down, she wasn't actually sure *what* was feasible. Numbers and plans floated around her head in a jumble. 'It would be a huge decision for me.'

As they made their way out, Nina felt a bit buzzy. The place needed work, a lot of work, but it was maybe what she'd been looking for. It was a project, a challenge, but it felt right.

'So, what do you think?' Ella asked as they stepped back into the sunshine.

Nina took a deep breath as she looked up at the building. 'I think I just fell in love with an old building full of junk.'

Ella beamed. 'I had a feeling you might say that.'

About ten minutes later, after looking around the outside as Nina watched Ella walk away, she felt a strange feeling of possibility. And just like she had when she'd first started her journey to Lovely Bay, she felt pure, simple, very easy hope. It was a feeling that had been missing from her life for way too long. Hope was becoming her new best friend.

5

Lost in a world of her own, Nina watched the moving platform slot into place on the other side of the station. A train pulled in, unloaded its passengers, and took off again. She observed a mismatch of people traipsing over the footbridge looking for the platform. The sign above her head flicked over to say that the train going the other way was approaching, and the track hissed, indicating that the sign was indeed correct.

A few minutes later, Nina was sitting on the train. As it started to make its way away from Lovely Bay and juddered over the tracks, her mind went back to the first day she'd arrived in town. Then she'd not really had a clue what she was doing or why she was there and she'd been travelling with a jagged slice running right down the centre of her broken heart. Then she'd been laden with all sorts, not just actual physical baggage, of which there was much, but also emotional, spiritual, and mental baggage and whatever else you wanted to throw in for free.

She smiled to herself as she thought about the Nina who had arrived back then. That Nina had been sad, down, and wondering about life all around. Things, however, had changed.

She hadn't felt as she had in the 'before Lovely Bay days' for ages as just about everything, but especially her heart, had healed. But now, going back the other way to London to complete the sale of the investment flat, she felt a bit upside down.

Had the jagged edge in her heart opened up again a tiny little bit? Even though she was happy as a pig in mud and very much looking forward to making her roots permanent in Lovely Bay, emotion was coursing through her veins at a hundred miles an hour. The sale of the flat truly was sealing the deal of a new life in Lovely Bay. A new life where Andrew really, really, *really* wasn't anywhere to be seen. He was now so much more than lost it wasn't even funny.

Trying not to think about it too much and determined to keep Andrew's memory a happy one, she opened her phone and went through her work emails. She'd started her little business, A Lovely Organised Life, almost by accident just after she'd moved into the cottage and had intended to start seriously looking for a proper job as her money had been fast running out. A friend of Jill, owner of The Summer Hotel, had heard what a good job she'd done with it and had asked if Nina would be interested in going to have a look at her house to see if there was anything she could do. Nina had gone along with an open mind, attempted to keep her shock at the state of the woman's house off her face, and had quoted accordingly at the huge amount of work involved.

The woman had almost bitten her hand off, Nina had hastily set herself up a shed-load of insurance and the following week had got stuck in. The rest, as they say, is history. Nina now had a small but thriving business and a waiting list as long as her arm. By way of social media, a few of her old clients in London had heard she was again up and running, and she now employed a local part-time to help her out with the actual day-to-day decluttering and invoicing and she was enjoying the challenge of the business side of things. Compared to her old, boring job, oh how things had changed.

After sending a couple of questionnaires to clients, scheduling a job, and doing a quote, she flicked over to her social media account. On a whim on the first day of the job for Jill's friend, Nina had propped up her phone in the, quite frankly, revolting kitchen, pressed the time-lapse button, and got on with it. That evening, astonished herself at the transformation to the kitchen in the day, she'd slapped on a few hashtags and posted the kitchen declutter video and had been more than surprised when it had received a fair few views.

From there, her social media presence had slowly trickled along. Nina had gathered that people at the other end of the country and the other side of the planet enjoyed watching decluttering and cleaning videos. Who even knew? She had been dropped, by way of a house in Lovely Bay, into a whole new world. One where she was thoroughly enjoying herself and earning money to boot. Can't be bad.

Her phone vibrated. Robby's name went across the screen. She swiped to answer.

'Hi, how are you?' Robby asked.

'Fine. Yep, good. How are you?'

'Good. Where are you?'

'Just about to change trains for the express service.'

'Are you feeling okay about everything?' Robby asked, referring to the fact that Nina was about to close on the investment property she'd had with Andrew. He knew how delicate the situation was. They'd discussed it a lot.

Nina leant back in her seat, feeling the train rumbling underneath her. 'Yeah, I think so. It's a bit odd, really. As we've said, finalising the sale feels like closing a chapter, you know?'

'I can imagine. It must be bittersweet. You've been quite quiet the last few days, too. I don't really know what to say to make it any better.'

'You don't have to. It's fine. It *is* bittersweet,' Nina admitted, watching the countryside blur past her window. 'But it's also a step forward and not back. I'm ready for more new beginnings in Lovely Bay, and to get that, I need to do this. Simple when you think about it like that.'

'That's the spirit,' Robby encouraged. 'And how's the train journey?'

'So far so good. A little delay at the last station; I'm not sure why because they didn't say anything over the tannoy, but nothing too bad. I should be there soon.'

'The joys of public transport, eh?'

'Works for me. I'd much rather be sitting here working than sitting in traffic on the motorway.'

'Good point. I'm doing just that. It drives me up the wall. The sooner the government sorts out the public transport system in this country, the easier it will be for everyone.'

Robby was meeting Nina in London after being up and out early on a job on the other side of the county. 'Oh, no, are you going to be late?'

'No, no. I factored in sitting in a queue of cars. I'll be there, don't you worry about that.'

'I bet you did.'

Robby inhaled a whoosh of air. 'Look, I've been mulling this over a lot this morning. I wanted to say that what you're doing is quite a big deal. Selling a property, especially one tied to so many memories, isn't easy.'

Nina sighed, feeling a mix of emotions. 'I know. I feel like it's time, though. Time to let go and move on, even though I hate it when people say that. Lovely Bay has been so good to me. I feel like I belong now and you know, you and me. It's a good thing. It has to be done.'

'Lovely Bay wouldn't be the same without you. I wouldn't be…'

Nina smiled. 'Aww, too sweet.'

Robby changed the subject. 'So what work were you doing?'

'A couple of quotes and questionnaires. I can't keep up with it fast enough.'

'Can't complain, eh?'

'Nope, it's keeping me busy.'

'You've really found your niche, haven't you?'

'I think so. It's strangely satisfying to help people organise their lives. It feels like I'm making a real difference sometimes. People get themselves into so much stuff and clutter and can't fathom a way out. Yeah, I have to say I love it. For now, that is.'

The train announcement interrupted their conversation, and Nina listened as the next station was called out. 'Oh, okay, that's me. My stop's coming up. Thanks for checking in. I'll text you when I'm nearly there.'

'See you soon. Love you, Neens.'

'Love you, too.'

As Nina got off the train, worked out what platform she was meant to be on, went up the steps, and back down the other side, she thought about the investment flat. She'd realised once she'd appointed the solicitor that she probably could have used a solicitor anywhere and not gone back to the one Andrew had used. But somehow, using the same firm and the London trip was a necessary step in closing that chapter of her life. It felt as if it had been a very long time coming indeed.

6

Nina stood with her head back and her chin up and looked at the gorgeous London building. It was a classic old Georgian property that had been converted into flats many moons before. Nina and Andrew had bought it when the area was still on the tatty, rough-and-tumble side. Now, it was far from it. The same as where her other flat was situated, the area had been gentrified to the hilt. She wasn't sure whether or not she liked it. Sure, the bay trees in pots were nice, the shiny black painted front doors, the fancy Dutch e-bikes tied to perfect railings, but something about it didn't feel right. Nina didn't know what at first until it came to her. It didn't feel that *friendly*. She tutted and shook her head. She'd become too used to Lovely Bay, where people spoke to you and smiled, and things were pretty and quaint. Where people actually knew your name, said hello and were interested in how you were going about your day.

She jumped out of the way as a food delivery cyclist zoomed past, nearly knocking her flying. He shook his head, looked over his shoulder, and shouted. 'Oi! Idiot! Watch it! Look where you're standing, love. It's called a pavement. Know what one of those is? People cycle on it, you know!'

Nina just blinked, thinking she was not his 'love' and half-thought about yelling back about the law concerning cycling on the pavement. She didn't bother. He was long gone anyway. 'Charming,' she said under her breath and made sure she stood closer to the edge of the pavement. Her phone pinged with a text.

Robby: *Five minutes away. Parking is a nightmare around here!*

Nina: *Okay. I'll see you outside the solicitors.*

Nina ambled along past the property where her flat was and made her way towards the high street. It also had been gentrified. Long gone were the kebab shops and pawnbrokers of old. A fancy greengrocer with a black canopy outside made a big deal of selling artichokes, and a boutique estate agent drowned in Farrow and Ball green. A few minutes later, Nina was standing outside the solicitors.

Robby came hurrying the other way. He rolled his eyes. 'How much does it cost to park around here? I had to use my credit card. Honestly, you can't make it up.'

'I know.' Nina gestured around. 'The whole area has changed exponentially over the years.'

'No wonder people are saying they are priced out of London these days. Parking your car alone is an arm and a leg. Anyway, how are you? Okay?' Robby kissed her on the cheek.

Nina was more than okay despite her nerves on the train and the feelings of closure on another chapter of her life. When she'd actually arrived and seen the flat's building, she'd known she was ready. It was definitely the right thing to do. She wanted and *needed* closure. She now just wanted it over and done with. Onwards and upwards with her new business and hopefully her new property in Lovely Bay. 'I'm good. Yep.'

'Let's get this show on the road then. All good to sign on the dotted line?' Robby joked and went to push open the door.

Nina suddenly wanted to go in alone. 'Actually, do you mind if I do this bit on my own? I know you've come all this way but...'

'Of course not. You know I said I was just coming along for the ride to see if you were okay. I don't need to come in. See you in a bit.'

'Thanks.'

'Ready?'

Nina gave a half-hearted smile. 'As ready as I'll ever be. Time to get on with it.'

Nina entered the solicitor's office and immediately felt as if she'd zoomed back in time. It was a place that held memories of a different life, a different Nina. Once she'd checked in with the receptionist, the solicitor, Mr Hargraves, greeted her with a professional nod. 'Ms. Lavendar, follow me.'

In the stark office with its shelves lined with legal books, a large mahogany desk, and certificates adorning the walls, Nina immediately felt as if she was in trouble. It was the kind of place where seriousness and importance oozed from just about everything. She remembered the last time she'd been in the room sorting out legal stuff after Andrew had passed away.

As they sat down, Nina glanced at the various documents laid out on the desk. This was it – the final step in letting go of a significant part of her past. Mr. Hargraves cleared his throat, breaking Nina's train of thought. 'So, we have everything prepared for the finalisation of the sale of your property. All we need now are your signatures in various places indicated here to complete the process.' He slowly pushed a posh-looking fountain pen across the table.

Nina nodded, picking up the pen. Her hand hovered for a moment before she signed her name in the places indicated by little pink tabs. She swallowed and pushed back the pen. 'Thanks.'

'There, that's all done,' Mr. Hargraves announced, closing the folder. 'You'll receive the final documents in the post.'

Nina exhaled, a weight lifting off her shoulders. 'Thank you.'

Two minutes later, Nina was standing back outside in the street. She'd made such a big deal of it, but it had been done in a flash. Robby put his hand on the small of her back. 'How was that? You alright?'

Nina nodded, 'Yeah. I'm good. It's strange, though. It feels like the end of an era.'

'It is, in a way. But it's also the start of something new. Lovely Bay, your business, everything. You've got so much to look forward to. Plus, you now have the pleasure of being stuck with me,' Robby joked. 'That has to be worth something.'

'You're right. This feels like closing a book.'

'That's because it is in a way. Right, I'm famished. Fancy grabbing some lunch?' Robby suggested.

Nina pointed down the high street. 'There used to be a pub on the corner there right on the intersection. It's got one of those light systems where you can cross diagonally. We used to sit there in the window with a drink and watch the world go by.'

'Sounds just right.'

About five minutes later, they were outside the pub. It ran through Nina's mind how the last time she'd been in the pub, she'd been with Andrew. She pushed the thought aside and followed Robby in. After getting a drink and a menu from the bar, they were sitting at the window bar on a couple of stools. Nina's phone buzzed.

Sophie: *How did it go? You OK?*

Nina quickly typed a response.

Nina: *All done. Officially no longer the owner of an investment property.*

Sophie: *Congrats! Big step, Neens. Proud of you. xxx*

Nina smiled at the message. It was true; she had taken big,

huge, gigantic steps, steps towards healing, growth, and a future she was starting to love.

Nina: *Thx.*

Sophie: *How do u feel?*

Nina: *Fine. Good. I needed it to be done and dusted. Bit sad, but fine. Thanks for caring. xxx*

Sophie: *Excellent.*

Nina: *Just at the pub. Speak to you later.*

Sophie: *Will do x*

After spending much longer than they'd thought they would people-watching across the funny junction and watching red London buses pass by over and over again, Nina drained her drink. 'Phew, that was lovely. Thanks for coming. I appreciate it.'

'Don't be silly. Here for you. Ready to head back?'

Nina nodded enthusiastically. 'More than ready, actually.'

Robby hopped off his stool as Nina stifled a yawn. He smiled. 'You look exhausted. It's been a big day already. Tired?'

'I am. I need to get home.'

7

About a week or so later, Nina was standing in the back of the deli in her apron, loading baskets of dirty dishes into the dishwasher. She'd been called in to help in the deli after a particularly busy secret chowder evening the night before when, at the last minute, Alice, the manager, had been called away. The result of Alice's emergency had been no clearing up in the kitchen and a lot of mess. Nina was quite the expert at clearing up mess and still helped out in the deli once a week or when needed. She'd already loaded two dishwasher loads, reset the back room, and sprayed the sides when Birdie hustled in. 'Thank you so much, Neens! I had so much to do at the chemist and then all this. I'm so grateful! Lifesaver.'

'Not a problem. You know me, I love me a bit of organising and clearing up.'

'How are you?' Birdie asked.

'Yep, good,' Nina said, standing up straight, putting her hands on the small of her back, leaning back and stretching her neck.

'Everything okay with you? You seem a bit quiet.'

'Yes. Lots on my mind.'

'Like what?'

'Remember that place I went to look at on the harbour?'

'Old Johnny's place?'

'Yes. Someone is now interested in it, but they've offered a laughable amount of money because of the state of the place. Ella called me to give me the heads up. Now there's someone else in the running I feel like it's made my mind up, and I want to go for it.'

Birdie's face crinkled. 'So, what's the problem?'

Nina made a wincing movement with her lips. 'It just feels like a huge thing. I don't know, I've never really done anything like this before on my own.'

'Did you offer anything?'

'No, not really, though Ella knows my budget. We talked about it, and she said the price was negotiable but not as low as what the other party offered. I wanted to take my time but now this has happened.'

Birdie inhaled, then blew the air out through her teeth. 'Are the other party Lovelies?'

'No, they saw it on the internet. Investors from Manchester, I think she said.'

'Right.'

'Yeah, so I just don't know what to do. I was speaking to my mum about it earlier, and she wasn't much help. I'm meeting Ella over there for a third look. Robby came with me last time, and he reckons to go for my life, but I just don't know...'

'I can come and have a look with you if you like. It might be good to get a different perspective.' Birdie winked. 'I'm pretty good at investment properties as it goes.'

'You're pretty good at everything, aren't you?' Nina fired back with a smile.

Birdie nodded and propped herself up on the counter. The Shipping Forecast came from the direction of her shoulder. 'Well, I've seen a few properties in my time. The key is to look past what is in front of your eyes and think about the potential and what you could make good. Easier said than done a lot of the time.'

Nina sighed, wiping her hands on her apron. 'That's just it. I can see the potential, but it's a big commitment. What if I can't turn it around?' She shook her head. 'What if it's all too much for me, you know? I feel a little bit out of my depth.' She suddenly thought about Andrew and how he'd always handled life things. Now she was doing life things on her own it felt a bit daunting. She wasn't going to mention him and all that, though. No one needed to know how without him around she still found certain things hard.

'You've got a good head on your shoulders, and you've turned around worse. Remember The Summer Hotel? You made that shine. I reckon you'd be fine, to be quite honest, but I get what you mean.'

'True. That wasn't my money, though. It feels different.'

'With this, you'll have Robby's support, so you're not doing it alone,' Birdie reasoned.

Nina nodded, feeling a bit more confident. 'You're right. It's just taking the leap, you know?'

Birdie smiled. 'Take it from someone who's leapt a few times – it's always scary, but sometimes, it's the best thing you'll ever do.'

'Yep. I want to do it on my own and be independent, but that also scares me. Nuts!'

'Why don't we go together? I'll give you my honest opinion, and we can brainstorm ideas. It's always good to have someone else to bounce things off. Someone who's not your partner or your mum, if you get what I mean. A bit more impartial.'

Nina's face brightened. 'That would be great, actually, as long as you don't mind.'

'Mind? Of course not! Not at all. You, me and the Shipping Forecast will go and work out what is what.'

Nina inspected one of the weathered old pieces of cladding by the barn doors of the property by the harbour as Ella stood and chatted with Birdie. The Shipping Forecast came from Birdie's direction. She studied the wide barn doors at the front and looked up at the tall floor-to-ceiling window on the second floor and the wonky-looking chimneys jutting out of the sloping roof. Everything her eyes landed on was weathered and sun-bleached and seemingly battered by the elements. The air was so crisp and full of salt that she could taste it on her lips and the noise from the boats in the harbour carried across the breeze. Ella led them around to the back of the building and opened the back door.

Birdie stepped in, put her hands on her hips, and looked up. 'Right, yes, hmm. They're all the same, these old places. I've been in a few of them in my time.'

Ella chuckled. 'I bet.'

Nina stood beside Birdie, followed her gaze, and looked at the high ceilings and dust motes dancing in the air as her eyes adjusted to the light. As the other times she'd looked at the place, it had a warehouse feel with its high ceilings, huge barn doors, and timber beams. One of the oversized, rusty industrial pendant lamps squeaked as it swayed back and forth in a breeze coming through the back door.

Ella smiled at Birdie. 'What do you think? First impressions?'

Birdie pinched her lips together. 'Good, workable, depends on what's upstairs.'

'You wait. The third floor is interesting.'

All three of them stood for a second and didn't say anything, taking in the expansive ground floor. Ella walked over to the barn doors, leaned down, yanked up a bolt, and scraped the door back a touch. Light and air billowed into the room. 'Imagine the possibilities. With some work, this could be an amazing space. I thought it from the second I first walked in.'

Nina nodded, her mind racing with ideas. 'It's got so much character. I *do* love it.'

Birdie chimed in as she walked over and touched one of the walls. 'Structurally, it seems sound and these beams,' she pointed upwards, 'they add character, and they look like they were reinforced at some point.'

Nina walked around the space, touching the weathered wood. 'There's a fair amount of work to be done, but tell me if I'm barking up the wrong tree. It feels like there is a lot of history in these walls. It's calling out to be given a new life.'

Ella agreed, 'Absolutely.'

Birdie craned her neck up to the industrial pendant lamps. 'These could be a feature. Imagine them restored...'

Ella nodded. 'Yeah, there are loads of things like that.'

Nina chuckled. 'Are we including the kitchen in that?'

They followed Ella, today in flat shoes, up to the second floor and then the third floor. Birdie squeezed in amongst the fishing junk. She shuffled down to the window and let out a low whistle at the view. With her hands on her hips, she gazed out at the harbour with wide eyes. 'Well, would you look at that? It's not every day you get a view like this. Living here never gets old. I'd forgotten what it's like up here and from this side of town.' She swore. 'It's outstanding.'

Ella squeezed up next to Birdie and leaned against the window frame. 'I told you the third floor had something special. You can see the entire harbour from here, and on a clear day, the horizon seems to go on forever. I was up here the other day showing someone else around and just couldn't believe it. You think you've seen it all...'

Nina joined them. 'It's breathtaking. I can already picture the sunsets from here.'

Birdie looked thoughtful for a second. 'This is the jewel in the crown. With windows like these, you'd want to wake up to this. Once there's no junk, that is.'

Ella nodded. 'Imagine waking up to the view every morning.'

Nina's eyes were fixed on the horizon. 'I'm sold.'

Birdie chuckled. 'I think anyone would be. I'm surprised it's not been snapped up already.'

'The work puts people off,' Ella said as she gestured around. 'Think of the space as a blank canvas. What else do you see here?'

Birdie pointed to the exposed beams. 'This ceiling shape could be a feature, and the lovely old dormer windows.' Birdie sighed, 'I might have to buy it myself. I could hide from the world up here, never to be seen again. I'd never have to dispense another drug in my life.'

Ella smiled. 'I have two interested parties. Ha! I love where this is going.'

Nina looked at Birdie. 'It feels right, doesn't it? Like I was meant to find this place and breathe new life into it.'

Birdie gave Nina a knowing smile. 'It does have a way of speaking to you. Places like this, they have a soul. As I said, that view…'

'It's got a lot of scope. Thank goodness they were zoned well.' Ella added.

Nina's mind raced. 'I can see it now.' She walked over to the other end of the room, where light peeked in through a dirt-smudged window. 'I would have to use what is here. There wouldn't be any budget for anything.'

Birdie chuckled. 'Tap your boyfriend up for some help. He's rolling in it. Ditto the O'Connors as a whole.'

Nina's response was instant. 'God no! I want to do this all myself.'

Birdie nodded. 'Joking.' She pointed down to the floor. 'In interior designer-speak, don't they call these reclaimed wood floors these days?'

Nina clapped her hands together. 'Too funny.'

'It ticks loads of boxes if you ask me.' Birdie said.

Nina nodded over and over. 'It's just what I want.'

'I take it that means you want to make a formal offer.' Ella laughed.

Nina nodded. 'Yes, yes, I think I do.'

Birdie chuckled and joked. 'Let's get this party started, people. Nina Lavendar, may I be the first to welcome you as a bona fide property owner in Lovely Bay.'

8

Accompanied by the Shipping Forecast, Nina and Birdie were walking along the harbour discussing the potential of the property. The air was filled with the salty scent of the sea, and seagulls swarmed around not too far in front of them. They were engrossed in conversation about the costs of getting the property spick and span when Nina looked up to see a figure appearing, seemingly out of nowhere, close to where they were walking. As Nina focused, she couldn't place the woman for a second. Then she realised it was the woman, Lindsay, who had spoken to her before when she'd been outside the cottage sweeping and tending her hanging baskets.

Lindsay sort of hovered at the edge of their path, and as they approached, she stepped forward, not fully blocking their way but making sure she was seen. Nina was surprised when Lindsay acknowledged Birdie with a smile.

'Oh, hi, Birdie.' Lindsay's tone was sickly sweet, and unless Nina was imagining it, her eyes were so intense they were scary. All Nina's vibes were screaming at her from the back of her head.

Nina was taken aback by the direct approach and how

Lindsay had completely interrupted them. Birdie, however, didn't miss a beat. Her tone was short, tight, and clipped. 'Lindsay.'

Nina felt *monumentally* awkward. The air could have been cut with a knife. 'Hello again.'

Lindsay jumped on Nina's comment. 'Nice to see you, Nina. How are you?'

'Good, thanks.' Nina gestured back towards the fishing sheds. 'We've just been to look at a property.'

'Right! Amazing! Yes, I heard that you were interested in that.' Lindsay's gaze shifted between Nina and Birdie.

Nina didn't feel comfortable. Birdie's body language wasn't helping. She assumed Lindsay knew that she'd looked at the property because of the way news travelled around Lovely at lightning speed whether you liked it or not.

Lindsay continued and gesticulated to the harbour. 'Nice spot. Lovely Bay is such a small, friendly little place, too.'

Nina was completely thrown by Lindsay and her tone. Her words appeared to be laced with an odd familiarity that didn't sit right with Nina at all. She blinked and put it down to the fact that even after having lived in Lovely Bay for a while, she had a long way to go until she was initiated to the same level as those who referred to themselves as Lovelies.

Birdie stepped slightly in front of Nina, her body language protective. 'It *is* nice here, yes, thanks.' Birdie's voice was cool; her frostiness towards Lindsay completely threw Nina. She'd never heard Birdie sound like it before.

Lindsay's smile faltered for a moment, and then she continued with her overly friendly composure. 'I loved my time here before. It was just so nice, so yeah, I decided to come back for a bit.'

Lindsay's tone was innocent enough, but there was a really strange undercurrent. Unless Nina was hearing things, there was something she didn't know. She kept her mouth shut as she sensed Birdie's tension.

'Is there something you want?' Birdie asked, her voice unfriendly and short.

'Actually, I was wondering...'

Birdie interjected before Lindsay could continue, 'We're actually quite busy today. Got to get on.' Her tone was firm and abrupt.

Lindsay nodded and stepped aside. 'Of course, I'm sure we'll bump into each other again,' she said and turned towards Nina. She locked eyes with Nina in a way that made Nina's skin crawl.

Nina frowned and shook her head as Lindsay walked away. She turned to Birdie with confusion written all over her face. 'What was that about? Do you know her? Who is she?'

Birdie sighed, watching Lindsay's retreating figure. 'Let's just say I did know her, but it's not something I fondly remember. She's bad news. If she's back in town, it's not for any good reason. Hopefully, she's just visiting.'

'What? What does that mean? She's bad news, is she?'

Birdie tutted. 'Look, just steer well clear. Enough said. Hopefully, she won't hang around too long if she's got any sense. No one here likes her, put it that way.'

'Is she one of the people I've heard so much about whose face doesn't fit?'

'That's putting it mildly,' Birdie replied, her tone serious.

Nina wasn't sure what to say. Birdie wasn't in the mood for joking. 'Right. I need to keep out of her way, do I?'

Birdie nodded. 'Yep, take it from me, you most certainly do.'

9

It was a few weeks or so later, Nina watched the wheels on Sophie's pram as she and Sophie strolled in the direction of the harbour. Sophie was filling her in on something that her husband Nick had done to irritate her and they were on their way to walk around the harbour property, which Nina was just about to take possession of. Since the day she'd been to see the property for the third time with Birdie, Nina'd had her formal offer accepted and things had moved fast. It was as if everything had aligned, and it had all been meant to be. Her offer, which was higher than the investors from Manchester but lower than the asking price, had been good, and it had moved at lightning speed from there. Now, it was nearly time for push to come to shove.

Sophie held her face up to a sky patchy with clouds, sunshine, and a hazy mist. 'Gosh, it *is* lovely down here on the coast. I seem to think that daily or even hourly. What took us so long?'

'Don't ask me. I'm the same!'

'Do you miss your London life at all?' Sophie asked.

Nina thought for a second. She didn't really, but sometimes she did feel as if maybe she missed the hustle and bustle, the trains, the red buses, and the option to have a lot of culture at her fingertips. Not that she'd ever utilised any of it anyway, so she wasn't sure what she was actually thinking. 'Yes and no. It's more that I *think* I miss things, and then I think, well, actually, I didn't ever do that anyway. There are so many things I haven't seen in London and now I'm not there, I feel like I want to go almost as a tourist, if you see what I mean.'

'Exactly. I do precisely the same. It's bizarre that I've seen more of London now that I don't live there than I did then.'

Nina nodded and continued with a chuckle. 'Like I imagine myself cycling around and going over Southwark Bridge on a bike with a coffee in my hand. More chance of pigs flying. The fumes were awful, the other cyclists were a nightmare, and people yelled abuse at you if you got too close to them. That happened to me every single time I went out on my bike.'

Sophie cracked up laughing. 'Hilarious. I imagine myself on a summer evening sitting outside that pub we used to go to over near Covent Garden.'

'Thing is, we hardly ever did that because of the tourists.'

'I know.'

'And then I imagine myself sitting at the top of Primrose Hill looking over London and the amazing views. It *is* nice up there.'

'The problem is it was a right faff to get there,' Sophie noted.

'You're not wrong.'

'Ahh, I do miss it, though. Nothing a quick trip to my flat won't solve.'

'How is that?'

'Yeah, no change.'

'I don't get how you can just let it sit there when it could be bringing in an income.'

Sophie certainly didn't get it. She hadn't buried her husband.

'Yeah, I know.' Truth be told, Nina couldn't face packing up the flat, moving Andrew's clothes from the wardrobe, or doing anything with it at all, really. Which was precisely why it had sat there and festered once Nathan, the bloke who had moved in for a bit, had gone back to his own flat. She was lucky it had been paid off with the life insurance. It wasn't as if it was costing her any money, well, not much, but it wasn't *making* her any money either. It was an issue she simply didn't want to face.

'I guess it will happen in time.'

'Yes, it will.'

Sophie bumped the pram wheels up the pavement and widened her eyes at the harbour. 'Ooh, yes, better than the pictures you sent me the other day. Nice.' A few minutes later, they were standing with their heads up, looking at the building's sloping roof. Sophie nodded. 'Yeah, love it. I said it the first time I came with you, but it was chilly that day. It's amazing today.'

'I hope it's better than the pics once I actually get in and get going on it.'

'Too late now.'

Nina gulped. 'Yep.'

'You'll be fine once you get the keys and move in.'

'That won't be for a while. There is a lot of work to do.'

'Slow and steady wins the race, don't they say?'

'I know. I sort of feel the opposite now, though. I'm raring to go. I want to crack on and get going on it.'

'I get it. I would be the same.'

A voice behind them made them both turn around. Robby kissed Nina and then Sophie on the cheek. He peeked into the pram. 'Aww, snug as a bug.'

'Yes and hopefully not going to be waking up for a while.'

Robby gestured to the building and addressed Sophie. 'So, what do you think?'

'Same as before, I love it,' Sophie answered with a beam.

'Ready to get your sleeves rolled up?' Robby joked. 'There's just a bit of work to be done and you did offer.'

Nina nudged Robby's arm. 'She has quite enough on her plate already.'

'I intend to help just so that I can leave my lot and get some peace. In fact, when that top room is up and running, I will be coming for a sleepover. Alone.'

'I thought it was your children who would be coming for a sleepover,' Robby joked.

'No, I am first in line. Mama needs some best friend time.'

Nina side-eyed, 'Since when did you start calling yourself Mama?'

Sophie laughed. 'I'm doing it to wind you up.'

'Good. I can't stand those Insta-huns with their Mama-this, Mama-that while they drink that stuff. What is it? Kombucha or something. Gross.'

'You sound like a right old grump today, Neens.'

'Do I?'

Sophie nodded. 'Yes.'

'I guess that's because sometimes I *am* one when I see all this rubbish on social media these days.'

'Hmm.' Sophie waved her hand around at the harbour and then back at the property. 'Speaking of social media. This is going to be great for your reels. You can do so many amazing before and afters. They already love your decluttering ones.'

'I know. I thought the same. I'm going to upload them daily and show the real hard work involved in getting this place shipshape.'

'Sounds like good viewing. I'll be watching with bated breath.'

'Me too.' Robby laughed. 'I'll also be watching... from my phone screen, not there doing it.'

Sophie shot back. 'Funny that, I thought you'd already been

earmarked for a lot of work. In fact, you're labelled as free labour on the spreadsheet.'

'Really. I think I'm busy for the next month,' Robby joked. 'Yes, that's right, I have loads of stuff on. I think I'm away on some overseas jobs too.'

Sophie laughed and nodded. 'You and me both.'

10

Nina, in jeans, a white shirt, and tennis shoes, stood next to Ella, the estate agent who was all dressed up in a fancy trouser suit and sky-high heels. Robby was to Nina's left, and Ella had a hand-tied bouquet of flowers in her hand. All three of them were standing with the water behind them and the harbour property in front of them.

Ella handed over the flowers to Nina. 'Congratulations. I hope you're going to love it!'

'Ooh, thank you so much!' Nina replied with a beam. 'Blimey, is this how you do property purchasing in Lovely Bay? You get flowers and the fancy treatment. Amazing. I'll have to do it again.'

'We do everything better in Lovely Bay.' Ella chuckled. 'You should have realised that by now. We simply don't do things by halves. It's how we roll.'

'Yeah, true. I should have known.' Nina agreed.

'So, here we are,' Robby said. 'A new chapter begins.'

Ella smiled and looked up at the building. 'Ready to get stuck in, our Robby?'

Robby blinked and shook his head. 'I don't think I have a lot of choice in the matter. I'm marked down for all sorts.'

Nina smiled. 'You can do whatever you like.'

Robby put his arm around her. 'Tell me what to do, and I'll make it happen.'

Nina zoomed to the moon.

'Aww, I need a Robby in my life,' Ella joked. 'Rightio, I'll love you and leave you. Enjoy and congrats, Nina. I'll remember this one. Nice working with you.'

'Thank you. I don't know about enjoy! It seems like a lot to take on now.'

'Ahh, you'll love it. I'll be back to check up on your progress.'

Nina followed Robby down the side of the building to the small yard behind, put her arm over the gate, slid back the bolt, and pressed down on the latch. The gate opened with a creak, they walked over the somewhat depressing yard with its funny little mossy, slippery steps and she fiddled with the keys to open the back door.

'Will I be carrying you over the threshold?'

In an instant, Nina was by the door of her flat. Her mind raced. Andrew had done exactly that when they'd bought it. Instead of making Nina sad, however, she smiled fondly. She laughed and stepped in. 'I think I can manage. I don't need carrying, plus I don't think you'd be able to pick me up.'

Robby made a whooshing sound as he followed Nina in, sucked in air through his lips, and looked around. 'Sheesh.'

Nina zoomed around. 'What? Are you thinking what I'm thinking?'

'I don't know. What are you thinking?'

'That we have a lot of work on our hands. Oh dear, it suddenly looks dreadful.'

Robby nudged an old fishing net with his boot and dust flew up into the air. His straps jangled. 'You're not wrong there.'

Nina half spoke to herself, half to Robby. 'I must not get

buyers' regret. I must remember at all costs to look at the bones of the place. I must remain calm and in control.'

'Formulate the plan, stick to the plan, execute the plan.'

'I am beginning to think the plan was made in cloud cuckoo land.'

Robby squeezed Nina's elbow. 'Worst case scenario is you rent it out, remember? Keep that front and centre.'

Nina nodded as if trying to convince herself. 'Yes, yes, that's right. Or have it as a hot desk place for digital nomads and use the upstairs for storage for the business. I need to keep that in mind.'

Robby walked over to the far side and ran his hands over the barn doors. 'Or we'll run off into the sunset together and leave all this to itself. That is another plan of attack. Or you move in with me. There are lots of options as we discussed before you signed on the dotted line.'

Nina swallowed as she felt her heart sink. 'Right now, that's looking like quite the attractive option. I might be moving in with you. What in the world have I let myself in for?'

11

Both Nina and Nancy were wearing white disposable hooded overalls. Sophie was kitted out in a similar get-up; only hers was bright orange and even less attractive. Nancy and Nina had spent the morning cleaning the ground floor of Nina's new abode whilst Sophie, with the help of Robby, had made multiple trips up and down the two sets of stairs, emptying the attic room.

Nina yanked the straps from the backpack vacuum off her shoulders and leant the vacuum up against the wall. Nancy followed suit. Nina rolled her shoulders around, winced, and rubbed the back of her neck. She walked over to her phone, where it had been propped up recording a time-lapse of their progress for her social reels. She pressed the red button to stop the recording and put her phone in the pocket of the suit. 'You see, in my mind's eye, it didn't look like this when I first looked around. I must have been hallucinating or drunk. One of the two. There's so much dust and dirt. What was I thinking? It's bad.'

Nancy grimaced and pulled the hood down on her disposable suit. 'What did you envision? I'm having trouble seeing it, too, at this moment in time. Blimey, this is hard work and I thought I was fit.'

Nina widened her eyes. 'I saw myself sitting at a lovely desk doing my quotes and talking to customers on the phone with the sun shining and the view of the harbour at the end of my nose.' Nina looked out at the pouring rain, grey, angry sea, and even greyer sky. 'This isn't living up to my expectations in any shape or form. Thank goodness I now know that Lovely has four seasons in a day. It's grim today. Flipping weather!'

Nancy harrumphed. 'Hmm. I'm having the most trouble with the sunshine part of that scenario. It feels like it's been raining for weeks.'

'It *has* been.'

'True. Which has made this job a million times harder. Blooming rain, rain, rain for days!'

Nina nodded. 'I just didn't realise how big the place was. It's not exactly a cottage and so much bigger without the junk. I should have remembered that from my experience with The Summer Hotel. Everything takes so long.'

Nancy walked over to the window, wiped her sleeve across the glass, and peered outside. 'Well, the good thing about Lovely weather is that it's predictably unpredictable,' she joked. 'We'll have sunshine by the end of the day with any luck.'

Nina scanned the room. 'Hopefully. A bit of sunshine will brighten things up.'

Nancy looked back. 'Today, I think, has broken the back of it, though.'

'Yep. I can see the light. I keep telling myself once it's all done, this place will be incredible. It's just getting there; that's the mountain to climb. I should know that in my line of work. It just feels so different when it's your own and you've dumped your savings into it.'

'Oh yes. I felt the same when I moved into the cottage. I was literally asking myself what I had done. You'll get there.'

'I hear you.'

Nancy shook her head. 'But the high ceilings, these old beams, and the location. There's character here that you just don't find in new builds. It's the same as the cottages. Gosh, I looked at so many places back in the day, and it was that old one that took my fancy.'

Nina pushed off from the wall. 'Exactly. And that's what drew me to this in the first place. The history and, of course, location, location, location. It's just hidden under years of neglect and dust at the moment. Can't see the wood for the trees! Oh, well...'

Nancy gestured to the clear canister on the back of the vacuum. 'A lot of the dust is now in there. How many of those have we emptied this morning? I've never seen dust like it. It must be because it's right on the harbour.'

The conversation was interrupted as Sophie and Robby entered the room, their arms laden with boxes. Sophie, in bright orange overalls, looked slightly more upbeat than Nina. 'You should see the attic now. It's almost empty. Found a few old vintage glass floats that might be of interest.'

'Could be a nice touch to the decor, a nod to the building's past,' Robby stated.

Nancy chuckled. 'It's like we're in one of those home renovation shows. You're doing something most people only dream about, Neens.'

Nina nodded. 'There is that. The last reel I did had thousands of views. People find it relaxing watching other people work apparently. Who would have known? YouTube has an army of people watching other people clearing up.'

Sophie set down a box and leaned against it, wiping her brow. 'From abandoned fishing hut to stunning coastal home – I can see the headlines already.'

Nina sighed. 'I have so many ideas. Just not much time, energy, or money.'

Robby interjected. 'It won't be long. The structural work is solid, and the foundations are there. We knew that from the word go.'

Sophie agreed. 'Just need to keep plugging away at it. Little by little, it'll come together.'

'Yeah, one step at a time. Today, we finish cleaning. Tomorrow, we start planning the rest of my life,' Nina joked.

Nancy started to pull off her suit. 'I'm going to have to call it a day.'

'Thanks so much for helping, especially with what you've got on this evening.'

Robby frowned. 'Where are you off to? Anywhere nice?'

Nancy's face crumpled. 'Nowhere nice unfortunately, well, not really, sort of. My friend with cancer I was telling you about who used to work at the station. They've decided to get married, in case, well, you know...'

Robby nodded. 'Right, yeah, sorry. Oh, well, I hope that goes as well as it can do.'

'I never thought I would be saying that.' Nancy shook her head, 'Yeah, so I'm not sure if it's going to be sad, happy, or what. I guess a bit of both.'

'You just don't know what's around the corner,' Nina said. 'I know from experience.'

Sophie shook her head and sighed. 'Life sure is full of surprises. That's for sure.'

'That's why they wanted to get married now because everything is up in the air.'

Nina knew that only too well. In her case, life's surprises hadn't always been nice ones. 'Indeed. What lies ahead is anyone's guess.'

Robby picked up a huge black bin liner full of rubbish. A funny look crossed his face. 'Hmm. It absolutely is.'

12

It was a couple of weeks or so later. Nina had gone from going hell for leather to get the new place cleared out and clean to taking things a bit more slowly. Now the guts of the job had been done, she was left with a shell that still needed a lot of effort to make good but it was a decent enough palette to work from.

Whilst working every day for her small organising business, doing the odd shift in the deli, and packing up the cottage, she hadn't had much time for much at all. She was sitting in the kitchen of the rental cottage with the back door open, surrounded by boxes, when she heard someone shout from the end of the garden. 'Come in. The gate's open,' she called out the back door.

A minute later, Nancy was standing in the kitchen. She looked around at the cardboard boxes. 'How are you getting on?'

'Really well.'

'Gosh, it's all go with you right now, isn't it? You haven't stopped.'

'I know.'

'What are you doing tomorrow?'

Nina frowned. 'You already asked me that yesterday.'

'Oh, did I? Sorry. Brain's not in gear. Just asking.'

Nina squinted. 'What are you up to?'

'Nothing. No, no, nothing at all. I was just wondering if you had a day off or not. You said that your job was cancelled and you were going to leave the painting until next week.'

Nina nodded. 'Yes, but I think I might just crack on. No time like the present. I have loads to do so I might change my mind on the painting.' She waved around at the room. 'I've got all this to get sorted too.'

'Right. So you're still good for Lighthouse Drinks, are you?'

Nina wasn't sure she was. She'd had a busy week, Robby was away on a job and not sure how long it would take him to get back, and she half-fancied simply sitting at home with her feet up, eating fodder and doing absolutely sweet nothing. Lovely Drinks was an important local event, though, and in the time she'd been in Lovely Bay, she had committed to attending, which had cemented her into the infrastructure of the community. 'Ahh, look, if you don't mind, I'm going to play it by ear.'

Nancy seemed to flap a little bit. 'Right, umm. Err, okay.'

'You don't mind, do you?'

Nancy seemed agitated. 'I, err, actually, I really need some help with the set-up this time.'

'Oh,' Nina frowned, 'I thought you said everything was sorted when I asked you before.'

'Did I?' Nancy flapped her hands.

'Yes, remember? You said you and Birdie had been working on getting everything sorted up in the lighthouse and you were good to go.'

'Oh, yes, yes, no, I, umm, I didn't mean that bit.' Nancy scrambled for words, 'I meant the drinks, yes. They are what I need help with.'

'Right, you need some help with the drinks set-up, do you? Okay.'

'I do, yep, definitely.' Nancy nodded as if not only trying to convince Nina but herself, too.

Nina narrowed her eyes. 'I thought you said Birdie was helping and the drinks had already arrived.'

'She was. She's not well.'

'She was fine when I saw her earlier.'

'It came on quickly.'

'Okay, yes, then I can help.'

Nancy clapped her hands, 'Excellent!'

'Good. So what do you want me to do specifically?'

Nancy coughed, and then she cleared her throat. She flapped her hands again. 'Oh, you know this and that with getting the drinks ready.'

'This and that? Anything in particular?'

'Umm.'

'Will the lighthouse be open?'

'No! No, no, no. That won't be open. Not at all.'

'I assumed that's why it's a busy one this time because everyone loves going up there.'

'Just general help. Yes, that's it *general* help.' Nancy clarified.

Nina repeated Nancy's words with a lilted question at the end. 'General help?'

'Yup. Exactly.'

'So what time will you need me there for this *general* help?' Nina put her fingers in the air to mimic quotation marks around the word general.

'Like I don't know, six?'

Nina wrinkled her nose. 'Won't everything have been done by then?'

'Not this time, no.'

Nina regarded Nancy with a tilt of her head. 'Six seems a bit late for setup, doesn't it? Usually, these things are done in the afternoon. You always say early worm and all that.'

Nancy fidgeted with the hem of her shirt. 'Well, yes, usually. But this time, it's different. Some last-minute changes, you know how it is.'

Nina raised an eyebrow. 'Last-minute changes? That's unlike you. You're always so organised where the Drinks are concerned.'

Nancy took a deep breath. 'It's just been... hectic. With Birdie out of the picture suddenly, things got a bit scrambled.'

Nina crossed her arms, unconvinced. 'But still, what exactly needs doing at six? The event starts at seven-thirty, doesn't it?'

Nancy nodded, her eyes darting around the room. 'Yes, yes, it does. It's just some final touches I need doing. You know, making sure everything looks perfect.'

'You're being vague. What's going on? You're not usually like this about it.'

Nancy sighed. 'Okay, I'll tell you some of it. It's just that there's this surprise element to the evening. I wanted to keep it under wraps, but it's causing more stress than I anticipated.'

'A surprise? For the event? Who for?'

'Yes. It's something special, but I can't really talk about it. I just need an extra pair of hands...' Nancy sounded *really* agitated.

'Okay, happy to help. Ooh, a surprise for someone. I can't wait to see who.'

Nancy swore. 'I promised I wouldn't tell anyone. It's not a surprise for someone as such but a community surprise. Yes, that's it. Sorry, it needs to stay a secret from everyone. Including you, I'm afraid.'

Nina nodded slowly. 'Not a problem. I'll keep schtum. A community surprise, eh?'

'Yes, yes, that's it. It's going to be a great evening.'

'I'm sure. Now is there anything else you can share about this 'general help' I'll be providing?' Nina chuckled.

Nancy hesitated for a moment, and then she was definitely cagey. 'Nope, not really. Just the usual.'

Nina laughed. 'Sounds all *very* mysterious. But alright, I'm in. I'll see you there at six.'

As Nancy left the kitchen, Nina turned her attention back to the boxes around her, shrugged, and went back to her packing. To be frank, she had so much going on she wasn't really interested in the surprise, whoever it involved anyway. Probably just another one of the weird little Lovely traditions she'd become used to since she'd moved in permanently. She was just looking forward to a few hours off and a couple of nice drinks and a chat. That was more than good enough for her.

13

It was the next day and the day of the drinks at the lighthouse. Nina'd had more than a day of it. She'd had a problem with one of her clients, she'd been to paint the second-floor bathroom at the harbour property, and she'd packed up more things from the kitchen cupboards in the rental cottage. She'd showered and put on a nice top with black jeans and had just finished blow-drying her hair when her phone pinged and then pinged again a few times. Three messages from three different people, all at the same time.

Robby: *Just checking, you're good for later.*
Nina: *Yep, see you there. Where are you?*
Robby: *Currently sitting in traffic*
Nina: *Oh dear.*
Robby: *I might be late.*
Nina: *Not a problem. I'm getting there early to help.*
Nancy: *Change of plan. Don't need you until 7.15 now.*
Sophie: *Have a nice time tonight.*

Nina frowned. Weird, she'd not told Sophie she was going to the lighthouse for drinks, she didn't think.

Nina: *Thx. Will do. Are you OK, Soph???*

Sophie: *Fab, yes, thanks.*
Nina tapped on Nancy's message.
Nina: *I thought you needed me to help????*
Nancy: *All good now. Don't need you until later. Just make sure you're not late.*
Nina: *So u do need me or u don't need me?*
Nancy: *I do need you, but not until then...*
Nina: *OK. See u soon then. x*
Nancy: *Yep, make sure you're on time.*

Nina frowned. Nancy was acting quite strange about the drinks. She'd been antsy about it, borderline hyper the day before, and now she'd changed her mind. She put it down to the surprise. Not sure what was going on, and now, with time to kill, she went downstairs and made a cup of milky coffee. She started to pack another moving box and then sat drinking her coffee whilst she watched a YouTube video on a makeover on a farmer's shed in Oklahoma.

She was doing a quick last wee before strolling to the lighthouse. As she got up and had just flushed the chain, her phone slipped out of her hand and dropped straight down the toilet into the pan. For a second, she just stood and stared at it, unsure what to do. After a moment of shock, she quickly reached into the toilet, her face twisting in disgust. At least the water was clean and she hadn't dropped the phone a few seconds before. She grabbed her phone, shaking off the water, wrapped it in a towel, doused it copiously with disinfectant wipes and hoped it wasn't completely ruined. Shaking her head and with no time to dwell on it, she washed her hands a few times, walked back downstairs, grabbed her bag, put her phone wrapped in a tea towel in her bag and headed out the door.

She took big gulps of the fresh, cool evening air as she strolled down over the green in the direction of the lighthouse. As she walked along, wondering whether or not her phone was going to work again, she thought about the odd vibes she'd felt from Nancy. Deducing it must be something to do with the lighthouse funding and dismissing it, she put it out of her mind.

As she approached, the lighthouse took her breath away as it stood out against the twilight sky. Her mind flew back to the first night she'd been to the lighthouse when she'd not been in Lovely Bay very long. She'd ended up at the top, looking out over the fantastic view and had then kissed Robby. She smiled as she thought how far she'd come since that night. She remembered how amazing he'd made her feel, how she'd begun to feel alive again, how her heart had started to heal.

As she got to the lighthouse building, she assumed the event was going to be in the old hall and made her way there. Seeing no signs of life at all and going back around the other way, she made for the other hall just under the lighthouse itself. As she made for the hall, she poked her head around the door at the bottom of the lighthouse. Nancy and Birdie had been busy. Fairy lights were strung around the entrance lobby, music played in the background, and she could see little flickering lanterns on every step going all the way to the top. Someone was clearly being treated to a nice time. The surprise must be enormous.

As Nina approached the hall, she spotted Nancy, who appeared to be darting around, attending to last-minute details. Nancy caught sight of Nina and rushed over, her earlier agitation seemingly replaced with relief. 'Oh, Nina, you're here! Thank goodness. Fantastic. Just in time.'

'Just in time for the surprise. Exciting!'

Nancy stopped dead in her tracks. 'What surprise? What do you know about the surprise?'

'Errm, nothing. You wouldn't tell me anything. Remember?'

'When?'

'Yesterday. Are you okay? You seem all out of sorts.'

'I'm absolutely fine! Right, come on then, let's get you a drink. Come on, hurry up!'

'You don't need any help now?'

Nancy nearly growled in her response. 'No!'

Nina didn't say anything, frowned, and walked into the hall. The usual suspects stood around drinking. Clive and Colin were both standing together with drinks in their hands. Nina walked over, stood next to them and said hello. Someone put a glass of bubbles in her hand, and she chatted.

'Bonsoir,' Clive said with a beam. 'You're looking well.'

'Looking good, Nina! What a good night for it,' Colin bellowed.

'Good for what?'

Colin gestured with his drink. 'Oh, you know, the Lovely Drinks.'

Nina lowered her voice. 'What's the surprise this evening? Do you have any idea? Nancy is beside herself. She wouldn't let on.'

Clive frowned. 'No idea what you're talking about. Not heard anything myself.'

'Yes, I think it's to do with the funding or someone's birthday or something.' Nina frowned. Everyone seemed to be in the dark about the surprise, or they were all very good at pretending. She sipped her drink, scanning the room for any hints of what might be planned, but apart from the extra decoration in the lighthouse itself, nothing seemed any different from usual.

Her phone pinged from inside the tea towel in her bag. She let out a sigh of relief that it was still working.

Robby: *Running late. I'll be there when I can.*

Nina: *No worries. x*

Just as she was putting her phone back in her bag, Nancy came up to her, still antsy. 'How are you?'

'Good. Is everything okay with you? Did you get everything sorted in the end?'

'Yes, mostly.'

'When's the surprise?'

'Oh, no, not until later. I actually *do* need a hand now.'

Nina frowned. 'Oh, right, yep, what with? I thought you just said everything was done?'

'Just up at the lighthouse there. Birdie needs a hand with, err, something.'

Nina gave her drink to Clive. 'Rightio, lead the way.'

When they got to the bottom of the staircase, Nancy suddenly turned around. 'Oh, I forgot my phone! Ahh, I'll just pop and get it. You go up.'

'No, no. I'll wait.'

'Go up!' Nancy screeched.

Nina nodded and started to climb the spiral staircase, the flickering lights casting shadows on the walls. Everything seemed strangely quiet, and she wondered where Birdie was. Stopping for a second, she leant over the staircase, her heart pounding from the climb, to see if she could see Nancy. With Nancy not in sight, she continued making her way to the top.

As she reached the top, the doorway into the lighthouse room itself framed a scene that took her breath away. Whoever was going to be surprised was going to absolutely love it. The entire space was twinkling with lanterns and fairy lights. Through the glass, the sea stretched out beyond the windows, and the light painted silver streaks across the water. Nina paused by the door for a second and nodded, taking it all in. Nancy and Birdie had done a very good job. Wondering what else could possibly need doing, she took a few steps in and frowned. Robby was standing on the far side of the room.

'Umm, what are you doing here?' Nina looked back towards the doorway and jerked her thumb downwards. 'Did she collar you into helping on your way in? I think she's losing the plot over this. You must have only just arrived. Hang on. You said you were going to be late.'

Robby had a strange look on his face; his hands were behind his back, and he didn't smile. 'No, I mean yes.'

Nina narrowed her eyes. 'Whose birthday is it? She said it was a community surprise, but that must have been a red herring.'

'What?'

'This must have been decorated for a surprise birthday or anniversary or something.' Nina looked around, stepping nearer to the windows. 'It really is incredible. They should rent this out for occasions if you ask me. It would be a good way to get in some extra cash for the building fund. Do you reckon? They're always harping on about how it needs funding.'

Robby took a step towards her. 'It's not anyone's birthday.'

'Ahh, right. What is it then? An anniversary or something special?'

'It is something special, yes, or should I say it's for *someone* special. You are special, Neens.'

Nina side-eyed. 'Thanks. You're being weird. What's going on? What's all this for?'

Robby took a deep breath. 'Nina, from the moment you arrived in Lovely Bay, I loved you.' He paused, reaching into his pocket.

'What in the world?' Nina's hand flew to her mouth. She gasped as the realisation of what Robby was doing dawned on her.

'You're my best friend. I can't imagine my life without you in it.' He held out a small, open box. A ring sparkled under the lights. 'Will you marry me, Neens?'

Nina stared at the ring for what felt like a decade. She shook her head over and over again. She couldn't believe it. She'd been well and truly surprised. So much so, in fact, that she couldn't quite compute it all. Married? Did she actually want to get married? She wasn't sure. She was well and truly on the spot. Tears welled up in her eyes. For a second, she was totally and utterly overwhelmed and rendered speechless. Suddenly, all she could see was Andrew. She put her hand out to the window ledge to steady herself. She placed her left hand on her chest, sucked air in through pursed lips and closed her eyes.

'Neens?'

Again, at first, she didn't say anything. Then she heard her voice come out in a whisper. 'Yes.'

With that, a cheer erupted from her left. She turned to see Nancy and a few others who had sneaked up the staircase to witness the proposal. Nina, still in a daze, looked down to see Nancy leading a small group into the lighthouse room as Robby hugged and kissed her fiercely.

'Congratulations!' Nancy squealed. 'I am *so* happy for you.'

'Thank you. I, umm, I can't quite believe it.' Nina laughed.

'We got you good, didn't we? You had no idea! None at all!' Nancy exclaimed, hugging her tightly. 'I have been a nervous wreck!'

Nina felt so emotional she wasn't sure whether to laugh or cry. She could barely speak. 'You certainly did. I had no idea. None! I thought it was a bit much for someone's birthday. Has everyone been in on it?' She turned to Robby as she spoke, addressing him too.

Robby looked a lot of things but mostly relieved. 'I wanted it to be a surprise. A moment you'd never forget.'

'Mission accomplished,' Nina managed to say. She was struggling to believe what had just happened was real.

Clive raised a glass. 'Congratulations! To Robby and Nina.'

'Cheers to that!' Colin added. 'Congrats!'

Birdie hugged Nina. 'I nearly had a heart attack getting all this ready. Thank goodness it's over! So happy for you. Congratulations.'

Nina laughed. 'I did wonder what was going on.' She was totally overwhelmed and found herself repeatedly glancing at Robby.

Birdie continued. 'We wanted to make sure it was perfect. We couldn't be happier for you both and especially for our Robby.'

'Thank you.'

'How does it feel to be getting married?'

Nina's smile was radiant. 'It feels perfect. Like everything has finally fallen back into place.'

14

Nina sat in The Drunken Sailor and watched as Nancy stood at the bar with Sophie. She fiddled with the diamond on her left hand so that it caught the light overhead. It twinkled and sparkled back at her. She shook her head for what felt like the millionth time about Robby's proposal that had taken her completely by surprise. Not only had the proposal itself surprised her, but her response had been a shock, too.

She'd not even thought about getting married; not even a sniff of it had crossed her mind. It hadn't been on her radar in the slightest. In fact, before Robby's proposal, it was as if marriage was a thing for the other Nina; the one before she'd moved to Lovely Bay. She always thought about it in the past tense as something that she'd done with someone else, which, to be fair, was true. She just assumed that she wouldn't be doing it again. Ever. As if it was all a foregone conclusion. Now, not only had she said yes to doing it again, but deep down inside, she was over the moon about it. Someone else was, too; Sophie could barely contain herself. When Nina had phoned Sophie to tell her the news, even though Sophie had known precisely what was going on, she'd squealed and whooped with joy.

Nina smiled as Sophie and Nancy made their way back from the bar. Sophie plonked a gin and tonic on the table in front of Nina and sat down. 'So, here we are! I cannot tell you how excited I am by the news. I can't wait to start the planning. Bring it right on, is what I say. Hooray and then some. This is the best news ever!'

Nina nodded her head and widened her eyes. 'Same. Sort of.'

'Sort of?'

'The planning bit isn't filling me with joy.'

Nancy sat down. 'It's such good news.' She put her drink down and another one on a mat beside it.

'Just think, if I hadn't seen that post on Facebook.' Sophie mused. 'You never would have even known about Lovely Bay, let alone moved here.'

'Good point. You are the one who started it all, Soph.' Nina noted.

'In fact, you have me to thank for all of this.'

Nancy chortled. 'Not quite.'

'I did tell you many, many, *many* times that you needed a change of scenery and look what happened.' Sophie chuckled. 'I was right all along. You owe me big, Neens. Huge. Massive.'

Nina also chuckled. 'It's always been that way in our relationship. You're right and I'm wrong.'

'In this case, I was definitely right. I am so right that you now have a sparkly rock to show for it.'

'You so were.' Nina agreed.

'How many years was I telling you for? Can you remember or have you conveniently forgotten? It was like I was banging my head against a brick wall.'

Nina was never going to forget how grim Sophie's Friday night calls, complete with the Pity Smile were. There were many years of long calls behind her that she'd very much like to draw a line under and put in her past. At least these days, the phone calls were long gone. 'At least five.'

'There you go. Look what happened when you took my advice. Actually, I'm a life guru. I should take it up as a job.'

Birdie came bustling in the door and, together with the Shipping Forecast from her shoulder, rushed over to the table and sat down. 'Evening everyone. Sorry, I'm a bit late.' She grabbed Nina's left hand and studied the diamond. 'Ooh, again big congrats. It's gorgeous. Oh, yes. Now I do like that. Hmm. Perfect.'

'Thanks. I love it.' Nina said as Birdie sat in front of the drink Nancy had put down before.

Birdie lifted the drink up and toasted, 'To wedding bells in Lovely Bay.'

Everyone toasted, and Sophie then leant forward. 'So, actually, have you decided anything? Like when, where, and how? Will it be in Lovely Bay, or I don't know, at your Mum's or near Robby's family?'

Nina shook her head and turned her lips upside down, 'Not really thought about it yet. It was all such a surprise.'

Sophie's eyes sparkled. 'Well, you said on the phone you didn't want a long engagement, right? So, we should start organising! Everything gets so booked up. Lovely Bay has some beautiful spots for a wedding. I think it would be nice right here, but I'm not the one in charge.'

Nina nodded; the reality of planning a wedding was starting to sink in. 'Yes, I did say that. I just want it to be simple, you know?' She felt funny about too much fuss. In a weird way, she thought it was because of Andrew, almost as if she didn't want to do the traditional rigmarole again. But then, on the other hand, she wanted to make a massive deal about it because it was just that to her: a huge, gigantic deal. Her feelings and emotions were totally confusing. 'Quick and not too fussy are my initial thoughts.'

Nancy leaned in. 'Simple but beautiful. The best way. Lovely Bay is always magical.'

Birdie chimed in. 'What about the reception? The Drunken Sailor here could host a cosy gathering. It's got that homey feel, and the food is great.'

Sophie looked around and nodded. 'Yep. It could work for a local feel...'

The pub certainly didn't really grab Nina. She needed to think about it for a bit. 'Maybe. Or I think just a party or something?'

'Did Robby have any thoughts? What did his family say?'

'His mum was beside herself with it,' Nina stated. 'I think she'd given up on him ever settling down with anyone.' She rolled her eyes. 'Now she's got me to contend with.'

Sophie patted Nina's hand. 'How lucky she is.'

'I don't know about that.'

Sophie sighed. 'It's going to be so beautiful. Nina walking down the aisle, celebrating, and having a party. I'm getting teary just thinking about it!'

Nina laughed. 'It feels unreal. I can't believe we're even sitting here discussing it, if I'm honest.'

Nancy sighed. 'You knew nothing either. It all started because of my friend with cancer and their wedding.'

'Yes, he said that was the reason he started thinking about it.' Nina replied with a nod.

'He had a right bee in his bonnet.' Birdie added.

Nancy raised her glass again. 'To Nina and Robby's wedding.'

They clinked glasses and Nina felt a surge of gratitude for the women around her at the table and for the place that had become her home. So much had happened to her in such a short time that part of it didn't feel real. She knew one thing that was going to happen; she was never going to look back.

15

Nina kissed Robby on the cheek, stood on the pavement as he got in his work van, and waved as he drove away. She turned around, looked at The Summer Hotel, and shook her head at the For Sale sign swaying back and forth in the wind. The Summer Hotel still hadn't sold. To be quite honest, Nina was amazed someone hadn't snapped it up. Yes, it was a lot to take on. Yes, it had a fair amount of heritage red tape around it. And yes, it was, to all intents and purposes, a money pit. However, in her opinion, it was also oozing something money couldn't really buy. She'd had quite a few conversations with Ella about it, and overall, the reason Ella believed no one had bought it was because no one had fallen in love with it enough. Plus, no one had been prepared to take a punt on whether or not, in the long run, it would actually be able to make money as a business.

Nina knew not a lot about the business of running a hotel, but she was sure it would be a success. Not that she was going to be taking it on anytime soon. She was still looking after it for Jill, who was still gallivanting around the globe on a jet plane, and she was invested in what happened to it.

Pushing open the gate, she smiled when she remembered kneeling on the ground and yanking out dead plants and weeds for all she was worth. She recalled jumping back in fright at a nest of spiders and wondering how crawling around the garden of an old hotel had caused her to discover muscles she'd never actually known she owned. Now, via both her effort and her contracting work out to various people, the place was very different from when she'd arrived with her suitcase trailing behind her. If buildings could show emotion, it felt as if The Summer Hotel was now smiling a little bit at the same time as sighing as it stood patiently waiting to be loved.

She walked around the left-hand side of the building, passed the door to the kitchen garden, peered in the scullery as she walked past, and started to make her way through the garden. Loads of little things looked back at her, reminding her of the first few weeks she'd spent in Lovely Bay; a beautiful old weather vane, a bird table choking in ivy, a pretty bench with a slightly wonky leg.

She inhaled and held her head up to the sky for a minute and then stood right in the middle of the lawn and looked around. She loved the feel of it all; the house looking down from the right, the river down at the end, the sea in the distance, the buildings of Lovely poking up into the sky. Such a shame that no one else had felt the same way as she had and was interested in calling The Summer Hotel home.

As she checked a few things, deadheaded some flowers, and monitored how bad a leaking tap was down the side, she thought about getting married. Now Robby had proposed, even though it was completely out of the blue, she couldn't really wait. The problem was *where* it was going to take place. At least *he* was easy, but *she* wasn't. Not at all. In fact, she was adamant that it had to not only be right but perfect in every way. She couldn't explain why, but it was something to do with Andrew. If she was going to be getting married again, if it was that special, that important, and that right for her, it had to tick all the boxes and do all the things. The thing was, she wasn't really sure what that entailed exactly.

Nina wasn't tickled by any of what she felt were normal wedding-y things. Did she want a big white dress? Possibly or maybe not. Did she want to walk down an aisle? Not that bothered. Been there done that, hadn't ended quite as she'd thought. Did she want a church and an organ? Neutral. A formal reception and a top table? Almost definitely not. Was it a spiritual thing for her? Not really. Did she want fancy cars and buttonholes? That would be a no.

She'd thought a lot about alternatives. A trip to the Caribbean to get married on a beach. An outdoor wedding and glamping had come up on a wedding site, and she'd found herself watching YouTube videos about weddings on a cruise. A fancy dress wedding in a castle in Scotland. None of them had grabbed her. Not even anywhere near close. In fact, every time she'd opened a wedding site, she found herself going a bit cold. It all seemed so fake, so *bothered* and cheesy. Or was she just no longer in her twenties and not buying into the fairy tale anymore? Or maybe she was just bitter and twisted. Maybe years of grief had done that to her.

Nina muttered to herself as she walked down towards the river. Just as she was pulling open the gate, and letting her eyes run over the shells on the river beach, she heard a rustling. June, the neighbour and Robby's aunt called over, 'Hello. How are you?'

'Good. You?'

'Very well. What are you up to?'

'I just came in to check on everything and see how the garden was. There's a tap that needs fixing.'

June looked back towards The Summer Hotel. 'Looking good, is it not? I'd buy it. I'd have a little empire down here then.' June laughed at her own joke.

'It is. I was just thinking that myself.'

June pointed over towards the river bank. 'Won't be long until the flowers are out down that way. I love it when they're out and the days are long.'

Nina nodded. 'I thought they might be. I remember last year. It was breathtaking out here, in the evenings especially. I love it down here with all the wildflowers and seashells.'

June looked upwards to where the sun peeked through clouds. 'Make the most of it. It's going to rain shortly.'

Nina glanced up at the sky, noting the darkening clouds on the horizon. 'Yup, looks like we might get quite the downpour. Hopefully, it'll hold off a bit longer until I'm gone.'

June nodded, squinting up at the sky. 'Yes, it's been threatening all morning. The garden's certainly not thirsty, though, what with all the rain we've had. It feels like it's been raining cats and dogs for weeks.'

Nina agreed as she looked back towards the garden. 'Everything's so lush and green, but we could do with a few days of sunshine.'

'It's always like this at this time of year. We seem to get these sudden showers from nowhere, or so it seems. I think they come in from off the coast. It makes everything so fresh, I suppose.'

'True. There's something refreshing about a big old dollop of rain. Cleans everything up and makes the colours pop.'

June agreed. 'The smell. There's nothing quite like the smell of rain on the soil. Brings out all the scents of the garden.'

'I love that too. It does make you appreciate nature a bit more when everything is lush.'

'Yes, indeed. And it's good for the soul, too. A reminder that everything renews. I wish I could say the same for me,' June joked.

'Too funny.'

June gestured to the hotel garden. 'Your efforts with the

garden have really paid off. It's looking beautiful. Remember how bad it was before you got to work?'

'Thank you. I'm happy with how it's come around, especially now that the gardener comes. Keeping on top of it is the answer.'

June smiled. 'It just goes to show what a bit of care and attention can do.'

Nina laughed. 'I'll have to remember that.'

June gestured to the river and the garden. 'There's always something nice to look at down here. Then there are all the flowers and shells and everything. So nice.'

'Definitely. That's why I moved here permanently.'

'Funny that. I thought it might be to do with a certain man I happen to know.'

'No idea what you are talking about.' Nina laughed.

June nodded towards her house. 'Right, must get on. See you later.'

'Will do. See you.'

As Nina pottered down towards the river, her mind zoomed back to the year before when the whole of the far part of the hotel's garden had been full of wildflowers. Poppies had swayed in the wind and taken Nina's breath away. Back then, she'd felt as if she was blooming as she'd finally let go of the grief that had swallowed her whole since Andrew had passed away. Now, she felt completely different. Alive. As she stood lost in thought, remembering the flowers and her feelings, her mind wandered for a bit. She squinted, imagining the wildflowers, and smiled. Thank goodness for Sophie, the Facebook post, and the man who had started a chain of events that had saved her life.

16

In jeans, her Blundstone boots, and an oversized shirt, Nina strolled along beside Nancy with the sky and marshland stretching out ahead of them. She vacuumed up the fresh air and colours and, as usual, couldn't quite fathom that the scenery around her was as good as it was. She'd walked by the river, around the bay, on the beach, and through the marshes many times since living in Lovely, but the ever-changing weather and sky still took her breath away. A tapestry of greens and blues and smudges of white blurred all around. As she looked ahead, the colours were punctuated with a labyrinth of wooden boardwalks just about as far as the eye could see. All of it as the name itself; lovely.

Nina inhaled the scent of wet earth, wildflowers, and the water meandering through the grasses and reeds. Dots of colour burst here and there, and the sound of water layered with the birds. As they strolled and made their way over a boardwalk, Nina felt far removed from life, as if she and Nancy had been plonked down into a whole other world. A world where life was pared back and really, really slow.

Reeds swayed in the breeze, little oddments of suspended

clouds stretched away, and small obscured pools of water reflected the sky. Both stopping for a second, Nina watched a dragonfly dart over the water, its wings iridescent in the light, and in the distance, a heron stood still as if wondering quite who they thought they were to be disturbing the peace.

Nina felt as if she was leaving her life behind as the further they meandered, the quieter it became. Nancy suddenly put her hand out for Nina to stop. She pointed to the left and whispered. 'There we go.'

Nina turned to where Nancy had pointed to see a couple of otters slipping in and out of the water. Standing still, they watched in silence as the otters swam and went about their business. Then, oblivious to their audience, they disappeared into the reeds, leaving ripples on the water's surface.

Nina smiled. 'That never gets old. I *love* seeing them. They are so sweet.'

'Me too, and I've lived here all my life. It still, to this day, feels like a treat to spy them here and there.'

Nina sighed. 'I feel so lucky to have all this on the doorstep. So lucky.'

Nancy chuckled. 'You don't miss batch-brewed coffee out here in the sticks, then?'

'Gosh, no. I wouldn't go back if you paid me.'

'Ahh, but it's nice to be able to get around easily up there. To be able to hop on a train and see the rest of the country. I love going out for the day and seeing what's what. We have such a beautiful island to explore and so many lovely things in the UK.'

Nina nodded, but truth be told, she was quite happy to stay right where she was and not go anywhere at all. Lovely Bay would do her for a while. 'I think I'm quite happy here, to be honest.'

'There are worse places to end up,' Nancy said as she led the way over a bridge.

'Indeed, there are.'

'So, what's the latest with the wedding planning? What's sorted?'

'Nothing other than the fact that we've done the official legal stuff and just have to wait for that to come through. It was the first thing we did. That was the easy part.'

'Right.'

'I have nothing to wear, nothing planned, no venue, and not even a buttonhole sorted. Not that I'm having buttonholes or anything traditional anyway.'

Nancy pursed her lips and nodded slowly. 'I'm thinking you might need to get a wriggle on if you're wanting to get it in before the weather gets chilly again. It will soon roll around. Before you know it, there will be mince pies in the shops and Jingle Bells in our ears.'

'Yup. I know. I thought the same. Time is marching on.'

'So, no dress, no venue, and no plans?' Nancy clarified as they navigated another stretch of boardwalk. 'From the person who organises for a living. Interesting.'

'Exactly. I've got the fiancé, at least. That's a start, right? I've got one thing sorted. Oh, and the legalities. So that makes two things.'

'A very good start. Let's think about this. What's your ideal setting for the wedding? You've mentioned wanting something simple, so at least you know that.'

Nina paused, looking out over the marshes. 'You know what? I keep coming back to the idea of being outdoors. I was thinking that the other day when I was speaking to June in the garden. There's something about being surrounded by nature, like this, that feels right. Maybe it's because for so long I didn't have that. I don't know…'

'Lovely Bay has plenty of beautiful outdoor spots. The beach, the marshes here, or even down on the river at the RNLI club.'

'Mmm.'

'The Summer Hotel's garden would be nice. Shame you can't have that.'

'The Summer Hotel,' Nina repeated. 'It's where it all started.'

'True that. Not really the place for a wedding party, though, is it?'

'Nah, I suppose not.'

'What about the rest? You mentioned a dress. Any thoughts on that?'

Nina shrugged. 'I want something special, something that feels like me. God knows what that is. I've hunted online and found nothing so far.'

Nancy smiled. 'You'll know it when you see it. It's your day, so you have whatever you like. Go for your life.'

'You're right. I want it to be precisely what I want, not just a collection of 'should-dos' and what we all think is the way to do it.'

As they approached the end of the boardwalk, they paused, taking in the scenery. Nancy sighed. 'Imagine saying your vows, that's if you are having vows of course, with a backdrop like this. It doesn't get more personal than that if you ask me.'

'Better than some musty old church.'

'The Summer Hotel has that beautiful garden. It's meaningful to you, and it's right here, in the heart of where you've built your life, and it's pretty much free. We could have a party and throw in a wedding,' Nancy joked. 'I'm very good at organising drinks and stuff, as you well know.'

'Yeah, in a way, it's sort of symbolic, isn't it?' Nina mused. She imagined a garden party with the sun out and the River Lovely in the background. 'The place where I started my new chapter, now becoming the spot where I start another, even more significant one.'

'Exactly! Have a word with Jill.'

'I might, you know.'

'I can't see why she wouldn't say yes, can you?'

'No, but you never know. It's up for sale and everything. She's not going to want a party there. I don't know. Nah, it's not really right.'

Nancy joked and laughed. 'Let's move back to the dress. Maybe a trip to the city could be fun. A special day out.' Nancy suggested.

Nina laughed. 'A shopping trip does sound like fun, I think, or it could end up being a nightmare. I might just look online. Not sure. My mum keeps threatening to book into one of those wedding dress shops.'

'What's Robby's input on the matter?'

'Pretty laid back about it all. He just wants me to be happy.'

'Aww, nice. I really think you should speak to Jill about The Summer Hotel's garden.'

'I'll give her a call,' Nina agreed, feeling a surge of productivity. 'We'll just keep it small and intimate. God knows what his mum will say. I think she was thinking about inviting half of the country.' Nina laughed at the thought of Robby's mum wanting to invite loads of people to their wedding. 'I can just imagine her guest list. It would probably stretch all the way from here to France.'

Nancy nodded in agreement. 'Well, it's your day, not hers. It's important to keep it about you and our Robby, what you both want. It's about making memories that you'll cherish, not about pleasing everyone else.'

'True,' Nina said, her mind wandering to Robby's mum. She was lovely, really, and had welcomed Nina into the family with open arms. 'I think she just wants to celebrate. She's been waiting for Robby to settle down for so long.'

'She probably wouldn't care if it was in a shed then.'

Nina nodded thoughtfully. 'I think I'll have a bit of a heart-to-heart with her when we go round for a roast at the weekend.'

'Good idea. What will Robby say?'

'He wants it to be just about us and not a big fuss. You know what he's like. Not the best at parties and stuff like that.'

'Honestly, a wedding in the garden at The Summer Hotel sounds idyllic. It's so you. Plus, with the river and the sea as your backdrop, it'll be stunning.'

'Possibly.'

Nancy joked. 'You're welcome. I'll pop my bill for the wedding planner services through your door.'

'Ha! I can't afford you.'

Nancy rolled her eyes. 'Oh, alright, I'll give you a freebie. As you know, Lovely Bay takes care of its own.'

'In all seriousness, it does.' Nina sighed. 'I'm so glad I ended up here. It's changed my life.'

'And now it's giving you a wedding,' Nancy said with a wink. 'Let's get planning. We've got a garden party to organise. You know what? The wildflowers will be out. Wow, that would be stunning, actually. The colours and the scents would be incredible. Very you.'

'It would make it feel even more connected to Lovely Bay.'

'We could put fairy lights in the trees and have tables set out under the stars. Birdie could cater.'

'Yeah, nah. I don't want the Shipping Forecast as a backdrop, plus she's a guest.'

'True.'

As they headed away from the marshes and back towards Lovely Bay, Nina felt as if she was getting somewhere. She wasn't sure about The Summer Hotel, but she was settled on Lovely Bay itself. So that was one thing sorted, at least.

17

With a moving box full of crockery from the kitchen in her arms, Nina hooked open the front door of the rental cottage with her foot, stomped the few steps out onto the pavement, and made her way towards Robby's work van. Robby was away in Bath working on a building with his team and had left her with his work van to use to move a few boxes from the rental cottage to the harbour property. The plan was to do the move bit by bit here and there to avoid a removal company. She stepped off the pavement onto the road behind the van and slid a box into the back. As she closed the doors behind her and just as she was walking back towards the front door, she saw Lindsay coming the other way.

Lindsay, seeing Nina, quickened her steps and smiled. 'Oh hi, how are you?' Lindsay asked.

'Good thanks, how are you?' Nina replied, cursing herself for asking how Lindsay was after Birdie had told her to steer well clear.

'Yes, I'm well.' Lindsay turned towards the cottage and beamed. 'How are you getting on?'

Nina didn't really want to interact with this woman in the

strange, obnoxiously bright, trying-to-be-expensive-but-failing-miserably, animal-print top. 'Yep, good, thanks.'

'What are you up to? You're moving out, are you?' Lindsay asked.

Nina felt a shudder inside. This Lindsay appeared hyper-observant somehow, as if she was frantically analysing every little bit of what Nina said and did. 'I am, yes.'

Lindsay turned and looked up at the 'To Let' sign poked into the tiny front garden. 'The estate agent told me it was going to be up for rent. I'd really like to live this way.'

'It's a lovely place to live. You said you knew Nancy, didn't you?'

'Yes, yes, I do. Well, I used to know her.'

'That's nice.' Nina wondered why Nancy hadn't mentioned this friend of hers but didn't really think much about it. There was definitely something odd about this woman, but she wasn't sure what. She seemed to be around all the time, too. Almost as if she'd engineered it. Nina put the thought out of her head. *Ridiculous.*

Lindsay really wanted to chat and pressed on. 'So, how have you been getting on with packing up and moving? It's always such hard work, I think.'

'Yes, fine, thanks. It's a bit tough doing it all on your own.'

'On your own? Robby's not helping you then?'

Nina frowned and wondered how this woman knew about Robby, but she didn't say anything. Nancy must have mentioned it. Everyone knew everyone's business in Lovely Bay. 'I'm okay. I've been on my own for a long time; it's fine.'

'Right, you've been on your own, have you?'

'Yes, I have.'

Lindsay was clearly trying to keep the conversation going for as long as she could. 'So what have you got on for the rest of the week?'

Nina felt as if the question was totally inappropriate. She

shrugged. 'Oh, you know, this and that. What about you?' She found herself asking, even though she didn't want to know the answer.

'Nothing much, you know how it is,' Lindsay said with a smile, pushing her limp, thin brown hair out of her eyes. 'I might pop down to the pub. I'm on my own at the moment too so, you know, it's a bit sad really. It gets quite lonely, but it is what it is. It's hard when you don't have any…'

Nina nodded. She definitely knew what that was like, but she could tell Lindsay was playing the sympathy card. She so wasn't interested in sympathy cards. She'd had enough of her own to last her a lifetime. Lindsay really gave her the creeps. Nina didn't engage in the loneliness topic. 'Yes, right, well, okay, look, I must get on. I've got a lot to do still.'

Lindsay wasn't going to give up lightly and continued. She took a step forward and rested her hand on the fence, and with the other hand fiddled with the high neck of the cheap ugly top. 'So how have you found this place? What about the heating and stuff like that? Has it been good?'

Nina didn't want to continue the conversation but nodded anyway. 'Yes, yes, fine. Everything has been great. It's a really nice spot, so handy for the shops and a nice view here behind the green.'

'So handy for the shops,' Lindsay echoed. 'Sounds perfect. Must be nice, being so close to everything and yet living in a cottage with a green in front of it.'

Nina shifted uncomfortably, keen to end the conversation. 'Yeah, it's ideal, really. Anyway, I better crack on. Lots to do and all that. You know what it's like when you're getting ready to move.'

Lindsay, seemingly oblivious to Nina's attempts to close down the conversation, lingered a minute longer. 'Of course, don't let me keep you. I'll let you know how I get on with the viewing when it happens.'

Nina's smile was polite but not really that sincere. 'Well, good luck with the viewing then. See you around.'

Turning on her heel, Nina headed back into the cottage. She could feel Lindsay's gaze on her back as she went in. The strange encounter had left a sour taste in her mouth, but she wasn't sure why. There was something unsettling about Lindsay's keenness, her probing questions felt too pointed and way too intrusive for casual conversation. Nina made a mental note to mention Lindsay to Robby when he got back.

Once inside, Nina stood for a moment as her brain percolated through the conversation. She brushed it off and decided it was nothing. Just someone who was a bit lonely and wanted to make small talk. Nothing wrong with that.

18

'Right, you're sure you'll be okay with that?' Robby asked with a serious look on his face.

Nina raised her eyebrows. 'I think I can manage.'

'You're not convincing me,' Robby said as he nudged the edge of a cordless spray painter with his foot.

'DIY has never been one of my natural skills.' Nina waved the paint sprayer instruction sheet around. 'This has been an interesting learning curve. In fact, there have been loads of things I've had to learn since moving here, power tools being one of them and a lot of them are rubbish.'

'A bad workman blames his tools.' Robby joked.

'According to this, it paints a wall eight times faster than a brush, saving time and effort.' Nina began to read from the pamphlet. 'Big surface projects like ceilings, exterior sidings, walls, and fences get a consistent finish with any coating. Ha! It sounds so easy.'

'So, in theory, you should have this whole place done by the time I get back from this job.' Robby said, gesticulating his hand around the room and referring to his trip to a National Trust property where he and his team of workers would be dangling off the side of a country house for the best part of a week.'

Nina swallowed. 'I didn't quite say that, but it's a cordless, battery-powered spray gun that you point at the wall. I'm all over it. What could possibly go wrong?'

'Okay.' Robby tried to keep a straight face. 'Let's break this down. The main thing is the battery is fully charged for it to work efficiently.'

Nina flipped the spray painter over and checked the battery compartment. 'Yes, it's all charged up. I made sure of that last night. It's just the actual spraying part that seems daunting.'

Robby nodded. 'The trick with these is to keep a steady hand and maintain an even distance from the wall. You don't want to get too close or too far away.'

'You seem to know a lot about these.'

'Try using a cordless device when dangling from a piece of rope.' Robby laughed. 'We don't paint things, but it's the same theory. Hold it something like this much away.' Robby held his hands out in front of him. 'Ten to twelve inches, thirty centimetres or something.'

'Right.' Nina looked at Robby sceptically. 'What about the speed? How fast should I move?'

'Steady, but not too slow. You want to avoid drips,' Robby joked. 'No drips or droopiness. It's a slow dance.'

Nina giggled as Robby moved his hips. She gulped, but didn't let him see. She really did like those hips and how they performed. 'A slow dance with a paint sprayer. Now, that's something I never thought I'd hear, and I thought my life was bad when I was in the flat.'

Robby continued. 'Overlap your strokes slightly, that way, you won't miss any spots.'

Nina nodded, absorbing the information. 'Overlap, steady speed, ten to twelve inches. Got it. And what about corners and edges? I'm guessing the slow dance doesn't quite cut it there.'

'You'll be fine. I'll be back before you know it.' Robby pretended to be serious. 'I want it all done and dusted by the time I'm back so we can start to move in.'

Nina walked Robby to the door, the instruction sheet still in hand. 'Hopefully, by the time you get back, you'll be walking into a freshly painted masterpiece. Or, at the very least, something that doesn't look like a disaster zone.'

'I have every faith in you. It's just paint. Worst case scenario, we repaint. No disasters here.' Robby kissed her and turned to leave. 'Right, I'll message you when I get there. Have fun.'

Nina turned back to the room, sprayer in hand. 'Fun? Not my idea of fun. Alright, let's do this.'

As she prepared the sprayer and filled it with paint, Nina went over Robby's advice in her head. 'Battery, check. Steady hand, check. Slow dance moves, check,' she recited, trying to pump herself up for the task ahead of painting the harbour property. It was going to be a long day.

As she fussed with the sprayer, she thought about Robby's words about them moving into her place. The one thing she hadn't liked about the proposal was the fact that it changed things about where they lived. She sort of wanted to keep her property to herself, but she wasn't sure why. There'd been a slightly heated conversation about it. Something kept telling her that she didn't want to move into Robby's house. Just as when she'd first moved permanently to Lovely Bay, it didn't feel right to her. Deep down, she couldn't put her finger on why, but she assumed it had something to do with Andrew as a lot of things had been in her life.

After a lot of debating, they'd settled that they'd live in Nina's new place, see how it went and put Robby's up for rent then work it all out further down the track. Best laid plans.

Nina mulled it over as she fussed with the sprayer and then found herself repeating Robby's mantra in her head like a meditation chant. 'Battery check, steady hand, slow dance moves,' she muttered under her breath, aiming the sprayer at the wall. The first press of the trigger hissed and sent a mist of paint across the surface much faster than she anticipated. The air was blue. There wasn't a lot of dancing going on. More a clumsy shuffling and quite the fair share of swearing. Nina frowned at what was in front of her. It looked nothing like the wall on the side of the sprayer box. The paint coverage was uneven, with some areas dripping while others seemed barely touched.

She stepped back to assess her progress and let out a frustrated sigh. 'This is harder than it looks,' she said to the empty room. 'Why am I doing this to myself? How did I get here?' She pressed the trigger again and aimed. The more she tried to correct her mistakes, the more she seemed to make. 'What was I thinking? What the actual?'

Determined not to let the sprayer win, Nina pressed on, reminding herself that before she'd moved to Lovely Bay, she'd had little choice but to get on with doing things herself. She continued to talk to the empty room. 'Robby's going to need a blindfold when he comes back.'

An hour or so later, she'd sort of mastered it. It was nothing like dancing, not even close. She had to keep her core still to hold the sprayer up and gently move it back and forth. It looked easy, but holding her arm at the angle made it ache and hurt. As she stood outside with a cup of tea for a break, she glanced at the instruction sheet again, wondering if there was some crucial piece of advice she'd missed. It seemed to her to be a lot harder than it appeared.

Once she'd finished her tea and was back inside, it didn't look quite as bad as when she'd been critically assessing it, and slowly but surely, the room began to take on a more uniform colour; though far from perfect, it was an improvement. Nina convinced herself that perfection was overrated anyway and that the place was at least now clean. There was one way of looking at it; the only way was up.

~

Several hours later, with paint splatters dotting her face and hair, Nina stepped back to evaluate her work. The walls were indeed painted, albeit with a few runs and missed spots here and there. She spoke to the wall for about the fiftieth time that day. 'Not quite a masterpiece, though it is now sanitised.' She felt as if there was white paint everywhere.

With her hands on her hips, she nodded to herself. Not bad, not bad at all. She ticked an imaginary accomplishment box rather pleased with herself. She had tackled something out of her comfort zone and while not exact, she'd managed to crack on with it and make a significant change. It seemed there were many changes now in her life.

As she surveyed the room, her phone buzzed from her pocket buried under her paint-splattered overalls. She carefully wiggled her phone out of her pocket, trying not to smear paint on the screen. It was a message from Robby.

Robby: *How's the painting coming along? Should I prepare for a surprise when I get back?*

Nina chuckled and typed a response, her fingers leaving faint white smudges on the screen.

Nina: *Let's just say you might not recognise the place. It's a work in progress.*

Robby: *Need me to call in a professional rescue team?*

Nina: *I think I've got it under control. Just needs a bit of touching up here and there. Defo a second coat. Or third.*

Just as she was finishing texting Robby, there was a bang on the barn doors at the front of the building. Nina wiped her hands on her overalls and hurried to the door. Before she'd opened it, she heard the Shipping Forecast and knew precisely who it was. *On behalf of the Maritime and Coastguard agency. There are warnings of gales in Viking, Dogger, Fisher, Trafalgar, Hebrides, and Faeroes.*

Birdie held up a brown cardboard box with green printed words on the top. 'Handmade biscuit delivery. It might have reached my ears that you are in need of sustenance.'

Nina stepped aside and pulled the door back fully. 'Ha, how did you know? What a day! I am in need of something, true. You're not wrong. Come in, I'll put the kettle on.'

Birdie stepped in, taking in the freshly painted room. Her chin dropped, and she made exaggerated blinks. 'Wow!'

'What do you think?'

'It's not half bad. It's got character, that's for sure.'

Nina chuckled. 'Is that a diplomatic way of saying it's a mess? My painting technique could use a little work.'

'You're joking. You've done loads.'

Nina gestured to the spraying contraption. 'It's that thing. You just point it and go or at least that's what it says on the box. It's a bit tricky to get it right.'

Birdie frowned. 'No cord. What will they invent next?'

'I know, right? Tea or coffee?'

'I'll have a tea, thanks,' Birdie said as she put the box of biscuits on a dust sheet-covered table and peered more closely at the sprayer. 'I've heard about these, but I've never actually seen one in action. So, it's as simple as pointing and painting?'

Nina laughed, 'In theory, yes. In practice, it's a learning curve. Robby likened it to the ones they use at work. Said it was a slow dance with a bit of rhythm needed to avoid drips and misses. Much easier said than done. My arms are feeling it.'

Birdie raised an eyebrow. 'Interesting advice.'

'Something about maintaining a ten to twelve-inch distance from the wall and moving at a steady pace,' Nina explained, demonstrating with a slight sway.

Birdie chuckled, shaking her head. 'I can just picture it. You slow dancing around the room with a paint sprayer all day long.'

'It's been an adventure, that's for sure.'

'This place is transforming already.'

Nina glanced around the room, noting the brighter feel the new paint brought. 'It is, isn't it? I'm starting to see it come together, even with the imperfections.'

Birdie shook her head. 'Look how far you've come.'

'I know. It's been quite the journey. You almost wonder what might come next.'

Nina made a cup of tea and they then sat on a couple of upturned paint buckets. Sipping their teas, the conversation naturally drifted from the painting specifically to Nina's wedding plans.

Birdie dipped a biscuit into her tea. 'What's the latest on the nuptials?'

'Nothing to tell on that. At least nothing you don't already know. Now we've decided on The Summer Hotel that's one thing sort of done.'

'Have you heard back from Jill yet?'

'Not yet. I'm hoping she agrees. It would be perfect – intimate, scenic, and it holds a special place in my heart, you know? It's strange; I kind of feel like I healed there.'

'Maybe you actually did, as it goes.'

'Hmm, maybe that's why I love it there. There's something about it I can't put my finger on.'

'Shame you didn't love it enough to buy it.'

'I was *never* going to buy it. For a start, I don't have that sort of money.'

Birdie nodded. 'There are ways and means.'

'Ha, yeah, not enough of them. No, I'll just hopefully have a wedding party there.'

'It is gorgeous when the sun's out, I'll give it that. It'll make for a stunning backdrop. Jill's always been a fan of making the hotel a part of the community's happy memories, so I can't see there'll be any problem from her side.'

Nina smiled. 'Exactly. After everything that's happened, it feels right to start married life there.'

'If there is one thing I know, Lovely Bay has a way of making things come together just right, so it should work out well.'

'I hope so, I really do.'

19

From the podium, Nina looked over at her mum, her sister, Nancy, and Sophie. Sophie had a smile on her face, Nancy was chatting to one of the assistants, her mum nodded, and her sister was happily knocking back the free champagne. Nina was not happy. That was putting it mildly. She'd not fancied the high-end wedding dress shop in the first place, but her mum, as ever, had been absolutely insistent. Sophie had been too, really. Her sister had been positive, always a first, so Nina had just gone along with it. Now, after having tried on what felt like every possible wedding dress known to man and with no sight of the end, she'd had enough.

She slumped her arms in front of her as the assistant fussed with the bottom of the dress and then snapped a huge bulldog clip in the back. 'This is nice. Yes, it looks good. How does it feel?'

Nina looked in the gigantic gilt-edged mirror, and a flash of her first wedding came to mind. Andrew's happy, beaming face was right in front of her. She hated it when that happened. It was like a strange whack of grief but now nowhere near as potent as it once had been but still horrid. She shoved it away, smiled widely, and tried to sound both polite and interested. She so wasn't interested. She was also losing the will to remain polite. 'Mmm, no, I don't think so. Thanks for trying.'

'I'll be back.' The assistant, head to toe in black, didn't seem in the least perturbed. She had the unenviable job of dealing with the ups and downs of brides all day long. *Possibly the worst job ever,* Nina thought as she looked around as the assistant walked away.

The thing was, Nina abhorred the whole affair. First of all, she felt a hundred years old compared to the young women beside her. Secondly, clearly, and little had she known, nowadays people got ready for their wedding dress shopping as if that in itself was an occasion and needed an outfit. She'd so not been aware or ready for that. She'd shoved on black chino pants and a fairly nice top and called it a day. When they'd first arrived, she'd immediately known she wasn't dressed correctly. She'd also very quickly ascertained that the shop wasn't for her. One of the other customers whose appointment was at the same time had rushed up to her and asked her if she would consent to being on the video she would be uploading to TikTok. The woman had clearly just come from a make-up artist; her hair was beautifully blow-dried and complete with long, lush curls, and her entourage's outfits coordinated, all of it a neutral, bland, minimalist ribbed beige.

Nina and her party were definitely not coordinated in any shape or form. Nor was she done up; her hair was shoved up in a bun, and she'd done her make-up in the car.

Then there was the shop itself. Ultra-expensive, hyper-gleaming, shiny to within an inch of its life. She grimaced at the long, sleek black side tables with the too-green faux plants in fake grey paper pots, the vomit-inducing grey shiny floor, the assistants in grey or black knit dresses, and the grey rugs. Everything grey and black and fake.

Nina kept a smile on her face for the sake of her mum and

sucked it up. It seemed as if everyone else was having a whale of a time. Maybe Soph would tell her the truth when they got home. Her mum had booked the whole day, including lunch, and had been really looking forward to it. Nina felt as if she'd rather *do* anything and *be* anywhere else. Her frustration simmered beneath the surface as she watched the assistant disappear into the sea of white and ivory backed by grey, her steps muffled by the grey floor that did nothing to soften Nina's growing disdain for the entire process. She turned slightly, catching her reflection; the dress looked *horrendous*. Rather than the bridal gown of her dreams, as the shop liked to call itself, she looked ridiculous. The huge clumpy black clip at the back, meant to simulate the perfect fit, looked as out of place as she felt.

Her mum clapped her hands together. 'Yes, I like this one! What do you think? Like it? I think it's the best one yet. How does it feel?'

Nina managed a half-smile. 'Umm, not sure. Yeah, I don't know. Thanks, Mum.'

Nina caught Sophie's eye through the reflection in the mirror. Sophie did a little thumbs-up and eyebrow raise. Nina could tell there was an unspoken understanding between them that this was perhaps not what Nina had envisioned. Her sister, meanwhile, seemed to be in a world of her own, the champagne evidently more appealing than either the dresses or how Nina looked in them. Her sister's laughter was a bit too loud, a bit too forced, and she'd told just about the whole room how nice the free bubbles were.

Nina turned away from the mirror and looked at the dresses that lined the walls – each one more elaborate and expensive than the last. The assistant returned, her arms laden with yet another selection of gowns, each one promising to be "the one".

As Nina reluctantly stepped out of the current dress and into another, her mind wandered to the conversation that had started the whole wildflowers at The Summer Hotel thing. Nancy had coined it: simple and elegant. When she'd been strolling in the marshes with Nancy and later talking it through with Robby, she'd envisioned a ceremony surrounded by the people who mattered most and not much else. Not all the malarkey she now found herself partaking in. Mostly, she just wanted to seal the deal with Robby and get on with it.

In the little dream in her head, there had been nothing of the pretence and pomp of what she was witnessing in the high-end bridal boutique. Despite how she felt, the show continued to go on, but with each dress she tried on, Nina felt further removed from herself and the essence of what she wanted. It wasn't about the dress, flowers or the cars or white tulle or satin. She'd already done that the first time around. It hadn't ended well.

Part of her wanted to just run away and get married, just her and Robby. She knew one thing for sure: she wouldn't be finding a dress in the grey and black bridal boutique anytime soon. There really was no doubt about that.

20

Nina strolled down the pavement alongside Robby. He took her hand, squeezed it, and watched as the riverboat approached. The just-about-there moon reflected off the water, little lanterns swayed back and forth in the breeze, and fairy lights twinkled around the top of the boat. The engine hummed, water splashed against the jetty, and a couple of people chatted as they sat on the bench at the end, waiting for the riverboat to arrive.

Once on, Nina took a seat at the front of the boat, pulled her bag around to the front, put her phone away, and just sat for a while, not saying anything and taking in the scene around her. It was a warm evening, the light was just right, and Nina and Robby were on their way to a secret chowder event. Life had been worse.

As the riverboat chugged in the direction of where The Summer Hotel was located, Nina smiled and turned to Robby. 'So, I've finally been invited to one of the most prestigious events in Lovely Bay,' she chuckled. 'It's taken long enough.'

Robby replied with a smile, 'You have. It's totally because of me and not because of anyone else. Remember that.'

Nina laughed. 'I will remember that the only reason I get invited to all sorts of things is because of you. That's right, isn't it?'

Robby joked, 'Yes, you'd better watch yourself, or you'll end up with no invites at all.'

Nina chuckled. 'How come this place is so highly regarded? I mean, we've been to loads now, but this is always the one everyone mentions.'

Robby shrugged and raised his eyebrows. 'I'm not really sure. It's one of the chowder events that takes place in a house. Maybe that's the reason.'

Nina queried, 'Why would that be then?'

'Because it's in a house, it's got more limited numbers and therefore it's more sought after? Who knows, really?'

Nina nodded. 'I see. That makes sense, I suppose.'

Robby put his arm along the back of the seat and shifted closer to Nina. 'Get ready to have a lovely evening. This one never disappoints.'

Nina nodded again. 'I will. How many people do you think are going?'

Robby shrugged again. 'No idea. Not many. All I know is that my aunt will be there and that the food will be out of this world. That's enough for me. Oh, and, of course, an evening with my fiancée. There's that.'

Nina raised her eyebrows in question. 'The food? What do you mean by the *food*?'

'What?'

Nina frowned. 'I thought there was only one type of food. I thought it was just chowder at these things.'

'Yeah, sorry, when I said food, I meant chowder. It will be amazing. Just wait and see.'

'So, if it's just chowder, what makes it so special that everyone wants an invite to this one specifically?'

Robby leaned closer and lowered his voice. 'It's not just any chowder. They say this one is a secret recipe passed down through generations.'

Nina rolled her eyes. 'Pah! They all say that. Birdie says that about ten times a day. Ask me how I know. She won't let you forget it.'

'The atmosphere of the event itself is something else. It's like stepping into another era, with jazz playing in the background and the house is, well, you'll see when we get there. Yeah, the setting helps.'

Nina's eyes went wide. 'Ooh, yes, June said the same.'

'You won't be disappointed.'

'So no one knows it's this one tonight apart from those of us who are going?'

'I assume not. That's the best part. The location is kept secret until the last minute, and you need a password to get in at this one. It's all very hush-hush, adds to the excitement.'

Nina laughed. 'A password? No, you don't, surely? Really? What is it?'

'That,' Robby joked, tapping his nose, 'is something I cannot reveal until we're on the doorstep.'

'I love the idea of a secret gathering. It feels like we're part of an exclusive club.'

Robby nodded. 'Hmm, I guess so. It harks back to a time when people gathered in secret and smuggling and all that. Maybe that's why...'

Nina leaned back, imagining the scene. 'I can't wait.'

'This one has live jazz if we're lucky.'

'I didn't realise chowder could be so... romantic.'

'It worked for you.'

Nina wrinkled her nose. 'What do you mean?'

'It was the first time we went out. Remember when you were peering in the window?'

How could Nina forget? She'd loved the night. It had been the beginning of pulling her out of a rut she'd been in for years.

There'd also been the fact that she'd absolutely loved being with Robby right from the word go. He hadn't disappointed one single bit. Straps. Now, she was about to spend the rest of her life with him. Ding-blimming-dong.

Robby chatted. 'We really need to make a decision about the reception and what we're going to do about the wedding itself.'

'I know.'

'Time is ticking on. We did the legal bit and then it's kind of come to a standstill.'

'At least we know it's in The Summer Hotel now.'

'Yep, but caterers and all of the rest of it. We need to get that organised.'

'We do. We'll make a decision by the end of the week one way or the other. Or we have to wait until next year when the weather will be warm again, and I'm not waiting a year.'

'No.'

They disembarked from the boat and strolled hand-in-hand towards the end of the road where The Summer Hotel was located. Nina had walked along the road many times and had heard all about the secret speakeasy chowder place, but had never been invited. Numbers were limited, demand was high, and according to just about everybody in Lovely Bay, it was booked up even before it went live. Nina adored being part of it and the Lovely Bay community; it was feel-good. People said hello to you as you walked along the street, you received smiles when the day was looking a bit grey, and sometimes it just felt nice to be in on things.

From the outside, the house looked like every other house in Lovely Bay. It was old, a little bit tumbledown, with beautiful shutters on the outside painted in white that had been weathered by the sea. The garden was quintessentially English and quintessentially beautiful, but other than that, quite unremarkable. From what Nina had heard, when she walked inside, all of that was going to change.

For a moment, they stood on the pavement, observing the house from the outside. It appeared very quiet. Robby extracted his phone from his pocket, swiped up, and tapped a few buttons. 'Okay, the password is noted,' Robby announced. 'We need to walk around to the right-hand side of the house.' He glanced up from his phone, squinted, and then peered back at the screen. 'A door halfway down leads into the side of the house.'

Nina frowned. 'I thought you've been to one of these before.'

Robby nodded. 'I have, yes, but that was in the winter, and the instructions for that one directed us to knock on the front door. This one is, hopefully, going to be in the back.'

Nina nodded and trailed behind Robby. He pressed the doorbell on the side, and after two minutes, the door swung open. Colin from the boat stood there, chuckling and arching his eyebrows as if awaiting Robby to utter something. Robby voiced the password. Nina giggled as she stepped in, with Colin opening the door wider.

'Welcome, our Nina and our Robby. Delighted to see you this evening. It's touch-and-go with the rain, but we'll see how it goes,' Colin greeted.

'Fabulous, thanks, Colin,' Nina said as she began to peel off her jacket and looked around. If the rest of the evening, and indeed the rest of the house, matched the entrance hall, she was in for a delightful experience. She gazed around, her chin nearly touching the floor and a peculiar flutter stirring in her stomach. The house was undeniably stunning. It was going to be a good night.

Nina surveyed the hallway, with its stripped floors and the colossal mirrors above a narrow shelf that sat about three-quarters up the wall beneath the highest ceilings. On the shelf, an array of jugs looked as if they'd been collected over time. A staircase with a hessian runner and brass rods led upwards, while three or four doors branched off the hallway. Colin led them through, opening one of the doors into a large sitting room. The room boasted three sofas, one in pale pink velvet, a massive fireplace, and beautiful gilt mirrors leaning against the walls. A chandelier hung from the centre of the ceiling, and through the doors at the back, Nina glimpsed willow trees swaying in the wind over a narrow orangery. She had to stop herself from gasping at the decor; the sofas, the paintings, the mirrors, and the high ceilings were all exquisite.

Stepping into the narrow orangery, the ambience changed dramatically. Tiny lights nestled in small glass jars illuminated the space as guests mingled, drinks in hand. A few nodded and greeted Nina as she edged towards the doors, taking in the sight. Outside, a series of vintage fringed sun umbrellas stood in a row above trestle tables, each adorned with distinctively English printed tablecloths. Rugs draped over the backs of chairs, and lanterns hung from the trees, their tea lights flickering. At the garden's end, a fire pit crackled away to itself. Shabby it was not.

Colin handed Nina a drink, glancing up at the sky. 'Looks like it might rain, but hopefully, it won't. Believe it or not, those umbrellas are actually rainproof, or so they say. More like drizzle-proof, if you ask me.' He laughed at his own joke and Nina chuckled.

About ten minutes later, she found herself seated outside next to Robby, with a man she didn't recognise on her right and a very pretty woman with her hair in an elaborate updo opposite her.

Colin brought out pitchers of beer and bottles of wine, placing them down the centre of the table. Robby poured her a glass and one for himself, passing her one. About ten minutes later, the chowder was served in the same small sourdough loaves as in the deli that were ubiquitous all over Lovely Bay.

After everyone had been served, Nina picked up her spoon and tucked in. Just as the first time she'd ever tasted the famous Lovely Bay chowder, her taste buds couldn't quite believe what had happened. The chowder was more than tasty; it was like something she'd never tried before, better than Birdie's, better than any of the chowder she'd had in Lovely Bay. She nodded, didn't say anything, put another spoonful in her mouth, and just continued to enjoy everything about the setting. The fire at the end, with smoke billowing up into the sky, the beautiful stars, the low lighting, the mix of people all on a mismatch of vintage chairs, the beautiful old tablecloths, the house in the background, and the tiny little lights flickering everywhere.

She whispered to Robby. 'Wow, I know why this has always been the one to get an invite to.'

Robby nodded. 'Yes, it's amazing.'

'I don't mean the food,' Nina said. 'I mean, look at it.' She gestured around her.

Robby agreed. 'It really is.'

He put his fork down. 'Do you know what? This is what we should do. Something like this. Just have the chowder in the garden of The Summer Hotel and leave it at that. We've been talking to caterers and suchlike when this would be just right. All we need is chowder. Everyone loves it.'

Nina frowned. 'What do you mean?'

'Well, you said you wanted simple and easy, and I don't really care. We could just go to the registry office and come back to Lovely for chowder, not some big elaborate meal with caterers and everything. It really would be as simple as that. Just a party, really.'

Nina mulled it over for a second as she looked around at the beautiful scene around her. 'It would work, yep. It wouldn't cost us much money and the setup would be easy. We could even ask Colin to help and maybe get the jazz guys to play, too.'

Robby nodded. 'Exactly. We just pay a few people to serve drinks and sort the chowder out. There are enough people in Lovely Bay who know how to do that, and it would all hook back to our first date.'

Nina giggled. 'That wasn't really a date.'

Robby shook his head. 'I'm calling it the first date. I saw you there, I asked you to come in there with me, and you said yes. Is that not a date?'

Nina chuckled again. 'I'm *not* calling that a date.'

'Okay then, whatever. But what do you reckon? Do you reckon it would be good to have something like this? It's what you said right from the word go. When you came back from that wedding shop, you said it was awful, and you wanted something different. Everything would be simple.'

Nina nodded. 'I wouldn't have to worry about anything. The wildflowers would be in bloom...'

'Think about it,' Robby said as Nina finished the rest of her chowder.

As the event went on, she *did* think about it, *a lot*. One of the things that was putting her off the whole marriage thing, in inverted commas, was that it reminded her of Andrew, and she felt so different now from her life that was Andrew. Everything about her felt different, and she kind of wanted her wedding to be different, too. She didn't want it to be in a church in a traditional way surrounded by all the things that people always did. She'd even thought about going for a curry after the marriage ceremony – but that hadn't ticked enough of anybody else's boxes; when she'd mentioned it to her mum and sister, her mum had looked as if she was going to faint.

But what Robby had suggested would work. It would mean that she wasn't so much doing the big white wedding thing again as she had the first time; it would mean that she was doing exactly what she wanted in her new life in Lovely Bay. It wouldn't cause her any stress, which was the most important thing. She certainly wouldn't have to go back to another one of those hideous wedding shops, stand on a podium with a massive bulldog clip behind her back, and worry about what people were thinking.

Nina thought about it for ages, and the more it filled her mind, the more she realised it was exactly what she wanted. In her head, she went over the email that Jill had sent her. She had been fine with using The Summer Hotel for a reception, so she couldn't see any problem there. The only real issue would be the weather, and even that, they could probably get around somehow. She sat lost in thought for ages as she finished off her drink and took in the surroundings of the beautiful house. Robby tapped her on the hand. 'Penny for them? You're miles away.'

Nina smiled. 'Am I?'

Robby nodded. 'Yes, you are. What have you been thinking about?'

Nina smiled. 'I've been thinking about exactly what you said. Wildflowers, chowder, a Lovely Bay garden, The Summer Hotel, where it all started off. It would tick all my boxes.'

Robby nodded. 'Works for me.'

Nina also nodded. 'Definitely works for me.'

Robby smiled. 'Let's make it happen, then.'

'Let's.'

21

Nina jogged along the pavement beside Lovely Bay beach following the instructions from the voice coming through her earphones. She felt as if the voice was now her friend even though she'd never even seen the voice and probably didn't ever want to. The voice had been with her since her early days in Lovely Bay and had seen her through a few things.

'Don't forget to breathe and have fun. Tall, soft, breath, fun,' the voice said. Nina had heard the same thing from the voice many times.

She chuckled to herself at how far she'd come in her running endeavours as she reflected on how long she'd been using the app. She recalled the first day when she'd tied on her trainers and taken to the path alongside the river, determined to at least give running a go. That first day had been a struggle and she'd barely been able to jog for the required minute in between the sessions of walking. As she'd plodded her way through, by the end of it, she'd actually felt as if she might collapse and have to get a random passerby to call someone to bring her some oxygen.

Now, though nowhere close to being an expert and still

considering herself an amateur jogger, she looked forward to her running sessions and made sure she completed them rain or shine. How far she had come.

'Remind yourself why you're here. You have the ability to run a long way. Feel the power of your body. Your body is an asset. It works *for* you and *with* you. It can do anything you tell it to.'

Nina's journey with running had been a rewarding one. In the first few weeks, she hadn't thought that, though, as she'd gritted and finished a sweaty mess, having wobbled in places she didn't know could wobble. These days, she still had her moments of doubt, but she could now run for vast stretches without gasping for breath and feeling as if she might combust. In actual fact, running had become more than just physical exercise; it was a way to clear her mind, let her brain empty out, and find peace in what was now quite a busy little life. Couldn't argue with that.

'Last run session coming up. Give it your best shot!'

As she approached the end of the bay that curved around towards the town, she took a turn and headed towards the harbour. Arriving by the water, it was bustling with activity; people waited to board boats, families with buckets and spades appeared to be heading in the direction of the beach, and the pub on the corner had its doors flung open and its patrons were soaking up the sun outside.

Running past the rows of old harbour properties to her left, Nina waved at an owner cleaning his front door and called out hello to the woman behind the counter of the little hut that sold fresh fish. Approaching her own property, she slowed to a cool-down walk and made her way over to the water. While stretching her calves, she noticed Lindsay, the woman she'd seen outside the cottage and whom Birdie had not spoken nicely about, to her left. Nina quickly looked away, pulled her foot up behind her, and made a huge deal out of stretching her quads and pointedly looking in the other direction.

Despite Nina's attempt to avoid interaction by turning away, Lindsay moved closer and stepped to Nina's right, greeting Nina with a beaming, overly friendly, and strangely unsettling smile. Nina pulled one of her earphones out of her ears. She couldn't quite put her finger on why, but she felt a nagging sense that something about Lindsay was off. Nina didn't know her from Adam and despite what Birdie had said, Lindsay seemed pleasant enough on the surface. There was a little voice and red flag popping up for Nina, though, and she sensed an underlying unease as she looked in Lindsay's direction. Trying to maintain a distant demeanour, Nina responded briefly. 'Hi.'

Lindsay seized the opportunity to chat. She beamed and turned her head to the side. 'How are you? How funny that I keep bumping into you! What a coincidence to see you down here again.'

Nina didn't want to get into a conversation. She made a little sound and shrugged her eyebrows a tiny bit. 'Hmm.'

Lindsay smiled again and looked Nina up and down, taking in Nina's black exercise leggings, crop top, and trainers. 'You look like you're really fit.' Lindsay gushed. 'What a figure.'

The one red flag that had been waving in the back of Nina's head turned into hundreds of them flapping madly right at the front of Nina's brain. She wanted to get away but smiled and nodded. 'Yes. Well, not really. I do my best. I wouldn't exactly call myself super fit, but it keeps me healthy.'

'It looks like you do more than your best to me. It looks like you're on fire. Gosh, talk about inspiring!'

'I do try.'

Lindsay smiled and pointed to Nina's headphones, clearly wanting to have a good chat. 'Do you listen to music for motivation? What's your secret?'

Nina did not want to engage but felt as if she'd been backed into a corner. All she wanted to do was run over to her place, slam the door behind her, and get away from this woman with the creepy aura, awful flowery-patterned, ill-fitting dress and overly friendly smile. 'I don't listen to music as such. I use an app for motivation.'

'Oh, wow, right. That's how you do it, is it? It must be the answer! What kind of app is that? I could have a go.'

Nina pretended she couldn't remember what the app was called. It wasn't that she'd forgotten, just that she didn't want to engage any more than she had to. 'I'm not sure. Actually, it's some... I can't remember the name of it.'

'Maybe I could have a go at something like that. I might end up looking as good as you do if I'm lucky!' Lindsay gushed. 'Where do you run?'

Nina wasn't happy about the questions, and she definitely wasn't going to be telling Lindsay where she ran. 'Oh, just, you know, all around here. If I'm feeling ambitious, I go up the hill to the church and back and by the water.' She immediately regretted telling Lindsay anything.

'Any particular tracks you take? Any recommendations for a good place to run?' Lindsay jumped in quickly and raised her eyebrows in question.

'No, no, you know, just anywhere. No specific route or anything.'

'How about the path down there beside the river? A lot of people run and walk there. Do you?'

Nina shook her head and lied, 'No. I don't.' She absolutely *did* use the path along the side of the river often, as many Lovelies did, but there was no way that she was going to tell this Lindsay that she used the path most mornings.

Lindsay continued in the same manner. 'I've always wanted to try running. It seems like you've got it all worked out. The thing is, I've always needed someone to show me the ropes, you know?' She left her sentence open.

It was clear that Lindsay wanted Nina to invite her to go for a run with her. There was no way Nina was doing that. She got all the wrong vibes from this strange woman and relished the time on her own when she went out to run. 'You just have to put one foot in front of the other. That's it really.' Nina turned and made as if to go.

Lindsay was having none of it. 'Actually, I was wondering if I might bump into you again. You have an organising business, don't you? What was it called again?'

Nina was taken aback and wrong-footed at the abrupt change in topic and the direct question. She was suspicious but also cornered. 'I do.'

Lindsay continued. 'So, how long have you had the business?'

'Oh, not that long.'

'Have you done well with it?' Lindsay asked.

Nina nodded. 'Yes, I have, thanks. Look, sorry, I *really* do have to get on. I've got loads to do.'

Lindsay smiled. 'Of course, sorry to keep you. I just thought it might be good to chat as soon as I spotted you. I've got a lot of decluttering to get done, so I thought I would stop you and have a word if I saw you.'

'Right.'

'Yes, sorry, I know you must be really busy with buying the property and getting married and all.'

Nina winced inside. This woman knew far too much about her. How did she know that she was getting married? The Lovely Bay grapevine had obviously told her. There was no way she was going to say anything; she just wanted to get away. 'I am busy, yep.'

Lindsay continued, not taking the hint at all. 'Do you think I could get a quote?'

Nina hesitated. 'Umm, yep.'

'I could send you the photos of what I want done if that would be easier.'

'Err, okay. I haven't got many slots available at the moment.'

Lindsay took her phone out of her pocket, swiped up, and tapped. 'Oh, that doesn't matter. If I text you the photos, we can go from there. What's your number?'

Nina hesitantly gave her phone number to Lindsay. As Lindsay tapped the number into her phone she seemed really pleased with herself. 'Excellent. I'll just add you now. Nina Lavendar. There we go.'

Nina really didn't want to interact with Lindsay any further. She didn't like the look of the woman, Birdie had been less than friendly to her, and she didn't like the way she hung around each time she'd had an interaction with her. All around, she didn't like the woman at all. She'd meant to say something to Nancy about it, but she'd forgotten. She made a mental note to say something. 'Sorry, as I said, I've got to go. I've got loads of work to do.'

Lindsay finally took the hint. 'No worries. It's been *so* nice to chat. So nice. Enjoy the rest of your day. I'll text you those pictures as soon as I get home.'

Nina nodded, hoping that Lindsay wouldn't follow up. 'Okay, great. I'll get back to you. I'm really busy at the moment, but I'll see what I can do.'

Lindsay nodded. 'Yes, fine. I've heard you're busy. I've seen it too.'

Nina frowned. 'Seen it? What do you mean? How have you seen how busy I am?'

'Oh, just on your Instagram, you know.'

Nina wondered how Lindsay knew about her Insta account. It must've been a local in the town who had told her, perhaps, or maybe in the deli or pub somebody had mentioned that she did decluttering. She thought about her card on the noticeboard in the lobby of the pub and the deli, but her cards didn't show her full details. Lindsay must have put two and two together and realised it was Nina's business. Whatever it was, and however

Lindsay had found out her name and her business, she didn't like it at all. The woman filled her with dread.

∽

Later that afternoon, Nina had completely forgotten about the interaction with Lindsay outside by the harbour wall. She'd spent too long finishing off some of the skirting boards in the attic room, sent off some quotes, and had a long conversation with the insurance company about changing her insurance policy for work. She was just making a cup of tea in the kitchen when her phone pinged. She looked down to see a number she didn't know, tapped on the messages, assuming it would be yet another spammer, and read a message.

Lindsay: *Hi, Nina, just getting back to you after our conversation today. It's so nice getting to know you. I am pleased our paths crossed. As discussed, please quote for the attached declutter. I have included pictures of my airing cupboard, wardrobe, bathroom cupboard, and dining room. Thank you so much, can't wait to hear back from you.*

Nina tapped on the downward arrow in the middle of the photos and waited for them to download. She squinted, used her finger and thumb to expand the first picture of the airing cupboard, and frowned. The airing cupboard didn't look too messy to her; in fact, it was quite organised. In her time in decluttering, she had seen a lot of messy spaces, rooms packed full of junk, kitchens overflowing with utensils and stuff not put away. This wasn't like that at all; it almost looked as if the airing cupboard had been ruffled up to make it look as if it was a mess. She downloaded the next photo and examined that one as well. It was the picture of the wardrobe in a very organised, clean, and tidy bedroom. The wardrobe was similar to the airing cupboard, as if it had been purposely made messy. By the time she opened all four pictures, it was clear to her that the house was in a good state and decluttering services weren't really needed at all.

Nina squinted as she drank her tea and wondered what this woman was up to. She didn't like her vibes, Birdie clearly didn't like her, and now she appeared to be making up things to try and get Nina to go and work for her. Very fishy indeed. She sat up straight as she realised that Lindsay had told her she was going to be viewing the cottage near Nancy's. Would someone who was just about to move be thinking about decluttering? She nodded; she knew from experience it was often the time when people wanted help. Maybe it was true...

She wasn't sure what to reply and going with her gut instinct, she sent a text back.

Nina: *Thanks for sending me the pictures. It doesn't seem to me as if you need much help. My jobs are usually a lot bigger. I don't really think it would be worth it for you.*

The little dots flashing on Nina's screen in response were instant.

Lindsay: *No, I really need you. I don't care how much it costs. I'm just not getting around to it at the moment, and it's really affecting my mental health.*

Nina frowned. *Really affecting your mental health? It's a messy airing cupboard.* She didn't know what to say to that. Before she had a chance to send a text, another one came in.

Lindsay: *Can you please get a quote to me as soon as possible and when can you fit me in? I don't mind when or if you need to charge express rates or something. I just want it done.*

Nina frowned again. This was really odd. This woman's behaviour wasn't normal.

Nina: *I'm really busy now for the next few months, so it will probably be near the end of the year anyway. Would you still like me to quote?*

Lindsay: *I'm really disappointed with that, actually, but yes, please send me a quote anyway.*

Nina: *OK will do. Thanks for your interest.*

Lindsay: *Yes, thanks, Nina. I'll wait to hear from you. Sure, I'll bump into you again soon anyway. Thanks again.*

Lindsay added a love heart, and Nina winced as she read through.

Nina put her phone down and shook her head. From her side of the table, she'd rather not be bumping into Lindsay anytime soon.

22

Once Nina and Robby had decided on chowder for their wedding reception, they had worked hard to make the details happen. They'd muscled to get everything arranged to ensure that they met the deadline for the appearance of the wildflowers and nice weather at The Summer Hotel. The best thing they'd done was to apply for the marriage licence right away as soon as Robby'd proposed. After that, there wasn't really that much that couldn't be sorted out. The wheels had been put in motion for a party in a garden in Lovely Bay with a jazz band, a few bowls of chowder and a prayer for good weather topping it all.

The Summer Hotel as the venue had gone down well with Sophie, who had clapped her hands and been over the moon. Nina's sister hadn't looked too impressed but asked what alcohol would be available, and Nina's mum, in the end, hadn't seemed too bothered at all. Everything had worked out well.

The most startling thing to Nina was that Robby had shown a very different side to him once he'd been on a mission to get things sorted. Since they'd met, Nina had been quite smug about how organised she was. She'd thought that she was the one who liked all her ducks in a row, but Robby had matched her and then some. Seeing the working side of Robby made her fall for him even more. He'd set up spreadsheets, taken everything on board, and more or less told Nina that all she needed to worry about was turning up. That was the sort of husband she could deal with any day of the week. Nina had laughed and teased him, saying that he would have to wait and see on the day if she showed up and followed through.

Not long after they'd got the go-ahead from Jill, a lot of the things to sort were done and dusted; they had a team organised who would be serving drinks, they'd bought a job lot of all-weather proof market umbrellas, trestle tables had been bagged from the church where June did the flowers, and Nancy would be providing vintage tablecloths and old English china from her mum's attic.

Things had quickly come together and Nina had let out a huge sigh of relief. The only thing left to decide was *who* in Lovely Bay was actually going to be in charge of the chowder. So many people had put their hands up and offered it had become a little bit awkward, and Robby and Nina had been unsure what to do for the best.

Nina mulled it all over as she strolled along on her way to help out at the deli. It was a beautiful day in Lovely Bay – the sun was shining, the sky was blue, and Nina was loving the warm weather. There wasn't a Lovely Bay striped coat to be seen anywhere as far as the eye could see.

As soon as she got to the back of the deli, she knew that Birdie was in residence. Even though Birdie had said she might not make it because she wasn't feeling well, Nina could hear the Shipping Forecast from the alleyway as she made her way through the gate and into the back kitchen. The kitchen, as usual, smelt fabulous, and as it normally was, it was immaculate. The whole place ran like clockwork via the systems that Birdie, followed through by Alice, had put in place, which meant that everything went smoothly for whoever was working. The dishwashers were humming away to themselves, three gigantic pots of chowder stood on the stove, and it looked as if things were ready for the speakeasy that evening.

Birdie bustled into the room. 'Neens, hello! Thanks for helping out. I'm so glad you're here.'

'No problem at all. How are you feeling?'

Birdie shook her head. 'I'm not too bad. Being a pharmacist helps when you don't feel well,' she laughed. 'I can dose myself up left, right, and centre.'

'Yeah, you don't look great,' Nina admitted. 'What do you think you've got?'

'No idea. I'll be fine,' Birdie replied as the Shipping Forecast played away from the speaker on a shelf to the left of them.

Nina shook her head and gestured to the door. 'Honestly, just go home. I can cope with everything here. Most of it looks as if it's been done anyway.' She turned around and looked around the small kitchen. 'What time is Alice getting here?'

Birdie turned her wrist over and looked at her watch. 'She said the train was running late, but she shouldn't be too long.'

'Where's she been?' Nina asked.

'She went up to see a school for one of her children and it ran a bit late. She's juggling so much at the moment. She does loads for me here, and I didn't want her to worry.'

Nina put her handbag in the cupboard not far away from the dishwasher, took a clean apron from a pile of them in a basket by the fridge, put the apron over her head, and tied it at her waist. 'So, really, it's just prepping by the looks of this,' she said.

'Yep.'

'Too easy. I can do it with my eyes shut these days.'

'Okay, well, I might stay for a bit, and then I'll go. By the way,' she said, 'have you decided what you're going to do about the chowder yet?

'I've had so many offers.'

'I know. Trust me, I've heard. What are you going to do?'

Nina shook her head. 'I'm not really sure yet.'

'Right, okay. Well, it wouldn't be a problem for us to do it. I'm offering again.'

'I know. The thing is, I want you there as a *guest*, not working.'

Birdie chuckled. 'Half of Lovely Bay wants to be there. I can assure you I can get a team together to make sure everything runs smoothly. I won't actually be working myself.'

Nina wasn't sure that was true. If Alice was out of the picture, Nina had been called in many times to help and save the day. She tilted her head to the side and considered for a second. 'You know what then let's do it.'

Birdie clapped her hands together and jumped up and down on the spot. 'Fabulous! I'm so happy. I really wanted to do this. Yes! I win! Points to me.'

Nina laughed. 'You're funny. Thank you. It's going to be the best chowder ever in Lovely Bay and the best wedding, of course.'

'Too easy. I will start to get the word out and get everything organised. It won't take much. We've done enough chowder events in our time in this town.'

Nina nodded her head. 'There *is* just one thing I'd like to request.'

'Of course. Anything! What's that?'

Nina laughed. 'I'm not really sure I want my wedding party to be accompanied by the Shipping Forecast.'

'Really? Why ever not? I thought you'd love that as the backdrop,' Birdie joked. 'It accompanies just about everything else that goes on in this town.'

23

Nina looked out the window as the train pulled into Lovely Bay station, slid past the moveable platform and edged closer to the stationmaster's house. She had spent the day in the town a few stops down from Lovely Bay decluttering someone's kitchen. Her little organising business was pottering along quite well, and she was pleased with its progress. It was never going to be up there with the Elon Musk's of the world but as a tiny, self-sufficient business that paid its way, it wasn't doing too badly at all. It paid the bills; always a bonus.

As the train inched to its stop, she picked up her huge work tote bag, scooped up her iPad and phone, and followed a man with a camera around his neck and his phone attached to a pole who was craning his neck to peer at the moveable platform. She smiled to herself as the man, completely oblivious to her, eagerly waited by the train doors, jigging from left to right in anticipation. Popping her phone and iPad into her bag, she passed another couple of trainspotters going the other way, then headed to the stairs, walked over the footbridge, down the other side, and waved to Nancy.

Nancy jumped up, opened the door, and peered out onto the

platform. 'Hello, where are you off to? Having a half-day, are we?' Nancy inquired and laughed. 'Don't think you can get away with anything around here. You have been seen. I'll be noting it down in the Lovely ledger.'

Nina laughed. 'Yes, I am. Friday afternoon, and I've spent a whole morning throwing away six-year-old cereal boxes and spices from the seventies. How are you?'

'How am I? Let me see.' Nancy rolled her eyes. 'Spending the day looking after trainspotters, sorting out lost schoolbags, and unblocking one of the toilets. Just another run-of-the-mill day at Lovely Bay station for me.'

'Sounds fun.'

'Could be worse jobs in the world, right?' Nancy chuckled.

'You could be a digital nomad,' Nina joked. 'You'd like to be one of those, wouldn't you?'

'Never,' Nancy retorted. 'Not on your Nelly. I'll stick with my job on the railway dealing with passengers and unblocking toilets on the side.'

They both laughed.

'Where are you off to?' Nancy asked.

Nina smiled. 'Actually, I'm going to meet Robby.'

'Ooh, nice. Where are you meeting him?'

'All going to plan, he should be on the boat. I don't know where we're going. It's a surprise.'

Nancy flipped her watch over. 'I just saw Clive; he's back from his French lesson, so he's doing the run today. We all know where Colin is.'

Nina laughed. It was a known thing that Colin went to a little place called Darling Island supposedly because one of the shops there did amazing coffee. Lovelies knew the real reason. 'Don't worry, I haven't forgotten, even though the timetable online says the ferry runs over lunch, I remembered it actually doesn't get going again until about two because he's off gallivanting down to Darling Island.'

'Well, now you're a Lovely you actually know how it works around here,' Nancy teased.

Nina felt heat rise to her cheeks. It was ridiculous, but she liked being referred to as a 'Lovely', and Nancy played on that. She just liked how it felt to belong and be part of the community.

'See you then. Enjoy the rest of your day.'

'See you. Have fun.' Nancy tipped the top of her hat. 'Be good, our Neens.'

A few minutes later, Nina was waiting at the jetty. She looked at the little weathered shed where Colin and Clive would often be standing and read the noticeboard. It held a jumble of business cards, notices, and all sorts of things of interest; a new Pilates class was starting in the RNLI Club, a local taxi firm had a special deal to the airport, and Clive was offering a lawnmower to any 'Lovely' who might need one. Nina felt a warm, cosy feeling surge through her veins as she realised that she was now part of Lovely Bay. It made her feel all sorts of good inside. As she watched the boat potter along, she saw Clive.

Clive smiled and called out, 'Bonjour!'

Nina chuckled to herself, and as the boat stopped at the jetty and he tied a rope, she responded, 'Bonjour! Hi, how are you today?'

'I'm good, thanks. Nice day for it,' he said, looking up towards the sky.

'Yes. Thank goodness. We've had too much rain these past few months.'

Robby waved from the front of the boat as Nina hopped on, walked towards him, and got comfortable. 'Hi.'

'Hi, gorgeous. Good morning?'

'Yep. Oh, I'm so looking forward to this. Where are we going?'

'I can't tell you that. Highly classified information. As I said.

It's a surprise.'

Nina looked down at the floor under Robby's feet, where a basket was wedged underneath the seat in front. 'Come on, just tell me.'

He laughed. 'Completely and utterly a surprise. You'll have to wait.'

'Oh well, I know it's not a surprise proposal. You already ticked that box, right? I'll just have to wait and see.'

About fifteen minutes or so later, they were at the stop at the mouth of the river nearest to the beach. Nina inhaled the salty fresh air coming off the sea as they walked along in the direction of Lovely Bay beach. 'Are we going to the bay?' Nina asked.

Robby shook his head. 'You don't need to know that.'

Nina laughed, and as they strolled along, the sea breeze whipped through her hair. They walked past where she thought they were going, the main beach of Lovely Bay, and strolled further to the far side, taking a path through some trees. Then went over gritty sandy gravel, through a small wooded area, up some stone steps, and back down the other side until they came to a small, almost private, and definitely deserted beach.

'I bet you haven't been to this one before,' Robby said with an expectant look on his face.

Nina raised her eyebrows in surprise; she didn't even know where they were, and she definitely hadn't been there before. 'Nup.'

Robby shook his head. 'Mostly only known to locals, and at this time of the year, not really that busy. Not on a Friday, at least.'

'You can say that again,' Nina replied as she looked around, spying only a few people on the beach; a family with a couple of toddlers sat behind a red and white striped windbreaker, a couple with camping chairs were tucked up near to a breaker, and another family with a huge picnic blanket had a disposable barbecue, sending plumes of smoke up into the air. Tucked on the far side, a small line of beach huts perched just above the sea, and the roofline of Lovely Bay sat just behind in the far distance.

Nina squinted and looked around. 'Wow, this is really nice. It's so quiet.'

'Thought you might like it,' Robby replied, holding up the picnic basket. 'This will help.'

A few minutes later, they were sitting on the beach on a striped rug. Nina had a drink in her hand, her head held up to the sky, and Robby was pulling things out of the small picnic basket. He secured the legs on a compact, low picnic table, put a bowl of salad on the table, and started to chuckle as he pulled out an insulated bag from inside the basket. Unzipping it, he lifted the flap and showed what was inside to Nina.

Nina peered in. 'It looks like a crumble.' She frowned, 'Where did you get that from? What in the world, did you make a crumble?'

Robby chuckled. 'I wish. I wouldn't even know where to start with a crumble. June made it.'

'June made you a crumble to take on a picnic?' Nina's voice lilted into a question at the end.

'She certainly did,' Robby replied. 'I get all the perks, me, and this insulated bag.' He patted the bag. 'Apparently, this will keep it warm for so many hours. Don't worry. I've got lots of instructions from Auntie June. You are experiencing a professional level picnic here. And there I was going to make a cheese sandwich.'

Nina giggled. 'I don't mind instructions from Auntie June. I'm surprised she hasn't been giving us directions on what to do with the wedding.'

Robby laughed. 'No, we've been lucky there so far.'

Nina took a sip of her drink and settled back onto the picnic blanket. 'How come I am being treated like this then? I'm not complaining. This is so nice.'

'I thought you deserved a bit of time off. What with the work on the house, your new business, and everything else. I thought we both needed downtime, away from talking to anyone about the wedding or the business or the house or anything else at all.'

'You're right, actually. It's been a bit of a whirlwind few months.'

Robby nodded. 'I think we're all set, though. Everything is done for the wedding, right?'

Nina smiled. 'I think so. And I think your spreadsheets and organisation have put me to shame.'

Robby laughed. 'So, everything is in place for the party in the garden? Tables are organised, chairs coming from the hall, Birdie doing the chowder, and staff serving drinks. Registry office is booked. My mum knows precisely what is what. What else?' Robby asked.

'Hmm, let me think. Oh, there's the small problem of a dress. I haven't got one I love yet.'

Robby smiled. 'I'm not getting involved in that. No can do.'

Nina shook her head. 'Not a problem. I'm sure I will get something sorted. If the worst comes to the worst, I'm going to wear that one that I got online even though I don't *love* it, it's nice. So, I think we're ready. You're ready, your mum is ready. Everyone's booked into various accommodation if they need to stay. We go off to the registry office with your mum and dad, my mum and sister, for the quiet little ceremony, and then have the party with the chowder, lots of drinks, and dancing under the stars later on that night. All too easy.'

Robby chuckled. 'Sounds like we're done and dusted apart from what you're going to rock up in.'

'It sounds like it,' Nina replied as she sat back and looked up at the wispy clouds trailing across a pale blue-white sky. 'I'll just wear the dress I ordered. It's fine.'

As quick as a flash and from nowhere, Andrew appeared. As often happened, he suddenly slammed into her mind when she was least expecting it. At least these days, it didn't happen very often, but he was still there, and she still sometimes felt a *tiny* bit sad. Not anywhere near as much as she used to, and the grief no longer had a hold of her, but sometimes he was just still around, front and centre, popping in and out of her life. Like he was speaking to her still all this time later.

Robby squeezed her hand. 'Okay?'

She nodded. 'Yeah, I'm fine.'

He squinted his eyes. 'Are you sure? You suddenly went very quiet. What are you thinking about?'

Nina wasn't going to bother to talk about Andrew, not that it was a problem between them, just that she didn't really want to change the mood. No one wanted to hear her keep going on about him, least of all Robby. She shook her head. 'Oh, nothing.'

'Are you sure it's nothing?' Robby insisted.

Nina was going to say yes then changed her mind. 'I just had a fleeting image of Andrew in my head. Sorry. The anniversary is coming up soon. It must be that.'

Robby nodded. 'I thought you might have done when you said about the date before. Have you been feeling sad?'

Nina shook her head. 'Not at all, the opposite, in fact. I don't feel sad about him anymore. I sort of feel fond memories and warm feelings, whereas before, I was so wrapped up in grief and hurt and sadness and pain that I couldn't remember things with fondness or happiness. Now that's changed.' Nina went quiet for a second. 'Because of you,' she added.

'I feel the same, even though what happened to me was a lot earlier, and I was a lot younger. I never thought I would meet anyone who, well, you know...' He stopped for a minute and then continued, 'I never thought I'd be with anyone who just made me feel like *me* again.'

Nina felt a prick of something in the corner of her eyes. She nodded. 'Same, same, same. Me too.'

24

In old, ripped jeans and a work shirt, Nina was in the new harbour property. She heaved herself up the timber stairs towards the third floor. She'd been working all day and was feeling it as she got to the top and stood looking at the room. Despite wondering when it was *ever* going to be done, she suddenly felt as if everything had come together. When she'd first bought the place, it had been covered in dust, cobwebs, and loads of junk. Now the junk was long gone, just a distant memory of one of the first few days when she'd taken possession. Not only was the place now free of junk, but the whole of the top floor was a beautiful, soft white. On the far wall, the old timber shelves that had stored fishing gear were a slightly warmer shade of white and now held pillar candles, a selection of photo frames, and a couple of plants. Nina was well on her way to getting the place sorted.

Across the room, she pushed up the beautiful sash window and stood for a while looking out over the harbour. Boats bobbed around on the water, the sunlight glinted off the sea, and every now and then, a seagull swooped down and landed on the back of a hull. After fussing with a sisal plaited rug that had been delivered the day before, she pulled a chair over towards the window and sat looking out at the same view, lost in thought. It was her and Andrew's wedding anniversary, and despite telling herself that she was fine and everything was okay when the date had flicked over on her phone, she wasn't very happy at all. She watched as Sophie crossed the harbour below, pushed open the window further, called out, and waved. At first, Sophie didn't hear her, so she called again. Hearing Nina's voice, Sophie peered up at the top of the building, put her left hand up to shade her eyes, and called out, 'Hello, how are you?'

'Yes, all good, thanks. How are you?' Nina replied.

'Fine.'

'Tea?'

'Yes, please. Love one,' Sophie replied.

Nina shut the window and made her way downstairs, and just as she was pouring hot water from the kettle into the teapot, Sophie came through the back door. She hugged Nina and then, holding her arms out and keeping her hands on Nina's shoulders, she raised her eyebrows in question. 'Are you okay? I know this is a sad day.'

Nina replied, 'Yes, I'm fine. Honestly.'

'Really?' Sophie replied, her eyebrows still raised in question. 'You seem very off.'

'No, I'm fine,' Nina repeated, as the Pity Smile Nina hadn't seen for a long time landed back on Sophie's face.

'Not the best day for you, is it?'

Nina shrugged and flapped her hand a little bit. 'I'm okay. I'm used to it. It's just... I've had a lot going on, and I seem to be strangely full of emotion, which I didn't think was going to happen. I'm just a bit fragile around the edges.' She shook her head and closed her eyes tightly. 'I should be happy, not feeling sad again.'

'It's a big day full of lots of memories and *very* emotional.'

'Yeah, but it feels different this time which is throwing me. Is there such a thing as happy-sad?' Nina asked.

Sophie looked from left to right and made a funny shape with her lips. 'I don't know, but I suppose there is if that's what you're feeling. Super happy and super sad at the same time, especially on a day like this. It's good to acknowledge it. Feel whatever you need to feel.'

Nina swallowed and nodded. 'Yep.'

Sophie lowered her voice and pursed her lips together before she spoke. 'Andrew would be happy for you. You do know that, don't you?'

'He would be. I guess.'

'He loved you *so* much, Neens. *So much*. There is no way he would have wanted you to be as you were in that flat.'

'I know, and here I am about to marry somebody else and going in a way that I thought my life was never going to go.'

'It's staggering when you think about it.'

'The thing is it makes everything else seem just so final.'

'How'd you mean?'

'Andrew *really* is dead, isn't he? He *really* isn't part of my life ahead anymore. I know that sounds weird.'

Sophie nodded. 'Well, there's one thing for sure; he *really* is dead, Neens.'

Nina sighed, the anniversary had stirred up a strange jumble of emotions for her. It wasn't as if she'd ever been in total denial about what had happened, but when she thought about it and how she felt now, maybe she had been underneath it all. Perhaps she'd never really believed what had happened. Now that she was about to start a journey with someone totally different, in a completely different part of the country, surrounded by people and in a place her old life just wasn't part of, she now knew one hundred per cent that she had moved on. Andrew wasn't in this new life of hers. 'It's all very strange,' she said to Sophie. 'Who would've thought I would've ended up here?'

Sophie giggled. 'I would have because I kept on about it to you for years. Just imagine if you weren't here, you would still be in that flat, doing the same old thing, week in, week out. Moping around with that flipping ledge full of flowerpots. That thing used to drive me around the twist.'

Nina nodded. 'It's true. I think I would've still been doing the same if I hadn't come to Lovely Bay that day on the train and ended up bumping into Robby. I would still be going to work, making food, and being sad and lonely for the rest of my life pretty much. That ledge was one of the only things I let myself do and think about.'

'You would've been okay in the end. It's just that this prompted it to happen sooner. I think you'll still be sad about things like anniversaries and birthdays, you know. Actually, I think it's totally normal to feel like this, and if you didn't feel this way, it would be more concerning.'

'You really think so?' Nina replied.

'I really do. Anyway, we don't have to *forget* about Andrew. Maybe we can somehow make him part of the wedding celebration.'

'What do you mean?' Nina asked.

'I don't know. Like, add something of his, that you've still got, to the wedding. Just an idea off the top of my head.'

'Like what?'

Sophie looked up in contemplation for a second. 'Well, I don't for a second believe that you got rid of his clothes, so maybe something from those. A card in your bag or something? I don't know.'

Nina laughed. She was never going to admit that she'd stood in Andrew's wardrobe more than once and inhaled. 'I may still have them...'

'Well, why don't you try and maybe pop something into your bag, or have you got something from your first wedding you could have as a memento?'

Nina thought about the boxes in her flat where all her wedding stuff was carefully stored and labelled under the eaves. 'Actually, I think I've still got everything. All the cards, all the things from people. Obviously, I've got my dress. I had it especially dry cleaned and put away in a box.'

'There you are then. Sorted. Why don't we pop up there and have a little root through it? You could wear something for good luck. That could be a way of making Andrew part of it.'

Nina nodded. 'I'm not sure if it's a good idea or not. I'm not sure I can handle the memories of opening the box and feeling the pain.'

Sophie mulled it over for a second. 'Maybe, maybe not. It's there though if you wanted to try, isn't it?'

Nina nodded. 'I'll run it past Robby. Maybe I'll give it a go.'

25

As soon as Nina got off the underground train and stepped out of the station, she was flooded with memories. Good ones, bad ones, *different* ones. Suddenly, there she was all those years before, just younger, skinnier, and lighter in both body, mind, and spirit. Then she'd been excited about life ahead with Andrew and their new flat. Nina grimaced; none of those dreams had come to fruition. Death had darkened the door. It had taken Andrew and had given her a ride to a dark place she never wanted to end up in again. Now, she was about to embark on a similar journey but with someone entirely different. Life zoomed around, twisted, and turned in the most mysterious of ways.

As she neared the flat, the familiarity of everything struck her. The crack in the pavement where the tree roots from the garden of a block of flats had pushed through still hadn't been fixed by the council. The odd little dog-leg junction with traffic lights, where no one really knew who had right of way, was still congested with cars. The screech of an ambulance a few streets away wailed in her ears.

A few minutes later, Nina was at the front door of the flats, keying in the code on the pad. She walked slowly up the steps to the top landing she shared with Mrs Gilbert. She could hear Radio 4 blaring from Mrs Gilbert's flat, as it always did, and she closed her eyes for a second, hoping Mrs Gilbert wouldn't come out. While she was nice enough, since moving out and on, Nina hadn't really missed her. Everything seemed to be a drama with her and Nina wasn't really up for that.

Intending not to be seen, Nina hurried to open her front door, stood at the entrance, slipped off her shoes, and inhaled. The air was musty, and for a second, she paused and wondered what the smell was. Of course she knew what it was. Andrew. His smell hit her between the eyes. Was she going mad? Was she smelling someone who had been dead for a long time? Of course, it wasn't *actually* Andrew, but what she smelt was the life that had been hers and his. A smell from a place long since dead. It put her in a spin.

She stood for a second, inhaling with her hand on the ball atop the bannister, and wiggled it as she always did, and as ever, was surprised when it moved. Then, crossing the tight wool carpet she'd put in not long after Andrew had died, she took the first small step up, then the next two steps down, and stepped up again, and turned. She got to the top of the stairs by the dresser where she kept her keys, her phone charger, and various other paraphernalia and continued to smell the scent of her old life as it wafted around her saying hello.

She looked past the dresser to the two small low doors built into the wall that went under the eaves. Nina knew exactly what was in there, all of it labelled, all meticulously organised things from her old life. Photos, suitcases, holiday things, keepsakes, her wedding dress in the box from the dry cleaners, and her wedding memorabilia, all sorted into tubs. Half of her wondered why she'd kept many of the things she had.

Deciding that she needed a bit of time before delving into the depths of the eaves, she made a cup of peppermint tea and sat at the tiny kitchen table, looking out over what she had once called her balcony garden. Now, she saw it with very different eyes; it was just a ledge. The pots she'd at one time focused a lot of her energy on were still there doing their thing. The last time she'd come, she'd weeded them fully and pulled out anything that hadn't survived, and some of them were still doing okay. She let her gaze drift across the rooftops, lost in thought for a while, thinking about how different the grey sky and urban scene were from Lovely Bay. How her new life was nothing like the one in the flat where she'd been locked in a circle of grief and pain and not a lot else.

Once she'd finished her peppermint tea, she strolled into the bedroom and opened the wardrobe where Andrew's clothes still hung. For a long time, she just stared at the row of shirts and things, not really sure what to do. What sort of memento was she looking for? Unlike her wardrobe, not that there was much in there now, which was colour-coded to within an inch of its life, Andrew's side had always been messier and it still was. His shirts were together on the right, a couple of suit jackets in the middle. A hanging organiser that wasn't really organising much but a jumble of jumpers hung on the left, and a tie rack was messily piled with ties. The shelf underneath the hanging section held more piles of clothes, a big, old-fashioned plastic file he had carried around with him since university days, and his leather satchel he'd always used when he went to work was stuffed in on the left. Drawer springs twanged as she pulled open the heavy top section on the left and a black eye mask from a business trip fell onto the carpet. She picked it up, put it to her face, and inhaled. She shook her head, unlike what she'd felt when she'd first walked in, Andrew wasn't there. His smell was no longer on a face mask from a business trip on a plane.

She shut the wardrobe doors, letting them bang back into place, went back into the kitchen, made another cup of peppermint tea, and then, as she drank it, she sat in front of the doors in the hallway, looking at them for a long time. About fifteen minutes later, she got down on her hands and knees, pulled open the doors, grimaced at the hot, musty feel under the eaves, and crawled in. Apart from the fact that it was a bit dustier than the last time she'd been into it, the storage area was organised, and everything was in the right place. Her wedding stuff was exactly where she remembered, with her wedding dress on the far left, near the pipes. Crawling over, she spied the gold logo from the dry cleaners and dragged the box towards her, doing the same with the huge plastic storage tubs packed full of wedding things. Before she knew it, she was perched on the landing, unclipping the blue latches on top of the storage tubs and diving in.

She sat in a strange world as she opened card after card and read word after word. So many messages from so many people offering their congratulations and good luck for a future that had never turned out to be. Shaking her head, she felt bad at the fact that she had lost touch with a lot of the people in the cards since Andrew passed away, especially Andrew's family and his friends. Initially, it had just been too much for her to keep up with anyone. Then, people got on with their lives and slowly but surely they'd drifted away. She'd never really liked his family anyway, so there hadn't been too much incentive for her to keep the relationship going there and his and their friends had dropped off one by one.

A few minutes later, she opened the wedding dress box. Inside, reams and reams of tissue paper confronted her. It crinkled as she peeled off the first few layers, finally arriving at the dress, which was wrapped in a different stiffer paper, some sort of preservation paper, she assumed. She lifted up the paper and stared at the bodice of the dress for ages. It was just as she remembered it – a plain, very simple white dress with small sleeves and a princess-line top. Suddenly, she was back in the church, walking up the aisle, Andrew smiling at her from the top. She could hear the music and smell her perfume, Sophie was behind her, and her mum beamed from the left. Flowers everywhere. A beautiful old church. Smiley happy people. Music. Life. Hope.

She pulled the dress, struggling with its weight to stand up and look at it fully. The skirt hung in a few creases, but overall, it seemed to be fine. Turning it around, she heaved it over the bannister and fiddled with the poppers on the big bow that held the train onto the dress at the back. Then, taking it into the sitting room, she hung it on a hook, hoping the weight of it wouldn't pull the hook out of the wall, and carefully unclipped the gigantic train. She was left with a plain white skirt with a pretty top that clipped together to appear like a dress. Standing with her fingers scrunching her top lip back and forth, she stared at the dress for ages. Sophie's words went through her head about having something to do with Andrew at the wedding. She pulled at the waist of the dress, wondering whether or not it might fit. She perhaps would just about be able to squeeze herself into it if she was lucky.

A few minutes later, she was chuckling to herself as she stood in the middle of the sitting room. After stripping down to her underwear and letting the dress fall down to the floor, she unzipped the back of the bodice and skirt and stepped in, yanking and pulling the fabric over her hips. Then she held onto both sides and pulled the bodice up over her bra. Struggling, her arms behind her, she found the zip and tried to pull it up. About halfway up her back, she gave up.

Pulling up the bottom of the skirt, she walked into her bedroom and stared in the mirror. As when she'd first opened the box in the hallway, a mix of emotions flooded through her veins. But standing in her socks with the bodice half open at the back, something about it simply felt right. The more she looked at it turning this way and that, the more she knew that she wanted the dress to be part of her day.

If she could work out a way to get the dress altered, she'd be wearing it. Still part of her, still part of the Andrew and Nina story. Only now, Andrew was no longer there, but he would have loved to know that she was happy. He would've loved that she had found someone who loved her just as much as he had done back in the day. All those moons ago, she'd worn the dress with hope and anticipation in her heart to marry someone she'd loved the bones of. Now the dress was going to take her on a journey to do the same thing again. Just as nice bones. Even better straps.

26

Nina hung the dress back on the same hook in the sitting room, went down the stairs, slipped her shoes on, hurried across the landing to avoid Mrs Gilbert, and made her way out onto the street. A few minutes later, she was in a café not far from her flat. She ordered herself a cheese and salad sandwich with beetroot and a Coke Zero, took it to a table in the corner where she'd often sat when she'd lived in the area, and ate her sandwich, lost in thought.

Was it peculiar to wear the same wedding dress you wore to your first wedding the second time around? she asked herself. *Would it be strange to be wearing a dress she married someone else in when she married Robby? Would Robby be okay with it? What would her mum think? Would her mum have some little quip to say about it?* She wondered what Sophie would think and pressed Sophie's number on her phone.

'Hey, how are you?' Nina asked. 'Everything good?'

'Yeah, good, thanks. Just busy, got a lot on.'

'You sound tired. Is Nick away?' Nina asked.

'Yes, of course, Nick is away. When there's lots going on,

Nick goes away. That's pretty much how it goes,' Sophie replied with a teeny bit of sarcasm in her voice.

Nina rolled her eyes. As she'd suspected many times before, Nick was often away for work to get him out of doing things at home, not that it was any of her business. She didn't say anything about Nick in case she couldn't stop. 'Do you need me to come over and give you a hand?'

Sophie did not sound her usual upbeat self at all. 'No, I'm fine. I just need to get my act together and put my feet up later on. I'm just exhausted, to be quite honest. I underestimated how hard it is with three. It's a whole different ball game altogether.'

'It must be and you do most of it on your own. Honestly, just let me know if you want me to pop over.'

'Will do. Anyway, what's up with you?' Sophie asked.

'Well, let me tell you one thing; I think I might have found a dress.'

'What? Oh right, excellent news! I didn't know you were going shopping. Where have you been? Has to be better than that place we went to with your mum. I thought you'd decided to go with the best one out of that lot you ordered online. I know you didn't love it but...'

'I *haven't* been shopping. I did what you said. I came up to the flat to have a look through the wedding stuff to see if there was anything of Andrew's here that I could use on the day.'

'Right and you found something in a shop on the way there, did you?'

'No. I did find something, but I'm not sure if it's weird or not.'

'Hang on, sorry, crossed wires. What have you got of Andrew's? Are you going to be wearing one of Andrew's T-shirts under the dress?' Sophie asked with a chuckle. 'Neens, I *do* think that's a bit weird if I'm being honest.'

'Well, actually, no, that's the thing,' Nina said. 'I'm going to wear *the* dress.'

Sophie queried, 'Sorry, are you saying what I think you are saying? You mean the *actual* dress?'

'Yes, the actual dress. As in the dress that was in storage under the eaves. What do you think?'

'Sorry, let me clarify this. You mean you're going to wear the dress that you got married in for your first wedding for your second wedding?'

'Yup. Correct.'

'Right.' Sophie went quiet.

'You think that's weird, don't you?'

'Yes. Err, no, I don't know. Maybe a bit. Does it still fit?'

Nina laughed out loud. 'Is that a roundabout way of saying I've put on loads of weight since my first wedding?'

'No, no, we both have. I mean we're not in our twenties anymore, Neens. Sorry, I didn't mean it like that.' Sophie giggled.

'I tried to get the bodice done up, and I could get most of it all the way up. I don't know if it's because I can't do the zip or it's too tight, but I've examined it, and I think I'll be able to get it altered.'

'What did it look like?'

'I should have taken a photo. I detached the train bit, I don't know if you remember what it was like. It had that huge bow with the tiny sparkles at the back with the long train. Anyway, underneath that it's just a beautiful white dress, well a bodice and skirt. I think it will be good. What do you think?'

'Hmm. I can't see why not.' Sophie reasoned. 'Your mum is going to die.'

'I'll have to run it past Robby obviously. What do you reckon he'll say?'

'I'm sure he'll be fine with it. He's been super chill with everything else you've wanted in the wedding,' Sophie pointed out.

'Yeah, you're right. Well, as long as I can get the top of it adjusted, we're good to go. I'll send that other one back.'

'Wow, I didn't see that coming.'

'I know.'

'Interesting.'

'I have a dress I actually *love*.' Nina laughed.

Sophie chuckled. 'Best news I've had for ages. We're getting very close to everything being good to go. I'm surprised, but in a way, it feels good. I mean we were both at the first wedding, right? Why not the dress, too?'

27

Nina had struggled with the box her wedding dress was packed carefully away in when she'd had to cart it down the escalator to the underground train, but once she'd got on the main train to Lovely, she had tucked it in the seat beside her and hoped that the train wouldn't be too packed. As the carriages pulled out of the London station, the seats around her were half empty, and so all was good. It was like she was travelling with an old friend.

She patted the box, laughed to herself, and tapped her phone to call her mum to tell her that, as long as Robby didn't mind, she intended to wear her first wedding dress to marry Robby. She winced as her mum answered, wondering whether or not what she was going to say would go down well.

'Hi Mum.'

'Hello darling,' Nina's mum said. 'How are you?' The tannoy for the train made an announcement over Nina's head. 'Oh, it sounds like you're on the train. Have you been up to London?'

Nina nodded. 'Yes, I've been up to the flat.'

'How was it? Everything okay there? Any problems you needed to sort out?'

'Everything is fine. I went up to look at some stuff, actually, in the loft.'

'What's that then, darling?' Nina's mum asked with a mildly interested tone.

Nina swallowed. 'I went to have a look at some of the stuff from the wedding.'

Nina's mum's voice sounded confused. 'I didn't realise you had anything there for the wedding.'

'No, no, not that wedding, I mean not this wedding, my other wedding.'

'Sorry darling, do you mean to Andrew?'

'Yes, Mum, I do.'

'Sorry, what were you doing that for?' Nina's mum's voice sounded very uneasy.

'Well, it was Sophie's suggestion because I've been thinking a lot about Andrew the last few weeks because of the anniversary and everything. Sophie thought that perhaps we could encompass something from him into the wedding, like a little memento or my veil or something like that.'

'Hmm, really?'

Nina didn't like the sound of her mum's voice; clearly, her mum didn't think it was a good idea at all. 'Yep.'

'Right, I'm not sure about that darling, like you know how sad you were. Of course, anyone would be and it's taken a long time for you to get over it, so I'm not sure if that's a good idea or not. No, I'm really not convinced...'

Nina shook her head. Her mum didn't get it. She was never going to get over it nor did she ever want to. She *hated* it when people said she should be over it. Her mum was never going to understand that. Not many people did. 'No, no, Mum, it's fine. I think it's a good idea. It will make me feel okay about it all.'

'But what about Robby? What does he think?' Nina's mum asked.

'We'll find out.'

'I'm not so sure, darling. I'm not sure if I like the idea at all. Isn't it a bit morbid and strange? Won't it just make everybody sad? Yes, it's on the *ghastly* side. Awful, actually. Morbid.'

Nina shook her head; her mum was sometimes quite dramatic. She rolled her eyes, inhaled, and leant her head back on the seat. 'Well, this is what I'm thinking. I'm not just going to have a small memento, I'm actually going to wear my first wedding dress.'

Nina's mum made a noise between a squark and a howl. 'What? You've got to be joking! You can't do that! Why would you do that? No. Flat no.'

'I'm not joking.'

'Darling, I need to digest what you are saying for a second. Gosh. You were always odd, but this...'

'I think it's a good idea,' Nina replied. 'I've just been to the flat, I got it out and everything just felt right. It's *such* a beautiful dress.'

Nina's mum made a funny sound. 'That huge dress with the train that you married Andrew in?' Her mum's voice faded. 'Darling, I'm really not sure this is a good idea, as I've said a few times now. Maybe you should go and see a counsellor or something. Is that grief group you used to go to still up and running?'

Nina stopped herself from tutting. 'I'm not going to wear the train and all the bustle at the back. If you remember, that bit popped off. Underneath it, it's just a plain dress with an amazing cut.'

'Actually, darling, I do remember that. We thought it was a good idea at the time. Little did I ever think that it could be, well, you know, used in something like this. Repurposed. I mean that *is* all the trend these days, I suppose. Saving the planet and all that.'

'Mum, it looks like a completely different dress.'

'Anyway, darling, can I just ask this? I'm not being rude, but surely you don't fit in that anymore. I mean you've eaten your fair share since Andrew…'

Nina rolled her eyes. Couldn't make it up with her mum. 'It's fine, Mum. It just doesn't do up across the back where my bra goes. I think it'll be easy to adjust it. It has a zip underneath a line of tiny faux buttons, so I think it might work.'

'What about that one you got from that online place? That one looked lovely.'

'I know but it wasn't…'

'Darling, so between now and the wedding, you're going to get the dress adjusted and you have to talk it through with Robby about whether or not he's fine with it. Is that what you're telling me?'

'Yes, Mum, I am.'

'Okay, darling. Well, it's your wedding, and it's your life. Odd if you ask me, but then you always like to do things in your own special way. Always been the same.'

'Yeah, I think it will be good. I'm really happy to have made this decision.'

'Good, darling, good to hear. As long as you're happy, that's all I've ever been worried about.'

Nina sighed again; that was *so* not true. Her mum lived in a complete world of her own and didn't really let a conversation go by where she didn't tell Nina that Nina had always been, 'a bit different'.

'Look Mum, I better get going because the train is getting there and I'll have to get off soon.'

'Okay, darling. I'll tell your sister the news about the dress and let me know how it goes with Robby.'

'Will do. Bye, Mum. Love you loads.'

'Bye, darling.'

28

Nina looked at the riverboat timetable on her phone as the train approached Lovely Bay, noted that there was one every twenty minutes because of the time of day, and decided to hustle towards the river so that she could get home quickly. As the train passed the moveable platform, she picked up the box with her wedding dress, slipped her phone into her handbag, put her handbag on her shoulder, waited for the doors to open, and stepped onto the platform.

Unlike the times of the day when she normally took the train, which weren't commuter times, the train platform was fairly busy. Only one trainspotter stood watching the moveable platform, and everybody else hustled towards the footbridge. Juggling the big box in her hands, she made her way over the bridge, down the other side, past the stationmaster's office, and noting the closed door, wondered whether Nancy was on an evening shift. Slipping out of the side gate to take the shortcut towards the path leading down to the riverboat, she hurried along beside a couple of people she recognised as Lovelies.

As she got towards the jetty, she saw every other person

standing in one of the blue wax Lovely coats. One of Colin and Clive's assistants, also wearing one of the Lovely coats, stood in the little shed at the end of the jetty, tapping away into his phone and looking downriver. Lost in a world of her own, she was suddenly aware that Nancy was at the top of the queue. She walked up to her and started to chat as they got onto the boat.

Colin greeted them. 'Hello. How are you two today?' Colin pointed to Nina's box. 'Blimey, what on earth are you travelling with?'

Nina tapped the top of the box. 'A wedding dress.'

'I thought that was the talk of the town and you had one.' Colin laughed.

Nancy interrupted. 'Oh my! Have you found another one?'

'Sort of.' Nina laughed. 'I think I've found a solution to not loving that one I kept from the order.'

Nancy squinted and tapped the box. 'What's that then?'

'My first wedding dress.'

'So you're wearing the wedding dress you've already worn once?' Colin's eyes widened. 'The first time?'

'Where did you find that?' Nancy asked.

'I've been up to my flat. Sophie suggested that I have something from the first wedding.'

'Like what?'

'Sophie meant a memento or something. Well, anyway, when I went into the loft to have a look, I found my wedding dress, and here we are.'

Colin nodded. 'It's kind of romantic in a way, I think, maybe.'

Nancy didn't look convinced. 'Does our Robby know about this yet?'

Nina shook her head. 'No. I think he'll be fine.'

Colin nodded. 'Yes, you're probably right. He's not the kind of bloke that lets much worry him.'

'Why would it worry him?' Nina asked.

Nancy interjected. 'I don't know, maybe, you know, some people might think that it was a bit strange.'

Nina was *adamant* about wearing the dress. She was also more or less certain that Robby would be fine with it, too, otherwise she'd wouldn't have brought it back to Lovely Bay. Right from the word go, when she'd first blurted out about Andrew, they'd talked about him and how it affected her. It had never been a problem between them. She nodded. 'No, I think it will be fine. In fact, I think he will be pleased about it. It's not as if Andrew is anything bad from my past.'

'Totally agree,' Colin said and clapped his hands together. 'I literally can't wait for this wedding. It's going to be such a good party. Our Robby and our Nina, the love story of the century.'

'Aww, thanks. It feels that way for me, too.'

~

It was later on that evening, and Nina again found herself on the riverboat. Only this time, it was Clive in charge. He chatted away to Nina who was on her way to the stop nearest Robby's office.

After disembarking, she strolled along in the twilight, thought more about the dress, and wondered how Robby was going to take it. About ten minutes later, she approached Robby's office building and shuddered as she remembered what had happened when she'd first been going out with him a year before. She had popped down to his office to surprise him and had inadvertently overheard him talking to someone. She'd assumed that the person he'd been talking about was her and had been devastated to hear him say that he and her were just a casual thing.

Luckily, he'd been talking about someone else. It had been the first blip in their relationship and more or less the only one. Since then, they'd had a few little spats here and there, the odd bickering about something small and insignificant, but mostly, their relationship had just pottered along nice and comfortably, just as she liked it and wanted it to remain. She hoped the dress wasn't going to cause him to be upset. She didn't think so otherwise she wouldn't have gone ahead with it. She thought that she knew him well and it would be fine.

Robby had been away working on an office block on the outskirts of Bath. She walked around the back, opened the door, and found him at the end of the corridor, sitting in his office at the computer. He got up from the desk, kissed her on the cheek, and smiled. 'How was it? How did you get on at the flat? Everything all good there?'

'Yep, everything was fine.'

'Did you bump into Mrs Gilbert?'

'No.' Nina chuckled. 'I ran across the landing to the sound of Radio 4 and made sure that I kept well out of her way.'

'How was it in the loft?' Robby asked, cutting straight to the chase.

Nina smiled and raised her eyebrows. She blinked a few times. 'It was good, yes. Really good.'

'Did you find anything that might be good to include?'

'Well,' Nina said, pausing for a second. 'I actually did. I found something perfect.'

'Oh?' Robby replied, 'Like what?'

Nina stopped for a bit, pursed her lips together, and made a funny face. 'Actually, I hope this is going to be okay with you, but what I actually found was the dress.'

'Pardon. What do you mean?'

'I want to wear the same dress. My dress. *The* dress.'

Robby frowned and Nina panicked because of the look on his face. She felt all her muscles tense. She'd totally read the room wrong. He was not going to be okay with it.

'What do you mean, "the dress"?' Robby asked. The look on his face wasn't happy.

Nina faltered. 'I mean *the dress* that I wore when I got married the first time. That dress.'

Robby nodded. 'Okay. So that's quite a big memento from your first wedding.'

Nina felt her heart race and her stomach drop. That was the end of that. 'Okay, yes, sorry, umm, right. You think it's a bit too much?' Nina said with a wincing sound.

Robby frowned and turned his head. 'No, why would I think that?'

'Oh, I thought by your face that you weren't happy with that.'

Robby shrugged, got up from his desk, and took Nina's hand. 'No, I just didn't know what you meant. I couldn't care less if you wear a bin bag for all I care.'

'So you're telling me you're absolutely fine with it, are you? You don't mind? Not in the slightest?'

'No. What sort of dress is it? The whole big white thing? I thought you weren't going to go for that after the terrible time at the wedding dress shop. I thought the one you had was a much simpler affair.'

Nina inhaled. 'It is a white dress, but it's actually a bodice and a skirt. When I wore it before it had a huge train with a massive bow on the back, but that's all detachable. Without the bow, it's just a really plain top and a beautiful skirt, but it looks like a dress. It's almost exactly what I wanted and nothing like anything that I tried on in that hideous shop and nothing I've seen online. I can send that other one back.'

Robby nodded. 'Well, there you are then, sorted. Plus, it didn't cost me a penny.' He laughed and joked.

Nina shot back, 'You weren't paying for it anyway, so it wouldn't have cost you anything.'

Robby chuckled. 'Joking aside, so now we really are nearly done.' He moved around the desk and tapped his laptop. 'I can check that off on the spreadsheet then. Nina outfit: sorted.'

Nina laughed. 'You are funny. You're worse than me.'

'I like to be organised, Neens. It's how you get on in life.'

Nina nodded. 'Trust me. You don't need to tell me that.'

'So, you don't have any issue with it at all?' Nina clarified.

'None. Zilch. Do whatever you want to do. I'm just glad you said yes.'

29

A few days later, with the Shipping Forecast bellowing in her ears, Nina finished setting out the plates on the stainless-steel worktop opposite the dishwashers in the back of the deli. Alice, the woman who worked full-time for Birdie, had a problem with one of her children and had had to take her to hospital, so Birdie had called on Nina to do the prep for a speakeasy that night. Nina could have done without it, but as with everything in Lovely, she'd started to realise that people did things for each other when they needed help. If she wanted to be in on it, this was what was required to be part of the community. It was all very much give and take.

She checked in the walk-in larder that the correct number of sourdough loaves had been delivered, started laying out the plates and jugs and then walked through into the back room to check on the tables. Just as the first time she'd entered it, she was amazed at how nice it was, noted it needed a vacuum, checked on the glasses, and turned back around. Walking back into the kitchen, she took the two little steps down into the workroom, grabbed the Hoover, dragged it into the back room, plugged it in, and started to vacuum under the tables. About ten minutes later, Birdie came in with a harassed look on her face. Nina switched the Hoover off with her foot, put her hands on her hips, and frowned. 'Everything okay with you? What's happened?'

'Everything's fine,' Birdie replied. 'I've just heard from Alice, and she will be here later to sort the rest out. Her daughter has a clean break in her arm.'

'Oh dear, that sounds nasty,' Nina replied. 'I hope she's okay.'

'Yes, I know. That tends to happen when you fling yourself around on a trampoline. The amount of people who have been injured on a trampoline. I've seen it all in the chemist. I wouldn't touch one with a barge pole if it was me.'

'Yep, I've heard they cause loads of accidents,' Nina agreed. She flicked the button to coil the cable back into the Hoover, and they both walked into the kitchen.

Seeing that Nina had set everything out for the evening, Birdie nodded in appreciation. 'Thank you so much for stepping in and doing this. I had to be in the pharmacy today and our other pharmacy on the other side of Lovely had someone sick as well. If it doesn't rain, it pours, as they say.' Birdie raised her eyes. 'There's something in the air at the moment.'

Nina nodded. 'Sounds like you need to put your feet up.'

'I think you might be right,' Birdie agreed. 'That's business for you.'

'I'm learning that.'

'It's times like these when nice regular hours, holiday and sickness pay, and clocking in and out look very attractive. Throw in a trade union and I'm there with bells on.'

Nina laughed. 'It has its attractions. Anyway, what else has been going on with you?'

'Nothing, really, other than dealing with all these issues. I haven't got time! How is your business getting on?' Birdie asked.

'Good, I'm fully booked now until the wedding, more or less.

I can't quite believe how I've done nothing much to drum up business, but it's just taken off by word of mouth.'

'How's it going with those reel thingies you were telling me about? You said that you were getting lots of views on them,' Birdie said.

'Yes, no change on that, really. It's staggering how many people like to watch people cleaning and clearing up, though. I've put them up on YouTube now as well, so it's slowly building, but yeah, that's just a no-brainer. I don't think it's doing anything to promote me. I think it's word of mouth around Lovely.'

Birdie cocked her head to the side. 'So, are you making any money out of it? The social media stuff, I mean.'

Nina flicked her hand in front of her. 'No, not at all. Absolutely nothing much. You have to get to a certain number of followers before you can monetise it. I've done that now, but it's chicken feed, like pennies, if that.'

'Oh well, every little helps, as they say,' Birdie replied. 'These things seem to take off though, don't they? I watch this guy who talks about billionaires and what they do in their day-to-day life. It's quite interesting to see how people do things. Who would've thought I would be enjoying watching that? That took off so you never know.'

Nina laughed. 'Yes, it's a whole other world. I watch a man walking around the Scottish hills and the Yorkshire Dales when I'm on the sofa in the evening. It's so relaxing and I don't have to move a muscle.'

'There you go,' Birdie chuckled.

'And people are watching me go about my work day decluttering people's airing cupboards. Who would have thought?'

Birdie put her hand on her hip and winced a little bit. 'Speaking of decluttering, I've got a little bit of a delicate situation. You know the woman in the chocolate shop?'

Nina had been in there multiple times and indulged in the

chocolate many more times than she liked to admit, but she didn't really know the people in the chocolate shop. 'Well, not really. Obviously, I've spoken to her a couple of times.'

Birdie screwed up her face. 'You see, there's a bit of a problem. Out the back, their storage room is a complete mess and she needs help with sorting it.'

Nina smiled at the same time as thinking that she had no time at all, but there was no way she was going to say that to the person who basically ran Lovely Bay. 'Of course. How bad is it?'

Birdie screwed her face up again. 'It's really quite bad; you can hardly get in there. In fact, it's not really a storage room these days. It's just a load of junk that has been shoved in on top of each other.'

Nina shook her head. 'Wow, you wouldn't believe that from the front of the shop. It's amazing in there.'

'I know. I think it's one of those things where she's just so busy all the time, especially now they've taken on the extra shops, and it's just bottom of the priority list. It just keeps getting worse and worse with more and more stuff going in there.'

'Right, well, it shouldn't be a problem. Sounds like it's just a case of clearing things out.'

'Yes, precisely,' Birdie nodded. 'The thing is, it's getting to be a bit of a hazard in my opinion. You know, a health hazard. I don't know, but I feel like it is. You don't know what's in there, and it's right next door to my shops.'

'Yeah, there is that.'

'Do you think you could fit it in before the wedding?'

Nina was more or less fully booked, but there was no way she was going to say no to helping out a Lovely who was in a stitch. Everyone had been so amazing to her in the little town, and the way the system worked, you did things for other people when you could. If you were asked, you simply didn't say no. She'd worked that out in the early days. She'd have to juggle things around and change a few clients until after the wedding.

'Sure, sure, I can sort it,' Nina said, as if it was nothing. Internally, she rolled her eyes at yet another thing to have to fit in. *I only have a small wedding to organise,* she thought to herself.

She was super grateful to Birdie, though, who had helped her so much. Even the job at the deli, although she hadn't realised it at the time, had assisted in dropping her into the Lovely world, which had facilitated in healing the hideous grief that had strangled her when she'd first arrived in Lovely Bay. There was no way she was going to say that she couldn't help out. How bad could a storage room at the back of a chocolate shop really be? She'd soon find out.

30

Nina made a cup of tea, grabbed a couple of chocolate digestives, and walked back to the desk she'd set up in her new office area. The whole of the ground floor was now painted and clean, the windows shone, and light streamed through from the harbour. Nina hadn't really done much at all other than clear out the area and use the wonderful paint sprayer's skills to work its magic to sanitise and breathe new life into the whole of the downstairs area.

With not much time because of her actual day-to-day job and getting organised for the wedding, the only thing she'd really done on the lower floor was to sort out a desk. She now had two of them on either side of the main barn doors at the front. Placing them near the windows and doors had been one of her better ideas; the office overlooked the harbour and it made her smile every time she looked up from her laptop and gazed out over the sea.

Her desk and the one on the opposite side were actually old tables that had been found in the attic. Robby had stripped down the tops of the tables to their natural wood patina, and Nina had painted the legs in warm white. Once they were in place, she'd thoroughly enjoyed making the space her own; she'd placed a tall vintage reading lamp on the left of her desk, a bunch of flowers on the right, a pot with pens and pencils, and a few little baskets with all her stuff colour-coded and organised just so. Her workspace was about a million times better than what she'd had in the rental cottage when she'd started the organising business. In the cottage, she'd pretty much worked from her phone perched on the kitchen table and had never felt comfortable. Now, it felt like she had so much room she didn't really know what to do with herself.

The eventual plan for the lower floor of the building was to use it for storage for clients who might need a temporary place to put things and also somewhere she could keep her organising supplies in bulk. The commercial section of the property had ended up being much better than she'd thought it was going to be. It gave her somewhere to effectively work, with a beautiful outlook to boot. It made her old, past-its-best office block not too far from her flat and her tedious, boring job look a bit stupid, too. She was now doing something she loved for herself and reaping daily rewards left, right, and centre.

After answering a few text messages about quoting for jobs and sending an email to a woman in Lovely Bay who had sent her a bunch of flowers to say thanks for a job she'd done, Nina sat back in her chair and started to think about the wedding. Though she'd kept it entirely to herself, she'd had second thoughts about the dress and it being part of her second wedding. When she'd spoken to her mum about it, her mum had told her over and over again that she thought it was a bad idea. Nina hadn't agreed at all, but now it was getting close to too late for mind changes, she was wondering whether her mum was right. Her sister hadn't minced her words and had also told her that she thought it was a ludicrous idea. Not that her sister knew much; most of the time, she was half-cut anyway.

Mulling it over and wondering what to do, she picked up her

phone, flipped back the wallet cover, and tapped on 'Photos' in the albums. She scrolled and scrolled and then smiled at a photo of her and Andrew on their wedding day. A wave of emotion seemed to well up around her and grab her around the throat as she looked at the girl on her phone with not a care in the world. She couldn't seem to untangle herself from a multitude of emotions about her first wedding and here she was wearing the same dress as she started a new chapter. Why would she do that?

She shook her head to try and make sense of what she was feeling. Initially, she'd been so sure it was the right thing to do. Now, she was overthinking and questioning herself. It was as if her thoughts and emotions were knotted together, twisted up, vying with each other, trying to tell her she was doing the wrong thing to be wearing the dress again. Too many feelings, too much sadness. Guilt, that was in there, too.

There was also something else in the mix. An ending, not a moving on as such but a sliding to another place. The next part of her life was beginning. The dress being part of it seemed to accentuate that. She shook her head and tried not to think about it too much. It wasn't even worth going into. If she'd learnt one thing that had come out of the grief group, it was that despite what anyone said, what she'd lost because of what had happened to Andrew would never not make her sad. She shook her head and sighed and decided that she was overthinking. It was a dress at the end of the day. Robby was fine with it. She'd wear it and be done with it.

Just as she was ordering some work supplies she felt her phone vibrate in her pocket a few times, slipped it out, and looked at the notifications on the screen. She closed her eyes for a second, shook her head, and then sighed. Lindsay was again texting her. Since Nina had sent a vastly inflated quote to Lindsay in the hope that it would put her off, it had, in fact, had the opposite effect.

Lindsay had sent Nina multiple texts at all times of the day. Nina had replied, nearly every time, with one-word answers, hoping that Lindsay would get the hint. However, Lindsay hadn't got the hint at all; if anything, she seemed to be more insistent with her texting.

Nina tapped and read Lindsay's message.

Lindsay: *Hi Nina, how are you? Just wondering if you've worked out a date yet for the declutter?*

Nina shook her head. The woman wasn't going to take no for an answer. She read through the next message.

Lindsay: *If we can get this sorted, it would be great for me.*

Nina saw the dots indicating that Lindsay was typing so her fingers flew over the screen so that she could get in first.

Nina: *Yes, sorry, just organising my diary for after the wedding. I'll get back to you soon.*

Lindsay: *Btw, while I've got you, I wanted to run something past you. Remember when I bumped into you that day when you were jogging, and you looked amazing?*

Nina: *Yes.*

Nina gawped at her phone, wondering what was coming next.

Lindsay: *I wanted to ask if you'd be so kind as to meet up and go through the ropes with me, please?*

Nina raised her eyebrows and shook her head. There was no way she was going to help Lindsay. She felt herself frantically trying to think of a good excuse but couldn't come up with anything straight away.

Nina: *Look, sorry, Lindsay, I don't really have time at the moment. I'm hardly running much myself.*

Lindsay: *Oh, what a shame!!! I saw you run past me the other day... You see, I really need to get fit! Are you sure you couldn't just squeeze me in for a quick run????*

Nina shook her head again. This woman had the skin of a rhino.

Nina: *Nope. Sorry.*

Lindsay: *I wonder if you could maybe send me something then, perhaps some tips?*

Nina found herself typing back, even though she wasn't sure why.

Nina: *I'll see what I can do.*

Nina had no intention of doing any such thing. She watched as another text landed on her phone and then another one. She clicked the button on the right, waited for her screen to go black, and put her phone on the desk.

There was no way she was getting into anything with this Lindsay person; from the word go, she'd had the wrong vibes from her, and something about her and the way she was conducting herself over the decluttering turned Nina off immensely.

Nina couldn't quite fathom out what Lindsay's objective was, but it was as if she somehow enjoyed the chase. She didn't seem to realise that she was being given the cold shoulder. She just continued to send messages and try and bamboozle her way into a response.

If Nina had been in Lindsay's shoes, she would have got the hint pretty quickly and left it at that. Lindsay, however, seemed to have other ideas. She'd continued to message Nina and tried different angles to get a reaction.

Nina narrowed her eyes and nodded. Lindsay could try all she liked. The door was closed. Whatever the reason she was trying to get in with Nina, it wasn't going to work. Nina simply wasn't interested in any shape or form.

Most of all, where bright-clothed Lindsay with the off-vibes was concerned, Nina Lavendar really, one hundred per cent, simply didn't care.

31

Robby and Nina were standing at the back of The Summer Hotel after both having come straight from work to put the final plans in place for their wedding party. A light drizzle fell from a grey-white sky, and Nina was reminded of the day when she'd arrived in Lovely Bay when a fine rain had accompanied her journey ending up with her being wet through. Robby, in beige combat work trousers with straps, had an iPad in his hand and was looking around the garden. He tapped a few things and then looked up. 'You see, if the weather is like this we'll get wet.'

Nina replied with a sigh. 'I need to pray to the weather gods. Honestly, it all sounds good. But if it pours it's going to more than ruin it.'

'If it's *pouring* with rain, it just won't work. We'll get soaked even with those market umbrellas we've got – they're weather-proof, not downpour-proof.' Robby winced, 'I just don't think they will be good enough.'

Nina nodded. 'Colin said something about there being old-fashioned tent marquees for the Lovely Bay fête. He said we could use those.'

'You're happy with that?'

Nina shrugged and put her hands up in a gesture as if she had no idea. 'I guess so. We can't control the weather, especially not here. It could be raining, snowing, or foggy, for all we know. We get everything in a day in Lovely, don't we?'

Robby agreed, pointed towards the conservatory, and then down to the lawn. 'The trestle tables will run all the way through here and the conservatory will be open. If the forecast is for heavy rain the marquees will need to be set up over the top. That set-up *should* work.'

'Hopefully, heavy rain *won't* be forecast.'

'With any luck, but you never know in Lovely.'

'What else?'

'The kitchen and scullery for Birdie's people, so that's sorted.'

'Yes,' Nina agreed.

Robby looked down at the iPad again. 'And decoration. What about that? Is that organised now?'

'Yep. Same thing, really; it's all in Nancy's hands.' She turned back and pointed to the garden. 'Rows of trestle tables there, each with the vintage tablecloths from her mum, and the plates and china, coming from all manner of sources. Wildflower bouquets throughout.'

Robby smiled. 'You seem very chill about this.'

Nina shrugged. 'Do I? I don't think so. It's just a party, really, isn't it? We're doing the first bit in the registry office just with your parents and my mum and sister, so what's there to worry about?'

'True,' Robby nodded. 'I suppose it *is* just a party, really. A party with a sit-down bit.'

Nina looked around at the garden and The Summer Hotel. 'With the chowder in the bowls, it's not really much more than a larger speakeasy at the back of the deli,' Nina noted. 'And we know what a process that is, don't we? Birdie has everything organised to within an inch of its life, the same with Nancy on the decor front. Her cottage is absolutely beautiful, and we've done a Pinterest inspiration board, and really, it's just a load of trestle tables, so I don't think there's too much of a problem. It's the setting itself that's the thing.'

'When you put it like that,' Robby said.

Nina tapped the top of the iPad. 'And then, of course, there's you, Mr Organisation Extraordinaire. And I thought I was the one with the organisation business.'

Robby smiled. 'Well, I do like to have everything in my control. I've noticed you need to be quite organised when you are dangling from the side of a building.'

'Right, yes, that has a way of making someone organised, I assume.' Nina agreed.

Just as they were standing there discussing the chowder, Robby's phone rang. He took it out of his pocket and looked at who was calling.

'I'm going to need to take this. I've got to talk to this bloke about the Canary Wharf thing,'

Nina nodded. Robby cupped his hand over his phone's speaker and gestured to the road. 'I need to go to the van and check out the notes in there. I'll be back in a sec.'

Nina turned around and looked up at the hotel. She still couldn't believe it hadn't been bought by anyone, but as Ella, the estate agent, had said, it came with quite a lot of red tape. She stood for ages, just staring up at the windows wondering how it would go as an Airbnb business. She remembered when she'd first arrived at The Summer Hotel and walked into the kitchen and had never seen as much clutter in her life. How she'd cleared out Jill's aunt's belongings and got everything spick and span, and now here it sat, still without an owner and without anyone giving it any love. It was quite sad. She wondered what it would've been like if she had been able to afford it and instantly dismissed the idea. Even if she'd sold her flat, it was a huge thing to take on on her own. Although now, obviously, she wasn't on her own, but even so, Robby had his own very successful business and not a lot of time for much else. The Summer Hotel would be quite the undertaking for whoever ended up giving it a go. Gazing up at the building, she felt emotional. She had poured her heart into turning the place around, yet its future remained uncertain. Despite knowing it was unrealistic, part of her wished she could be the one to give The Summer Hotel new life.

Robby came strolling back through the side path with the straps dangling.

'Everything okay?' Nina asked.

'Yep. Just finishing off a few last things and making sure I've got the right team on that job. It's a complicated one.'

'Right.'

Robby followed Nina's gaze to the top of the hotel. 'What are you thinking about?'

Nina gestured up to the hotel's back windows. 'I was just thinking about this and how no one has bought it yet. I thought it would sell quickly. I guess you can never tell with a place like this.' Nina felt a pang, knowing how much work she had poured into restoring the old hotel. Part of her wished she could be the one to continue its legacy, but she knew realistically it was too big an endeavour and too much of a money pit. In a strange way, it felt like an old friend waiting to be brought back to life.

'Yeah, it's a shame,' Robby said. 'It would be a good place for someone.'

'It would,' Nina agreed.

Robby chuckled. 'We could sell our properties and buy this place together.'

Nina shook her head. *A bit of a pipe dream*, she thought. She thought about her flat in London, the one that was still just sitting there, not even earning any money. She knew that at some point she would have to do something about it, but it was still tied up in her old life and her grief. She knew it was a problem simmering under the surface but wasn't prepared to get on with it and deal with what it might throw up. There was no way she was going to sell it, that was for sure. She quipped back at Robby, 'You'd just need to sell a couple of assets from your property portfolio, wouldn't you?'

Robby laughed. 'I don't know about that. I think the price of this place is what puts people off. It's very expensive, really, because of the land value itself and the fact that it backs onto the river, and it's got its own little river beach. I don't think it will sell until Jill knocks something off the price. It's just too much of a gamble. It needs loads spending on it and you have to get approval from the council to make a cup of tea. I'd be hesitant to invest in it.'

Nina nodded in agreement. 'It's a lot to take on. As you say a gamble that may or may not turn a profit.'

Robby joked, 'Look at you, sounding all business-like now you've got your own small business.'

'Tell me about it,' Nina laughed. 'There's no point working for free. I learnt that in month one.'

'Do you know what? I haven't looked inside since you finished up on the hotel side of it.'

'Fancy having a look around?' Nina asked. 'Have you got time?'

'Yep. It would be good to see why it's not selling.'

A few minutes later, they'd gone through the tradesmen's entrance, made their way through the kitchen and the living quarters, and were standing in the hallway of what was considered the entrance to the old B&B. A beautiful old mahogany desk sat in the corner, a tessellated floor led to a large, wide staircase, and the panels beside the front door threw light onto the floor.

Nina opened a door into what would have been, in the B&B days, a communal sitting room. Tall ceilings towered over them, beautiful old ceiling roses and floor-to-ceiling doors looked back. A fireplace on the right-hand side, thanks to Nina, looked clean and well-cared for, and built-in bookcases displayed nice things.

Robby nodded. 'Gosh, it is beautiful.'

'Yup,' Nina agreed. 'It has some stories to tell in these old walls for sure.'

A few minutes later, they were on the first floor. Rooms led off a central hallway. Nina opened the door to one of them and remembered when she'd cleared and cleaned it for sale. She felt an odd attachment to the walls, floors, and surfaces she'd cleaned. As if as she'd got stuck in and worked, the place had let out a little sigh. She felt as if the same thing had happened to her, too. With each room, she'd healed and let go of some of the grief that had suffocated her for so long. Looking around she could vividly recall the emotions that had swirled around her in a fog as she'd got her head down and cracked on. An odd mix of hope, sadness, nostalgia, and looking forward. In a strange way, bringing The Summer Hotel back to life had brought Nina back to life too.

They walked over towards the window and looked down at the river snaking lazily down past the end of the garden. Nina sighed at the sight of it leading to the sea and the rooftops of Lovely topping it from the other side. A church spire punctuated the grey, white drizzly sky, and the lighthouse could be seen peeking its head out of roofs. A couple of boats chugged down the river in opposite directions and a swarm of birds swooped down into the water.

'Yeah, nice,' Robby agreed. 'Imagine coming here on holiday and waking up to this. It really is quite something from up here.'

'Yeah,' Nina said. 'It's very nice.'

'Shame it's still empty.'

'A lot of work for whoever ends up taking it on.'

'You up for it then now you've reminded yourself what it's like?'

Nina laughed. 'It all sounds good in theory, and yeah, I'd be up for it if someone dropped it in my lap or maybe I won the lottery and bought it with that, but no. And anyway, I've just bought a property. The one that we're going to be living in together. You seem to have forgotten that.'

'Oh, I don't know,' Robby said, laughing. 'It's just a bit of a dream. How nice would it be to live here where it all started?'

Nina puffed out a little stream of air through her lips. 'When you put it like that.'

32

Nina walked past Saint Lovely green with the sounds of the leaves on a huge old conker tree in her ears. The leaves rustled back and forth, a plane droned high up in the sky, and there wasn't a cloud to be seen. Nina was on her way to the chemist to first see Birdie, who was then going to take her around to the chocolate shop to start the decluttering job.

Nina had allocated a morning to work in the back room of the chocolate shop and had assumed that it wouldn't take a lot more than that. She'd delayed another job to fit it in and wasn't sure really what she was going to be greeted with, how much work there was going to be, and how big the job was at all. But deep down, a niggling doubt told her it might not be that straightforward. Birdie had talked about Nina doing the job for a 'Lovely price', as she called it, but Nina had heard nothing of it. The last thing she needed to be doing in Lovely Bay, to the people who had welcomed her, would be to charge someone to help out. She'd told Birdie, who had passed it on, that she would only charge at cost if she might need something like a skip.

Strolling through Lovely Bay, she pondered the wedding, who was going to buy The Summer Hotel and all sorts, as she got to the High Street and walked along the pavement. The familiar nods and smiles from locals warmed her heart, a testament to how well she'd been accepted in the third smallest town in the country. A couple of people raised their eyes in acknowledgement to her, and from the other side of the street, Clive called out, 'Bonjour.' A few minutes later, she walked past the deli, looked in the window of the flower shop for a few minutes, and pushed open the door to Birdie's chemist. The shop bell rang overhead, and as every time she walked in, she was taken aback at the lovely little chemist. No plastic shelving and horrid bright lights for our Birdie. She was enveloped in the quaint charm of Birdie's world. The Shipping Forecast played from the counter at the back. Birdie, in her white pharmacist coat, peered around a shelving partition towering with prescription drugs. 'Hi, how are you?'

'Good, thanks. It's a beautiful day. Long may it last. Everything good with you?'

'Yeah, just sorting out an order that's just come in. Ready for the chocolate shop? Wasn't sure if you were ready or not yet.'

'I certainly am.'

'Okay, so Lizzie is away, as we discussed, and we'll go in via the back door.'

Nina nodded. 'It all seems a bit hush-hush.'

Birdie shook her head. 'It is a little bit. I think there's a lot of stuff tied up in this back room with Lizzie.'

Nina nodded. From past experience organising homes, she knew old items often unearthed complex emotions and memories when it was least expected. And with Lizzie away, the secrecy around accessing the back room hinted that there were sensitivities to navigate. 'Yes, I've begun to realise that this is part of the job. Often, people's problems are tied up in their junk.'

'Yep, sounds like it. Right, okay, let me just finish this up and I will lead you out the back here and along.'

About five minutes later, with the Shipping Forecast accompanying them out through the back of the chemist, Birdie led Nina through a compact patio area, opened a gate, turned left, and walked into another small backyard area and to a door on the left leading to the back of the chocolate shop. The smell in the air alone told Nina where she was.

Just as they were stepping in, a young assistant wearing one of the chocolate shop branded aprons came out from the front of the shop and smiled. Birdie turned to Nina. 'Have you met Millie?'

'Yes, hi Millie, how are you doing?' Nina asked.

'Good, thanks. How are you? How are you getting on? You've bought a house over on the harbour, haven't you?' Millie asked.

Nina nodded. 'Yes, not really a house. It's an apartment over a retail or office area.' Nina was modest, downplaying the excitement she felt about the new place.

'Oh yes, I know the ones. It's really nice over that way. Good luck with that,' Millie replied.

'Thank you.'

Millie pointed to the storage room door. 'There you go, it's all in there waiting for you.'

Birdie lowered her voice. 'Is Lizzie okay with everything?'

Millie raised her eyebrows. 'Yes, well, she's not very happy about it, but we've got to get this problem sorted out.' Millie also lowered her voice to barely above a whisper. 'If you ask me, this is a health hazard. I'm surprised we haven't been in trouble yet about it.'

'Exactly, which is why I wanted to get Nina involved. She's an expert at this sort of thing.'

Millie nodded. 'Yes, I've heard about The Summer Hotel. You got that place spick and span.'

Nina smiled. Everybody in Lovely Bay knew everything about everyone, but it seemed as if her job at The Summer

Hotel was particularly well known. Millie, seeing the thought go across Nina's face, clarified, 'Oh, my mum lives down the same road, so we saw everything going on, and Ella is my cousin.'

'Ah,' Nina said. 'That makes sense. Well, if you know Ella, then you'll know that The Summer Hotel was a lot of work, but it turned out okay.'

Birdie smiled as Millie opened the door to the storage room. She tapped Nina on the elbow. 'Look, I have to get back on the double. I need to continue sorting out that order. I've got half of Lovely Bay arriving in a couple of hours to come and collect their medicines.'

'Yeah, see you in a bit. Thanks, Birdie.'

Millie sighed as she opened the storeroom door fully, and Nina was surprised to see so much mess. She had totally underestimated how big the job would be. From the street frontage, the chocolate shop was immaculate, and she hadn't realised the room in the back would be as big. She hid her surprise well and inwardly cringed at how much work there was ahead of her, so much for one morning of effort. This was more like a week, if not more.

What looked back at her were piles and piles of junk in what seemed to be an outer room, which led to an inner room. Junk looked back at her from every inch of space. A couple of modern-looking lamps with their wires trailing cables on the floor, a huge pile of blue, what looked like moving boxes, on the left-hand side. A Christmas tree wedged in the corner, a massive pile of shopping bags and baskets on top of what appeared to be garbage bins, and an empty box for the Christmas tree on the far wall. Timber Ikea racks, held piles and piles and piles of junk; stacks of cushions, what looked like a sleeping bag wrapped up in a bag, loads of bags stuffed full of newspapers, a child's wigwam with a dreamcatcher, a whole shelf full of old Halloween decorations, pumpkins, a skull, and more boxes of what looked like printer supplies than she'd ever seen.

Millie squeezed around two pieces of timber shelving stacked on their end, opened another door, and walked into another room where red metal storage units were also packed with junk. One shelf held various tins of paint and DIY supplies. Another looked as if it was stacked with old printer cartridges, reams of white paper, and on the left, old chocolate shop uniforms hung from the top of the red units along with loads of empty coat hangers bent out of shape.

It looked as if, at some point, somebody had tried to do something about the place because, on the far right, huge black storage tubs with yellow lids were stacked in a fairly neat pile, but that was the only part of the place that was neat. Most of it looked as if a small bomb had gone off. Three big red hard-shelled suitcases were stacked up near the roof. Huge black bin liners near the window appeared as if they were full of rubbish. Another Christmas tree in a wicker pot was wedged on a shelf, and there was another huge pile of pillows, these ones tartan, delivery boxes, and masses and masses of Christmas decorations.

Nina had thought she'd seen it all in her jobs, but this seemed to be as if people had literally opened the door, thrown stuff in, closed it again, and hoped for the best. It was a big job. Not that it scared her at all. She liked nothing better than to get stuck in, put her headphones on, listen to a podcast, and start clearing up. The problem was that she was trying to fit this favour in among her own business, organising a wedding and moving into a new house. She gulped at the sight of the work involved but didn't have a lot of choice but to get on with the job at hand; there was no way she was going to let anybody in Lovely Bay down, particularly not Birdie.

Nina was mentally assessing like crazy as Millie chatted away about the state of the room. Millie laughed and picked up a book from a pile on her right. 'For instance, I'm really not sure why Lizzie needs a "Scotland Real Estate for Beginners" book. Do you? I don't think she has much use for that in Lovely Bay.'

Nina chuckled. 'I've seen it all before, Millie. It's probably from when she didn't know what she was going to do with her life and thought she was going to be an estate agent.'

Millie picked up a broken trophy where a girl in a football uniform stood in gold on the top. 'And what about this trophy for a football team? Why is she keeping that?'

Nina nodded. 'Oh yes, we always find lots of trophies. You wouldn't believe how many trophies there are tucked away in people's cupboards. A whole army of the things.'

Millie laughed. 'Right, well, I'll let you get on, shall I?'

'Yeah, that would be good.'

'How long do you think it will take you?'

Inside, Nina was thinking it would take her a long time. She tried to play it down. 'Oh, not very long at all. I'll just keep coming back until it's all sorted.'

'Then I'll leave you to it then. Fancy a coffee or anything?'

Nina nodded. She could kill a cup of coffee. She needed the caffeine to get her through the rest of the morning. 'Yes, please. I'd love a coffee, thanks.'

Millie nodded. 'Coming right up. I take it you might like something on the side with that? Chilli chocolate, by any chance? Do you like the sound of that? Or salted caramel?'

Nina shook her head. 'I don't mind at all. I like the sound of anything from this shop.'

As Millie walked out of the room and made her way back to the front of the shop, Nina nodded to herself. She'd get stuck into it and see how she got on. There wasn't much else she could do.

33

Nina had taken the riverboat to the other side of Lovely Bay and made her way to Lovely itself. She was going to get her wedding dress altered and hustled along to make sure she was on time. With the dress folded up in tissue paper and carefully put into a bag, she made her way to the dressmaker. When she'd told Birdie about the dress and the fact that the zip on the bodice wouldn't do up at the top, Birdie had taken control of the situation saying she knew exactly what to do.

Birdie had gone on to recommend someone in Lovely who made bespoke suits for a living. Inside, Nina had wondered if Birdie was barking up the wrong tree but not knowing many people who did alterations and running out of time fast, she'd decided to plump for Birdie's recommendation and see how it went. Birdie had sent a few texts, got everything sorted, and Nina was on her way with the bodice to get measured and see what could be done in the short timeframe. There was nothing like leaving it until the last minute, very unusual for Nina but she had a funny feeling in the back of her head that everything would be fine.

Following her phone map and remembering Birdie's

instructions, Nina walked through one of the Lovely greens and smiled at what she saw. It was one of the bigger greens she'd come across, with a wide path through the centre, lots of trees, and small iron fences encapsulating areas full of shrubs. A man and woman walked towards her with a baby in a pram, a dog was running around off the lead, and a moody sky looked as if it was about to possibly pour with rain.

On reaching the far side of the green, Nina checked her phone to ensure she was in the right place, and stood by the edge of the green for a second, looking down a long road lined with large terraced houses. Huge trees edged the road, lots of chimney stacks poked up into the sky, and down to the left of the pavement basement French doors led onto small patios full of plants.

Nina squinted down the road as she ambled past perfectly cut hedges until she found the correct number. Before opening the gate she smiled at little white hearts and lanterns hanging from a tree in the front garden. Looking up at the house, a black railing encompassed a small balcony and to the left tucked in the corner, a huge palm tree looked as if it had been transplanted from warmer climes. She walked up to a pale blue, slightly on the shabby side, front door with a large circular brass knob in the middle and a little window pane just above.

A very pretty young woman with black high-waisted wide-leg trousers, a pretty white blouse, and long hair beamed as she opened the door. Nina didn't think the woman looked anything like a tailor, but you never did know. Birdie was hardly ever wrong about anything, so she went with it and smiled.

'You must be Nina,' the woman said with a smile.

Nina smiled back. 'I am. Hi.'

'I'm Faye,' the woman said. 'Nice to meet you.'

Nina smiled. 'Likewise.'

Nina then followed Faye up a very steep set of slightly grubby carpeted stairs to the first floor, where a small landing area led to another pale blue door. Nina wasn't sure what to expect; everything was a little bit on the tatty side and she was wondering if she'd made a bit of a mistake. As the door opened, everything changed. Nina raised her eyebrows in shock as she was presented with a stripped timber floor and an exposed brick chimney breast where, on either side, open shelving held all sorts of bits and bobs of sewing paraphernalia. A sewing mannequin stood on the left-hand side, a huge dresser was meticulously organised in perfect piles on the right, and baskets stacked in neat rows held impeccable lined-up rolls of fabric.

'Oh, wow! This is lovely.'

'Thank you. People are often surprised. It's nothing much from the street.'

'What a lovely workspace.' Nina commented.

'It is, especially when the sun is out.'

'Ha, yes.' Nina gazed around. 'How long have you been tailoring?'

'Overall, about fifteen years. I got into it in my teens.'

'Oh right, quite a while then.'

'Yes. I started in the industry while I was at uni. Then I moved to Parkley Street Tailors, you might have heard of them. Anyway, everyone moved to the same area after Carnaby Street changed. There weren't many females when I was training. I was the only one at the time in my shop.'

'I thought it was unusual when Birdie told me.'

'It *is* quite unusual, I guess, to see an under-30-year-old woman in the industry, but it is a really great thing to be part of.'

Nina peered at the old-fashioned equipment. 'It looks lovely.'

'I love the heritage and the idea of continuing on all these old-school methods that have been around for hundreds of years. We still do everything exactly the same today. Nothing's changed, so it really stands the test of time.'

Nina took a few steps towards a table where fabric samples were stacked in neat piles. Faye picked one up. 'These are all one hundred per cent wool, and they're all from the mills in the north of England.'

'Wow, I wasn't really expecting this,' Nina said as she looked around in astonishment and felt as if Birdie had really done her a favour to get her an appointment.

Faye laughed. 'Everybody says that. I work here some of the time now since Covid, but I still go up and down to London quite a bit.'

'Birdie said you were just fitting me or I should say *her* in as a favour, and you don't normally do dresses,' Nina mentioned.

Faye nodded. 'No, I don't, but if I didn't do this for Birdie, I'd be chased out of Lovely.'

Nina chuckled. 'You certainly would.'

Faye laughed. 'You work for her, do you? How long have you been with her?'

Nina shook her head. 'I don't really now, I just fill in. It must be really about a year or so. I just started off there helping her out, then I worked there for a while doing a few shifts a week, and then when I actually moved here permanently, my business took off.'

'Oh, what do you do now, then?' Faye inquired with interest.

Nina smiled. 'I have a little organising and decluttering business,' she gestured around Faye's room. 'Not that someone like you would need that, by the looks of this.'

Faye nodded. 'How does that all work then?'

Nina smiled. 'Well, it's quite simple really. I just go in and clear people's clutter. You'd be amazed at what a demand there is for it.'

'And do you clean as well?' Faye asked.

'Yes and no, depending on what it is, but if it needs it, then I will. I have someone working for me part-time now as well,' Nina said.

Faye smiled. 'Wow. So how did you get that off the ground then?'

Nina nodded. 'To be quite honest, it just took off by itself. I started off at The Summer Hotel, you know, over there on the other side. I was working for Jill, the niece of the owner, and it all went from there. You'd be surprised how many people have clutter that they have lived with for years and just can't face sorting out. That's where I step in. I love it.'

Faye nodded and her face changed. 'Actually, I wouldn't be surprised, because my mum was a bit of a hoarder, and not in a good way. I know something about that world.'

'Right, I see. Yes, I've learnt a lot about this since I've started my own business. There are a lot of people in a bad way because of hoarding. It's wrapped up with mental health you wouldn't believe it.'

Faye nodded. 'I would, actually, I think that's my mum's problem. I grew up in a really disorganised house.' She gestured around at her workroom, 'Which is why I think I've gone the other way. I'm a bit over the top about it sometimes, I'm not sure if that's a good way to be either.'

Nina nodded. 'Well, it's better than being surrounded by complete chaos, I suppose.'

Faye also nodded. 'Yes, I think you're probably right. So, what sort of jobs do you do?'

Nina gestured with her hands. 'Well, for instance, you know the chocolate shop in the High Street there?'

'Yes, I do. I love it in there, especially the chilli chocolate.'

'Yes, me too,' Nina laughed. 'Well, I'm in there in the back room, which hasn't been touched for years, and I'm sorting that out.'

Faye chuckled. 'Not a bad job, especially if you get paid overtime in chocolate.'

'So, yeah, that's the sort of thing I get, or I might get just a job to, for example, go and completely organise someone's wardrobe, or the kitchen cupboards, or declutter and sort out a dining room unit.'

Faye smiled. 'Wow. You must find all sorts in your job.'

'Yeah, I certainly do, and I love it.'

Faye smiled. 'Right, well, let's get on with my job and why you're here. Let's have a look at the bodice.'

Nina nodded, opened the bag, and started to carefully take the bodice of her dress out.

Faye smiled. 'So, what's the story with this then?'

'Well, I actually got married for the first time in this dress. It holds a lot of memories for me.'

'That's cool.'

'Yes, my first husband actually passed away suddenly.'

Faye's hands flew to her mouth. 'I'm so sorry to hear that. You're so young for that.'

Nina had heard the same words *many* times before. 'No, no, it's actually fine. Well, no, it's not fine, obviously it's not fine that my husband died. But I wanted him to be part of the wedding, but I wasn't sure how. Then I went to my old flat and searched out my wedding things, and then I came across the dress. Without the huge train that pops on the back of the skirt, I thought it would be just right, which is what led me to you.'

Faye held the bodice up to the light near the window and smiled. 'It's really pretty.'

'It is.'

'Well, this won't be a problem at all. Let's get you in and see how we go.'

34

Nina was at the chocolate shop. She'd cracked on with most of the first room, but the inner room was in chaos, a stark contrast to the neat and inviting shopfront customers loved on the other side of the wall. Pulling on a pair of gloves, she shoved her earphones in, tapped on a true crime podcast, and set out to tackle the mess head-on. If there was one thing that didn't faze Nina, it was a gigantic pile of someone else's clutter.

As she lifted the lid off the nearest box, she shook her head as she found a jumble of papers, some dating back not just a few years but decades. It was clear that no one had gone near the boxes in years. She sifted through the papers methodically and organised them into piles: keep, shred, and check and found herself chuckling at some of the old advertisements and order forms. She'd learned early in her decluttering days when she'd worked for a few clients on the side that the process was slow and tedious at first, which was why most people put it off. Once the hump was over, though, things normally rapidly improved.

As she worked and the podcast ended, her mind wandered

to her own life and the changes she had made. Moving to Lovely Bay, planning a wedding, starting a new business, taking on new challenges, learning to run—it all felt a bit like decluttering herself, getting rid of the old to make way for the new.

Several hours passed in what felt like a flash, and as often happened, one minute, it felt as if she'd got nowhere at all, the next, there was small but significant progress. The pile of boxes full of old papers slowly diminished as she filled bags with documents for shredding and recycling. Every now and then, Millie popped her head in to check on Nina's progress and deliver something from the front of the shop. Not a bad perk of the job.

'How's it going in here?' Millie asked, handing Nina a mug of coffee and a little plate of chocolate samples.

Nina took the mug. 'Ooh, thanks. Getting there. I had no idea there was so much stuff crammed into this room. It really did need a good clear out.'

Millie smiled. 'It's been a long time coming. Lizzie always said she'd get around to it, but there was always something more pressing to do. I think she'll be relieved, deep down, to have it sorted.'

Nina nodded, taking a sip of her coffee. 'Well, I'm happy to help. It's taken me a bit longer than I thought…'

'Yes, I can't believe just how much stuff was lurking in there.' Millie laughed.

'I know. I've found all sorts.'

'Well, onwards and upwards. Let me know if you want anything else.'

'Will do.'

Nina continued to work her way through the clutter and uncovered some interesting bits and bobs – old photographs of the shop in its early days, handmade signs for long-past promotions, and a collection of traditional chocolate moulds. By the time she'd had another coffee, some of the floor was visible again, and the piles of junk had been replaced with organised sections for things to keep, donate, or throw away.

Nina stood back, hands on her hips, surveying the room. She cringed at the fair share of chocolate she'd had via Millie's insistence as she swept the pathway in the middle of the junk. Then she put the dustpan away and picked up the tray with the various mugs and plates on which Millie had delivered her goodies. She then walked through the narrow inner corridor from the back room in the direction of the chocolate shop itself. As she walked, the atmosphere changed from what was little more than chaos to the staff area, which was immaculate, then past another small storage room until she pushed open the door to the shop itself. Her eyes flicked to the huge copper machine in the corner and the counter area where Millie was making a coffee at the same time as dealing with somebody on the phone. Seeing Millie was busy, Nina, still with the tray in her hands, walked around the counter to place it in the working area on the other side.

Just as she was turning right past the counter, the door in front of her to the street opened, the bell tinkled above, and Lindsay walked in wearing the same bright green blazer jacket with the sleeves rolled up that Nina had seen her in before and a pair of too-tight, cheap-looking grey jeans. Lindsay smiled so smugly on bumping straight into Nina she looked like the cat who'd got the cream.

'Hey!' Lindsay grinned.

'Hello.'

'I knew it! I knew I was right.'

Nina frowned.

'On your stories! I thought I recognised the chocolate shop logo in the junk you panned. Love a bit of sleuthing on the socials, ha!'

Nina felt herself go cold. Lindsay had examined her stories. What the actual? Who did that? 'Hmm.'

Lindsay was on a roll. 'Wow, you get everywhere, don't you? Lovely Bay has taken you in as one of its own.'

Nina didn't want to interact. She smiled and lifted her chin but didn't say anything.

'I'm guessing Birdie took you under her wing when you first arrived.'

Nina just nodded as she put the tray on the counter.

'How long do you think it will take you?'

'Not sure. Look, sorry, I need to get on.'

Just as Nina turned, Millie interrupted from the other side of the counter. Her face changed as she saw Lindsay. 'Everything okay?'

Lindsay grinned, 'Yes, thanks. Can I get a coffee and a salted caramel truffle for one of the tables in the window there?'

Millie didn't smile. 'Sorry, we're just about to close.'

Lindsay frowned. 'Oh, it says five on the door.'

Millie's face was like stone. 'The machine is off.'

Lindsay clapped her hands together, 'No worries. I'll have a tea then.'

'As I said, we're closed.'

Lindsay's face dropped. 'You're closed?'

Millie didn't miss a beat. 'We are just closing now.'

'So I can't get a tea?'

'No.' Millie's tone closed the conversation.

Nina felt awkward as she went to step around Lindsay to head out the back. Lindsay turned, yanked open the shop door and closed it with a bang behind her. Nina turned to Millie. 'What was that all about?'

Millie grimaced. 'Not having the likes of her in here.'

'What's wrong with her?'

'Best we just leave it at that.' Millie replied as she turned a few knobs on the coffee machine, then started to spray it with cleaner.

'Birdie didn't like her either.'

'No one around here does.'

35

It was a sunny, windy day without a cloud. Nina stood at a pedestrian crossing and looked up at the red man. She wondered how long the blue sky and sunshine would last, hoping that it would be a similar day on the day she got married, although without the wind, would be good. As she crossed the wind whistled around her legs as she watched a man with fins in his hand and a small bodyboard under his arm come the other way. Another man with a backpack squeezed between pedestrians to cross the other way and Nina found herself hurrying along towards the riverboat.

Once she'd arrived at the jetty, she sat on the edge of the bench waiting for the riverboat to come along, musing quite how she was going to finish the chocolate shop job before the wedding. She looked down towards the river path where a woman in a purple running top, hat, and bright pink trainers ran along. Her mind flicked to her own running journey where she'd gone from hardly being able to put one foot in front of the other to now running, if badly, a few times a week.

As the familiar putter of the engine filled her ears, she gazed out at the riverbank sliding by. The sunny weather matched her upbeat mood. She mentally went through all she had left to do for the wedding. She had to go to have the final fitting for the bodice and make sure everything was okay with the skirt of the dress. She had to pop in to see Beauty by Bianca to check the booking for having her makeup done, and she needed to check that the drinks were sorted. She felt a flutter of butterflies at the thought that all the meticulous planning was nearly complete. Soon, she'd be walking into a registry office towards a totally different next chapter of her life. With a start, she realised Colin was talking to her.

'How are you?' Colin asked.

'Good thanks, how about you?'

'Yeah, fine. Ready for the big day coming up?'

'We've still got a bit of time to go,' Nina said with a smile.

'It will come around quickly. You seem very chill, though.'

'It will do! We're quite organised. We've been to the hotel, everything is ready for that. We've got the marquees ready to go if there's an inclement weather problem. Nancy and Birdie have done their bit. It's a bit overwhelming to think it's nearly here after all the planning. It's all been so fast.'

Colin interjected, 'There will be if it's in Lovely, probably get hailstones.'

Nina forced a chuckle. 'Don't put that image in my head! I'm stressed enough about the weather as it is. I should know by now to expect anything here.' She bit her lip, eyebrows knitted with concern.

'You never know in Lovely. Just have to be prepared for anything and any weather, four seasons in one day. Well, you already know that by now.'

'Maybe I was crazy to have it outside.'

'Maybe you were,' Colin agreed. 'So, how are you getting from the registry office to The Summer Hotel?'

Nina shook her head. 'Haven't really thought about it too much. A taxi, I suppose, or we'll just drive.'

'I'll drive you if you like. On the way back, you could come up on the boat. That would be a nice way to arrive.'

Nina wrinkled her nose and shook her head. 'Hmm. I don't really want to be walking up the road in the dress and everything.'

'I didn't mean that. We could use the jetty down there,' Colin suggested.

Nina was curious. 'What jetty?'

'Private jetty to the left of The Summer Hotel.'

'Oh, that one. I didn't even know that was in use.'

'It's not, not officially, but it can be. I can easily pull a boat up there.'

'Wow, that would be a nice idea,' Nina said. 'What, and then we'd just walk up through the garden?'

'Yes, it would be lovely if it's a nice day.'

'Yes, it would, actually,' Nina agreed. 'I'll have a think about it. Thank you.'

Colin tapped the side of the boat. 'We've got enough of these beauties. We could use the old special timber one, my favourite one. It's a bit smaller, but it would get you here in no time.'

Nina nodded. 'Thank you. I'll run it past Robby and see what he thinks. Thanks for the offer, Colin, that's so nice of you.'

'Not a problem at all, you know the gig now. It's the way we do it down here in Lovely. Help each other out and everything. I've heard about what you've taken on in the chocolate shop.'

'Yes.'

'So how's that going, the big clear out?' Colin asked.

Nina rolled her eyes good-naturedly. 'Where do I start? I didn't realise it was going to be as big of a job as it is. It's amazing quite how much stuff has accumulated there over the years. It's literally floor-to-ceiling clutter in every little nook and cranny.'

Colin chuckled knowingly. 'I can imagine. Some people do tend to hang onto things.'

'That's an understatement!' Nina laughed. 'I see it all daily in my line of work. There was so much in there – old electricity bills from the nineties, ledgers from years ago and so much random stuff. Promotional hats, a mannequin torso, boxes of ribbons and doilies, an old shop till. You name it, I found it.'

Colin grinned. 'That sounds about right. You'll have your work cut out, getting it all sorted. Sounds like a right mess.'

'It really is. There's barely room to move back there. But I'm getting there, one shelf at a time. Found a few buried treasures, too, like an old commemorative tin of chocolates.'

Colin chuckled. 'If anyone can tackle that job, it's you. Just don't throw anything out without asking first, if I was you.'

Nina nodded. 'Oh, believe me, I've learned that lesson quickly! People sometimes have fits over things I think about purely as junk. Anyway, I'm making progress, bit by bit, and I love it, so it's all good. I find it therapeutic, which is how I got into it all in the first place.'

Colin gestured to the water. 'I feel like that about my job, too. There's nothing like being out here on the water day in day out.'

Nina gazed at the passing scenery and the ripples on the top of the breezy river. 'I have to admit, it feels good to take a break and be out on the water. It's peaceful. I always think it helps me reset on here, you know?'

'Happy to provide the relief! My boat here has soothed many a frazzled soul over the years…'

They continued chatting amiably as the boat puttered along. Eventually, the jetty Nina was getting off at came into view. Colin expertly steered the boat alongside, threw a rope around a mooring post, and held out a hand to help Nina onto the weathered planks.

'Thanks for the chat. I'll let you know about using the jetty at the hotel. Such a kind offer, thanks.'

'Of course. Best of luck getting that clutter at the shop under control. Don't work too hard.'

Nina chuckled as she stepped onto the jetty. There was a fat chance of that. She was fully booked more or less right up to the day she stepped into the registry office. 'I'll keep that in mind.'

She turned and gave a little wave as Colin released the rope and revved the engine, and watched as the boat slowly puttered off down the river, leaving a wake trailing along behind it. For a moment, she lingered and took in the river air and view on the nice day. The sun was shining, the breeze was nice, the river looked so pretty, and life for Nina Lavendar hadn't felt as good for a very long time.

36

It was not that long after Nina had been to the tailor to sort out the fitting of her wedding dress. Faye, the tailor, had taken it in her stride and said that it wouldn't take much at all to move the zip a tiny bit. The skirt fitted onto the bodice underneath, and so, with all being well Nina was more or less sorted. However, what wasn't sorted quite yet was her new property. She waved to one of the neighbours as she walked along the harbour front, then proceeded around to the back, slid back the bolt on the gate, and made her way inside. The whole of the ground floor was finished. Rather than the filth, dirt, and fishing paraphernalia she had been faced with when she'd first moved in, things had vastly improved. Now, everything was painted in a neutral white, smelt fresh, and was aesthetically pleasing to the eye.

Making her way up to the second floor, she crossed over and then took the steep, ladder-like stairs up to the attic room, which was going to be her and Robby's bedroom. To be frank, as far as she was concerned, the whole timing of Robby's proposal probably hadn't been ideal but she'd take it. She'd more or less had the property for five minutes when he'd decided to propose. They'd talked about his timing at length; he had suddenly proposed because of Nancy's friend with cancer, who had got married in hospital which had got him thinking of similar scenarios. Robby had told her Nancy's friend's situation had brought back all sorts for him, including when his partner had died in an accident years and years before. He'd said he had been determined that it wouldn't happen again without him having his ducks in a row. The marriage proposal was his lining up of those ducks.

In a way, it was good that Nina had already bought the property by the harbour because when they'd discussed finances, houses, and suchlike, Nina had been adamant that she remain fairly independent. After a bit of toing and froing, Robby had decided that he didn't really care less where he lived. So they'd decided to give the place on the harbour a go, which meant Nina had to get it sorted out, and fast.

Like the ground floor, the attic room was now clean. It had taken nearly a day just to remove the dust that had been left once the junk had been taken out and give it a good airing by opening the windows and doors at either end. Letting the sea breeze whizz through had done a better job than any air freshener from a supermarket ever could have dreamed about. Despite the sea air working its wonders, the actual ingrained lifelong dust had been stubborn and then some. Nina had spent a long time with an industrial vacuum on her back, hoovering the eaves, the floorboards, and everywhere else in between. Once it was dust-free, it had been painted with the spray painter in exactly the same few shades of coordinating white as the other floors and was good to go.

After seeing a picture on Pinterest of an attic room similar to the one at the top of her new property, she'd also decided to go with painting the floorboards white. Robby, Nancy, and Sophie had all thought she was mad, but now, as she stood at the top of the stairs looking over to the window on the other side of the room, she knew that she'd made the right choice. Beautiful white floorboards looked back at her stretching endlessly to the far side of the room topped with the view of the harbour from the windows.

The bed she'd found on Marketplace took pride of place atop the white floorboards; a black Victorian frame in a simple heritage design with a touch of brass by way of its finials. According to the person she'd bought it from, it had been handmade in iron and brass by a small bespoke bedmaker in Norfolk. It had taken a lot of work, carrying it piece by piece, to get it up the stairs, but now it was there, it took pride of place. On either side of the bed, bedside tables held huge lamps topped with pretty white and blue pleated shades. By the window, she'd placed lush palms in huge white pots whose leaves danced in the breeze coming in from the sea. Beside the pots, oversized lanterns were filled with pillar candles nestled beside a fishing basket filled with blankets.

Nina walked over to the bed, smiled, touched the top of a brass finial, and remembered how the lady she'd bought the bed from had told her that the brass details were meticulously hand-finished. Now, as she stood looking at it, she could appreciate the beauty and workmanship of the bed she'd found for a song. Everything else about the room was simple; the clad walls painted in a soft white, the floor in a similar creamier shade, the huge windows contrasting in another shade of white again, and the little French door down at the end, leading onto the Juliet balcony, was open and blowing a breeze right through the centre of the room.

Nina was exponentially pleased with herself at how the funny-shaped attic room had turned out. It could have gone either way but the neutral whites and simple decor allowed it to sing. Well happy at a job well done, she started to pull off the plastic covering on an extremely expensive and even more sumptuous mattress that had recently arrived. It was large, plush, thick, absolutely gorgeous, and had been quite the nightmare to wedge inch by inch up the steep stairs. She couldn't wait to have a good night's sleep on the new mattress at the top of the property with the sound of the sea whistling in her ears.

The small bathroom tucked under the eaves hadn't been quite as easy to sort out. When she'd first looked at it, she'd almost given up hope as she'd examined a vast covering of green, grimy mould just about everywhere she'd looked. The shape of it wasn't easy to work with either; eaves sloped down virtually towards the top of the toilet, and the old pedestal sink, which had seen better days, was wedged in under a beam. A strangely placed window in the back-facing wall, nearly on the floor, looked out over the rooftops towards Lovely Bay itself, and the bath, blocked in with pine cladding, seemed as if it faced the wrong way.

Nina stood and analysed the bathroom for a second. It had come a long, long way. With the beams, ceiling, and floor now painted white, it looked clean and fresh. New taps on the bath and sink were in place, and white, plush towels changed everything. The pine cladding that had surrounded the bath, the window, and encased the toilet was white and Nina had become well-versed in the correct chemicals to remove decades' worth of mould. She'd tried everything from non-toxic mould killer to a much stronger kettle of fish altogether. Everything she'd read had told her that white vinegar would be a fabulous alternative to more harmful chemical cleaners. White vinegar did absolutely nothing for the sort of mould she was dealing with. After trying everything and finally finding a solution via an industrial plumbing site, she'd parted with the cash on her credit card for some stuff that you shoved down the toilet and hoped for the best. After it had arrived she'd guiltily done just that with her fingers crossed and mask across her face. It had fizzed, and as she wondered if she was doing the right thing, it had shifted the green and done just what it had said on the tin.

Nina stood by the window, gazing over the picturesque harbour below. Her phone buzzed and glancing at the screen, she saw Robby's name and answered with a smile. 'Hey, you.'

'Hey. How's the attic coming along? You sound happy. I take it everything's good.'

Nina chuckled. 'It's looking amazing. I've just finished taking off the plastic on the mattress. It's all come together beautifully.'

Nina walked over to the bed. She laughed. 'I'm standing in our bedroom, looking out at the view. It's just so nice up here tucked away from the world.'

'The start of a new chapter, eh? Plus, you get a new husband thrown into the mix.'

'I'm a lucky duck,' Nina joked. She was joking but underneath it all she was far from having a laugh. Never a truer word said in jest.

37

Nina sat opposite Sophie in the first café in Lovely Bay she'd ever been to. They were there for a quick bite to eat before going to see Faye for the final dress fitting. Nina ordered a chowder, Sophie ordered a chicken sandwich, and they then waited while Sophie chatted about the fact that her husband, Nick, was, as usual, away again. Sophie held her hand on top of the pram handle beside her and wiggled it back and forth as she spoke, completely oblivious to the fact that she was holding a conversation, pushing the pram, and taking a Tupperware pot out of her bag all at the same time.

'Look at you, multitasking.' Nina laughed.

'I know, right?' Sophie said as she jiggled the pram more. 'She really needs to drop off to sleep otherwise she's going to be a nightmare later.'

'I wish someone would tuck me up in a pram, push me back and forth, and let me drop off to sleep.' Nina chuckled. 'I think I'd sleep for a year.'

Sophie laughed and joked, 'That's Robby's job, isn't it?'

Nina also laughed as the chowder arrived in front of her, and a sandwich was placed in front of Sophie.

As they delved into their lunch, they started to talk about the wedding. 'So, once we get this dress fitting finished today and *my* dress done, everything is in place, correct?' Sophie asked.

'Yes.'

'What about Nancy and the wildflowers?'

The plan was to pick masses of wildflowers from down by the river, turn them into gigantic wildflower posies, and pop them into huge jugs on the tables. Basically, Nina and Nancy had decided that there would be wildflower posies on anything that didn't move. Nina was more than happy with that. From the word go, she hadn't been interested in fancy florist decorations. 'She's got it all under control. I don't need to do anything.'

'Gosh, she's turned out to be gold in this. I'd better watch my best friend status here.'

'Ha. We've been together too long for you to lose that now,' Nina bantered. 'But yeah, it's funny how we just clicked.'

'I love it when that happens. Another good thing about Lovely Bay, eh?'

Nina mused and nodded. 'Actually, yeah, I hadn't realised that really.'

Once they had finished their lunch and were making their way to the tailor's, they crossed one of the Lovely greens, walked under a line of pretty ash trees, and made their way to the long row of terrace houses where Faye both worked and lived.

Arriving at the gate, they stopped outside, and Sophie wrinkled up her nose as she looked at the slightly tatty pale blue front door and huge palm in the corner. 'Funny place to have a tailor.'

'I know, I thought the same thing but wait until you get inside.'

Nina rang the doorbell, and a few minutes later, Faye opened the door with a smile. After sorting out the pram and getting everything upstairs, Sophie's eyes widened as they walked into Faye's workroom, where Nina's dress was fitted on the dressmaker's mannequin in the corner.

Sophie's hands flew to her mouth. 'Oh my gosh, it looks absolutely amazing!'

Nina stood right where she was. She couldn't believe it; on the dressmaker's dummy, the dress looked exactly what she wanted but somehow much better than she remembered. It was a plain skirt with a bodice, but the fabric and simplicity of the cut spoke for itself. 'Wow, it really does look nice on there. Thank you.'

Faye nodded. 'It's actually a beautiful dress, and it was really easy to alter. It should fit you very well.'

A few minutes later, Nina was standing in the dress, or what was actually a bodice and skirt. Faye was standing behind her, with pins on a pin cushion slotted onto her wrist, finishing off the last few adjustments. 'It fits you beautifully,' Faye noted.

'Yes, it does, doesn't it? I'm so pleased.'

'Wow, it's amazing.' Sophie nodded. Her voice caught at the end of her words. She blinked and shook her head. 'Oh my God, I'm so sorry, Nina. It just reminds me of everything... Of Andrew and what you've gone through.' Sophie swore. 'Seeing you in that, wow, it's totally taken me back.'

Nina nodded. 'I know. I had the same thought the other day. I suddenly thought I'd done the wrong thing, but now I don't at all. I love it.'

Sophie shook her head and waved her hand back and forth in front of her face, then rubbed her eyebrow and tried to push away a tear. 'No, no, not the wrong thing, the opposite, in fact. It's just made me realise how good you are now, how far you've come, how you dragged yourself out of, well, you know. It's amazing. And the dress... The dress is absolutely beautiful.'

Faye also welled up. 'I was thinking the same thing as I was working on it. It must have so many memories attached to it. It's a really beautiful thing to do. You should be really happy.'

Nina felt pricks of tears, too, so all three of them had tears in their eyes. 'Thank you, thank you. I hope so. I really hope I've done the right thing. I just feel like Andrew is with me, but in a nice way, rather than before when it was always so gut-wrenching and horrible. Do you know what I mean? My mum said it was weird.'

'Yes, I know. It's *not* weird.' Sophie affirmed. 'That's so true. It just feels right and nice. I miss him too but this, it's…'

Faye fussed with the bottom of the dress and patted it down. 'It's going to be the best day ever, and you're going to look like a million dollars. Lucky Robby, that's what I say.'

Sophie smiled and continued to wipe under her eyes too. 'He's very fortunate indeed. I hope he knows just how much.'

38

A couple of days later, Nina walked down the steps with her raincoat on, her basket over her shoulder, and her small umbrella in her hand. The steps through the park in the middle of Lovely Bay were slightly mossy, and the drizzly rain tapped on the top of her umbrella. A council worker wearing one of the Lovely coats stood by the door of his van, chatting on the phone as the rain plopped down onto the pathway. Everything around Nina appeared as if it had been sloshed with a wipe of lush, intense green. Water glistened off the tops of trees and a magnolia tree's leaves shone in the fresh coating of rain. Nina inhaled the air heavy with moisture, the lovely fresh smell of rain-soaked soil and grass mingled with wet flowers and leaves. She smiled as she watched nature doing its thing as she made her way through the park underneath her umbrella.

The rain pitter-pattered on top of her brolly as she stepped along the sheen of a wet pathway. Sparkling raindrops clinging to leaves and spiderwebs caught her eye as she made her way beside a bank of beautifully manicured beds. As she got to a small stone bridge, she stopped for a second and looked into the stream gushing down in the direction of the sea. Raindrops caused circles to appear on the surface of the stream and as she leaned over, water trickled over rocks, and the fresh, clean scent filled her nose. Strolling along happily, she walked past a sundial surrounded by rosemary bushes and pondered for a second whether or not she should sit on an undercover bench for a bit and just let the world go by. Deciding she didn't have enough time, she continued walking, enjoying the feeling of living in Lovely Bay. Stopping at a large patch of ferns, stretching out over an entire bed, she listened to the birds chirping above and wondered how long it would be before the weather changed again and the sun would come out.

Nina was on her way to the deli to meet Sophie for lunch, and being a bit early she'd taken the long way around, and once she'd arrived she stood outside under the awning on the pavement people-watching for a bit. She smiled as a woman in an all-black outfit with long, blonde hair and a red umbrella clumped past her in too high shoes. A man in an aqua blue anorak with yellow sleeves, clearly a trainspotter, and his wife in a white raincoat with the hood up strolled past arm in arm, and a man on a green bike cycled past with a concerned look on his face as if he was going to get very wet.

Once Sophie turned up, they'd gone in and sat down, and Sophie raised her eyebrows. 'So, you're not into a hen do where we all get drunk and run around in bridal dresses with sashes, then?' Sophie asked with a laugh.

Nina shook her head fervently. 'No, I don't even want a hen do as such at all.'

'You don't want me to get you a tiara and rude things from the sex shop and present them to the group at the table?'

'That would be a no as well,' Nina said with a smile. 'Not my scene, as you know.'

'Pin the tail on the donkey or the you-know-what on the muscly man.'

'Soph!'

'How about a fake veil and a plastic, sparkly tiara?' Sophie giggled.

'We didn't even have that last time, on my first wedding, so I don't know why I'd want one all these years later when I'm older.'

Sophie chuckled. 'We're not *that* old. Right, so you just want a very nice, very tame, sophisticated, and elegant meal with the girls?'

Nina nodded. 'Correct. You've got that in one. It's not that hard. It'll be really nice, just a beautiful meal with loads of lovely food and a few drinks.'

Sophie nodded. 'Works for me. So, are we talking chowder in Lovely Bay?'

Nina contemplated for a second. 'Do you know what? I think it might be good to go somewhere else.'

'How about over my way? You could all stay with me,' Sophie suggested.

'Yes, that would be lovely. When you say we could stay with you, what do you mean? Like including my mum and sister?'

Sophie nodded. 'Yeah, not that I think your mum or your sister will stay with me, but the offer is there. Nick's here that weekend we're talking about, and I'm going to get him to take the children to his mum's.'

It's about time, Nina thought but stopped herself from saying. 'Sounds good.'

'Who would've believed it? Neens getting married again. I'm so excited.'

'I know, tell me about it.'

'So, what are you two thinking about doing about names?' Sophie asked. 'We did talk about it but you hadn't decided…'

'Robby Lavender sounds quite good to me, don't you think?'

Sophie raised her eyebrows. 'Could be an option, I suppose. Thank goodness it's not like the old days any longer and we have to automatically take a man's name.'

'We're just going to leave it as it is. Can't be bothered with all that rigmarole.'

'I don't blame you,' Sophie said. 'So old-fashioned as well.'

'I'm just going to keep my name as it is. And anyway, I feel like "Lavendar" keeps a part of Andrew and me, if you see what I mean. I'm sorry if I seem like I'm going on about Andrew lately. It's just that this feels like a massive step for me, and then the anniversary. I hadn't expected it all to be such a jumble of emotions.'

'Don't be ridiculous! It's understandable. You've been through loads. I feel like I have too in a way.'

'Yep. Sometimes, I think that talking about him makes me seem so wrapped up in myself and selfish,' Nina shook her head.

'Nothing of the sort! You hardly *ever* mention him.'

'I feel like I do.'

'No, no, not at all. And even if you did, it's fine. That's precisely what best friends are for. That and organising classy hen nights.'

39

With a small bottle of gin nestled in a basket over her arm, Nina strolled along beside Nancy. It was a gorgeous warm evening in Lovely Bay, and they were on their way to one of the secret chowder speakeasies. Nina still hadn't quite got over the quaint little places, often hidden in someone's home, a commercial building, or in a location you would least expect, but she knew that she loved them. She smiled as they crossed the road, walked over towards the central green, went underneath the huge old tree, and started to head towards the main part of the town.

'So, where are we going?' Nina asked.

Nancy chuckled. 'Have you not quite yet realised that you're not allowed to ask that when you go to a speakeasy?'

Nina laughed. 'I thought by now I might be able to know.'

Sucking air through her teeth, Nancy then chuckled. 'You need to be fully initiated.'

Nina laughed. 'You mean, like, have a ceremony or something? Are you going to touch me on either side of my shoulders with a sword? Will I have to kneel and wear a robe? Are there any thrones involved?'

'Exactly,' Nancy giggled. 'Actually, we don't kneel here. You'll need to lie down on a marble slab, and we douse you in water, chant old folk songs from the area, and dance around you.'

Nina played along. 'Will the water be from the River Lovely?'

Nancy laughed. 'Yes, indeed. I think that's how it goes.'

'So, considering I'm marrying someone who is a fully sworn-in Lovely, when will this full initiation take place?'

Nancy nodded and laughed. 'When you have the ring on your finger, all sorts of new things are going to open up for you in Lovely Bay. Just you wait and see.'

Nina laughed. 'Like what?'

'You'll just have to find out, won't you?'

About ten minutes later, they crossed another one of the Lovely greens, went over a small bridge, and made their way up a narrow lane running up the hill.

'I don't even think I've been to this side of Lovely Bay before, not many times, anyway,' Nina said.

'No?' Nancy questioned.

'No, where are we going up here? What's up here?'

'Follow your nose.'

'Oh, I see where we are,' Nina said as they took a left turn and seemed to double back on themselves a bit and started going down again. 'We're heading towards the RNLI shed, aren't we?'

Nancy chuckled. 'We might be, we might not.'

Nina nudged Nancy with her elbow. 'We are, wow, what a setting for it!'

Nancy lowered her voice. 'A good setting, a really good setting, but not one of the best chowders in Lovely Bay in my humble opinion, but what would I know?'

'Oh, right. I see.'

'Never, *ever* let anyone know that, and definitely don't say it was said by me.'

Nina nodded. 'Secret's safe with me.'

A few minutes later, they were in the back of the RNLI shed in what looked to be some sort of storeroom. A timber floor was lined with vast custom-made shelving units holding dinghies, rowing paraphernalia, oars, and all kinds of things. Strings and strings of fairy lights ran between the shelves and were layered liberally overhead, old rustic tables were adorned with not much other than candles in jam jars, and Nina could see a small kitchen area off to the right. Everything was rustic, shabby, and very Lovely.

The place was busy with Lovelies already seated as Nina and Nancy weaved their way through the tables. A couple of people smiled and said hello. Birdie jumped up from the far end, kissed both of them on the cheek, and then they sat down. Nina put her bottle of Hendricks on the table, pulled two glasses towards her, and started to pour them both a drink.

About half an hour or so after they'd arrived, a few drinks in and they were chatting about this and that when the chowder arrived. Nina dipped in, raised her eyebrows, and lowered her voice. 'Tastes really good to me. I don't know what you're talking about.'

Nancy laughed and whispered, 'You're just not quite as advanced in your chowder palate as me.'

'I'm clearly not. This is delicious. I like it. I love this funny little tradition we have.'

'We have loads of them, don't we?'

'Yes, it takes a bit of getting used to,' Nina replied.

'I bet it does. It doesn't seem like that to me, though; I've lived here all my life.'

'Yes, you're lucky. Talking about living here all your life, I met someone recently who you know. I've been meaning to mention it to you for *ages*. I keep bumping into her and she gives me, well...' Nina trailed off, not sure whether to divulge her feelings about Lindsay.

Nancy put a spoonful of chowder into her mouth. 'Oh, right, yes, who? I hope they said nice things about me.'

'Lindsay? Do you know her? Actually, I also bumped into her when I was with Birdie when I first bought the property, but Birdie was quite strange. I've never seen her behave like that. I kept forgetting to speak to you about it.'

Nancy slowly put her spoon down on the side of her plate, didn't say anything for a minute, picked up her gin glass, took a huge gulp, and then put it back down. 'Right, so you bumped into Lindsay, did you? If it's the Lindsay, I think it is... Well, I only know one.'

'I did.'

'What did she look like?'

'Brown sort of lanky hair. I don't mean to be nasty, but cheap, bright clothes.'

'Oh, no.'

'Is something wrong with her? You're also reacting in a strange way. Birdie clearly doesn't like her. I assumed they'd just fallen out over something. She said she was a friend of yours. No, not a friend, an acquaintance, I think. Birdie told me to steer well clear.'

Nancy shook her head. 'Birdie was funny to her?'

'Yes. Very.'

'She's no friend of mine, that I know for sure. I can't believe she's got the front to come back here.' Nancy nodded. 'I suppose the time is up now.'

Nina looked confused but thought that maybe her feelings about Lindsay were along the right lines. 'I'm not sure what you're talking about. Who is this woman? What's wrong with her?'

'*Lots* is wrong with her. How do you know about her? Has she been hanging around you or something?' Nancy asked.

Nina frowned. 'Well, she does seem to have bumped into me

in a few places. She was outside the cottage, and she said that she knew you.'

'She doesn't really *know* me, but she did. She was a friend of one of the girls who worked in the kiosk at the station. Have you spoken about this to our Robby?'

Nina shook her head and frowned. 'No. Why would I? She did say she knew him but I didn't really think much about it. I thought she was just a Lovely, you know?'

Nancy took another huge sip of her drink. 'I don't know if I should tell you this or you should wait until you've spoken to our Robby.'

'You're not making much sense. What are you talking about? Just tell me. How bad can it be? *Who* is she?'

Nancy shook her head. 'Look, put it this way; she's trouble.'

Nina nodded. 'Yes, Birdie said the same. *Why* is she trouble? What has she done?'

Nancy sighed. 'It's a bit of a long story, but basically, she's a scammer. Simple as that. At least, that is what she would be called these days.'

Nina wrinkled her nose up. 'What? What do you mean? What sort of a scammer? What does she scam people out of? Money?'

Nancy sighed again. 'Not just money. It's not just about money. She's... Well, she's sort of really nasty, evil. I don't know what the word is. She takes joy from horrible situations. She plays on people who have had bad things happen to them. It became apparent that she thrives on doom.'

Nina was confused. 'What do you mean "she takes joy in horrible situations"? Did she do something horrible to *you?*'

'Sort of. She's just *generally* horrible,' Nancy replied.

'Right,' Nina nodded. 'Doom, you say. So, why would that be of interest to Robby?'

Nancy sighed again. 'I just don't know whether I should be telling you. You should ask him yourself.'

'Just tell me and then I'll decide,' Nina reasoned.

Nancy nodded. 'Well, okay. So, she preys on people who are either down on their luck or have had something terrible happen to them. She thrives on trauma, as it were. And not long after the accident with our Robby... Well, you know what happened there – she pursued him. And when it didn't really go anywhere, she sent him thousands of messages and emails, and it all got *really* nasty.'

'What? Oh my gosh, are you kidding me?'

'I wish, but no, I'm not,' Nancy answered. 'And then it got worse because it all came to a head, but then she took off as fast as she'd arrived. It was weird. Eventually, a few years later, somebody contacted Robby because she had done it to a few other people but it was a lot more serious. I'm not sure how they knew that Robby had been involved with her. There were solicitors involved and, I don't know, loads of things. It was in the papers. She'd scammed people out of stuff.'

'I can't believe it! What happened?' Nina asked.

'Long story short, it went to court, and she was not allowed to go near anyone involved, including our Robby, for five years. That would've been up ages ago, but she's obviously decided to come back to Lovely Bay for some reason. I'm not sure how she knew about you, though, but she's obviously put two and two together. She schemes you see.'

'She said something about Facebook...'

'But you don't post on Facebook, do you?'

'Not really,' Nina said. 'But I do have a few things on there about me and Robby; maybe it showed up on his profile somehow, and she got hold of it. Sophie's always on there and tagging me in stuff. I think Soph puts what she's got for dinner on there. Maybe somehow through that...'

'I do know you just need to keep *well* clear. Hopefully, she'll get fed up. I can't believe she's back here.'

'I don't know what to say,' Nina said.

'I know,' Nancy replied. 'It's awful.'

'I can't believe Robby hasn't told me about it.'

'I can. I don't think any of us wanted to talk about it once she'd gone. Especially when we found out what she'd done to other people. And there was somebody else in Lovely as well, but he's moved away now.'

'Right,' Nina said, feeling a bit put out. 'Robby hasn't told me any of this.'

Nancy shook her head. 'I honestly don't think that anyone has thought about it for ages. It was a long time ago now, and we all tried to put it behind us.'

'Right, yeah, I suppose. I thought he would've told me, though. It sounds very serious.'

'You'll have to ask him that.'

'Yes, I will.'

Nancy nodded. 'You'll need to let him know that she's back around. I'm surprised Birdie hasn't said anything. Has she mentioned it to you since?'

'No. Though, she's been all over the show and not well too, so yeah...'

'Hmm.'

'God, it sounds terrible. You look worried about it.'

Nancy nodded. 'Yes, it's not nice. Look, the best thing you can do is google it and have a read of the stuff that was in the paper. There are loads of things on the internet about it, even though it was in the early days of stuff being online. She didn't just do it around here, either. She did it to a few different people around the country but mostly along the south coast. I can't remember where she originally came from. Robby got off lightly, so there is that, I guess. He was included in the court case as a number, as it were.'

Nina nodded. 'Right, oh God, I'll google it later when I get home.'

'Yes,' Nancy agreed. 'Then decide what to do.'

After finishing their chowder, Nina and Nancy lingered over their drinks, the atmosphere dampened by the turn in conversation. The Lindsay thing zoomed around Nina's brain and she couldn't let it go. 'So, what do you reckon I should do then?' Nina asked, swirling the ice in her gin and tonic, her brows knitted in concern.

Nancy sighed, tapping her fingers on the table. 'Well, first things first, have a google. Then you should definitely talk to our Robby. He's the one who's been through it. He'll know best how to handle it, I guess. I feel bad that I've told you.'

Nina nodded, taking a long sip of her drink. 'Yeah, it's just a bit shocking, isn't it? I mean, to think she's been lurking around, knowing all this stuff about us. It can't be a coincidence.'

'It is,' Nancy agreed, her voice serious. 'You've got to be careful, Nina. People like Lindsay don't just change overnight. If she's back in Lovely, there's got to be a reason for it.'

Nina shivered despite the warm evening. 'I know. It's creepy, isn't it? To think she's been watching and waiting. Makes you wonder what she's planning.'

'That's why you've got to stay one step ahead,' Nancy said firmly. 'Keep your eyes open and don't let her get under your skin. Keep away from her and don't engage.'

Nina swallowed, thinking about the vast number of text exchanges she'd had with Lindsay. She didn't tell Nancy about the interactions. 'I will. I'm not going to let Lindsay ruin what I've got here. Lovely's been too good to me.'

Nancy smiled, raising her glass. 'To Lovely, and Nina.'

'To Lovely,' Nina echoed, clinking her glass against Nancy's. 'And to getting rid of unwanted pests.'

They both laughed, but Nina wasn't feeling too happy. She'd clocked the weird vibes from Lindsay from day one. She just hoped she wasn't going to find out more.

40

Nina typed Lindsay's name into the search bar and scrolled up. There were many entries, none of them made Lindsay sound very nice. In fact, it seemed as if she was one nasty piece of work. Moving back up to the top, Nina rested her finger on the mouse, right-clicked on the first link, opened it in a new tab, and did the same all the way down the results until she came to about halfway down the screen.

She took a sip of her coffee and started to read the first article from a daily national newspaper. Lindsay was clearly one shady character. There were eight men who had taken Lindsay to court and three women. As Nina clicked and scrolled agog, she realised as she took in the information that Lindsay seemed to have a formula that worked quite well; she would make someone her friend, try to scam them out of some money and then turn nasty when they wanted to get rid of her. She had done it time and time again, all along the south coast. Nina went cold as she waded through and read. She opened the next article and read the same as the third and fourth. By the time she got to the end of the tabs, she wasn't sure if she wanted to read more or not.

Nina sat in a bit of a daze as she read through. This was not a small thing. She was reading about an out-and-out calculated criminal who had not only committed lots of crimes but also had been reported in various online publications about other situations she had got away with. From what Nina could ascertain Lindsay had a well-thought-out strategy executed with precision time and time again.

Her heart pounded as Lindsay's unsavoury history unfolded further on her screen. The articles painted a picture of a woman skilled in manipulation, leaving a trail of betrayed friendships and legal battles across the south coast. Nina felt a chill run down her spine and wrapped her arms around herself, trying to shake off the unsettling feeling.

Nina couldn't believe that Robby hadn't told her. She remembered one of the things Nancy had said when Nina had first started seeing Robby. Nancy had said that Robby had been through quite a lot. Nina had always assumed it was just the death of his partner when he was young, but it seemed this was something, too. As she sat trying to get all the information to make sense in her brain, she was upset that he hadn't told her; it was a significant thing that had happened in his life. A bit strange that he'd keep it quiet if you asked her. She wondered why he hadn't talked about it. Maybe it was one of those things that was very deep down that he didn't want to come back up to the surface. That could be an explanation, she supposed.

The weight of scrolling and reading felt like a tonne of bricks in her stomach. The implication of the articles swirled in her mind. Every time she clicked, every article she opened had made her feel worse as she'd dived deeper into something she hadn't expected to find. As she sat trying to make sense of what she'd just read, everything around her seemed to shrink, and the walls felt as if they were closing in.

The more she thought about it, the more she realised that she just had to talk to Robby about it. She presumed that he wasn't deliberately keeping things from her. She closed her laptop with a sigh. She'd believed that Lovely Bay was this dream-like place where nothing bad ever happened, but maybe she wasn't quite so right after all.

41

Nina was up to her neck in bubbly water in the bath. It was the first deep bath she'd had since buying the property by the harbour. When she'd bought the place, the bathroom had needed a serious amount of work. She'd had to get the toilet replaced in the end, despite the amount of chemicals she'd thrown down it guiltily, but now it was a good place for a nice soak in the tub. She took a sip of her gin and tonic and mentally went through what still needed to be done for the wedding. Now, the dress was altered, it was at the dry cleaners and needed to be collected, but everything else to do with the wedding was arranged and there wasn't anything else left to do.

On the work front, she was very much chipping away at all her jobs, including the chocolate shop. It had been a long week where she'd been at the shop for a few afternoons organising the shelving units and final bits and bobs. She was most definitely feeling her busy week in her bones and the soak was doing its job.

With her phone propped up on the side of the bath, she stared at the top of the vintage medicine vanity unit where a Tom Ford perfume, matching body cream, and bath oil stood in a neat row. She shook her head and laughed. She'd treated herself to the scent for the wedding and the three little bottles with fancy lids showed how far she'd come in her journey. When she'd been in the flat deep in the depths of life on her own, her self-care had been more or less non-existent. It had been about all she could manage to make the effort to slap on a bit of E45 and wash her hair a couple of times a week. Now, here she was buying fancy, expensive scents, making semi-regular trips to Beauty by Bianca, the beauty therapist in town, and taking care of herself a lot more often than she ever had. The bath up to her neck was part of her newly found 'Take Care of Herself' routine. It had been a long time coming.

After about fifteen minutes of staring into space and thinking, mainly about the situation with Lindsay, her phone buzzed from the side. She answered a video call from Robby and giggled as he came onto the screen.

'Oh, nice view. I don't mind when my soon-to-be wife answers the phone in her birthday suit.'

'Very funny,' Nina replied. 'You can't see me, so...'

'I can imagine, thank you very much.'

'How are you? How did it all go?' she said, referring to a huge job Robby had been to in Birmingham where he'd collaborated with another company to deliver the contract.

'Yeah, good,' Robby nodded. 'I wish I was home, though. It's been a long few days. How are you getting on?'

Nina shook her head. She wanted to bring up the Lindsay thing. It was as if it was sitting between them like a huge elephant in the room. The timing wasn't great so she decided to keep quiet about what she'd learnt. 'Same, which is why you find me here. I've been in the chocolate shop. I seem to have broken the back of it now, so that's good. It really was a lot to take on at this stage of the game.'

'I did try to warn you about doing that, especially for free.'

'That's the way it works around here, isn't it?' Nina replied.

'Well, yes, for sure, but still…'

'Remember when you came to help with The Summer Hotel back in the day when I was first here? You said that that's what people do for each other in Lovely Bay. I'm just following suit. I don't want to get chased out of town by anybody.'

'Exactly, though I may have had a little bit of an incentive in helping you that day,' Robby joked. 'It's just that you seem to have bitten off a lot more than you can chew at this stage of the game.'

'I'm fine. All is good. I like nothing better than sorting things out. Anyway, everything is done for the wedding.'

'How did it go with the dress at the cleaners?'

'Yep, good. The last bit of the puzzle is in place. They said it shouldn't take long because it's in good condition. It just needs a bit of a freshen up. It was packed away clean, but that was years ago, obviously, as you know.'

'Yeah, right. Okay, so we are ready to go then. Time to get the deed done.'

'Yeah, all you need to do now is to marry me unless you've changed your mind, that is.'

Robby chuckled. 'Absolutely not. I cannot wait.'

42

The following evening, Nina and Robby were sharing a takeaway. He'd come in from work looking exhausted, and so she'd decided to wait until she spoke to him about the Lindsay situation.

As they finished the takeaway, he got in first. He put his knife and fork down and sat forward in his seat. 'There's something I need to tell you, Nina.'

Nina didn't like his tone. She hadn't heard Robby's voice like it before. 'Like what?' she said.

Robby hesitated, his hands clasped tightly together. 'Like a situation I didn't tell you about because I never thought it would come up, to be honest. No, actually, that's wrong. I didn't think. I haven't thought about it for years.'

Nina didn't know what to do. It was *clearly* going to be the Lindsay thing. Nancy must have said something to him. Did she say what she already knew or not? She decided first of all to pretend that she knew nothing about it, so she kept schtum.

Robby's voice was tense and tight. 'There was something that happened to me ages ago. To cut a long story short, it all started with this woman who had seen my name in the paper. Not that

I knew that at that point, but she tracked me down, and we went out a few times. I didn't really like her from the start, so I wasn't very enthusiastic, but she was *super* pushy, and basically, I couldn't get rid of her. She didn't take the hint, and it got really horrible.'

'Like, how do you mean?'

'She just didn't give up and wouldn't go away. Then she said she was desperate for money. I basically paid to get rid of her.' Robby shook his head. 'I still can't actually believe I did that.'

'You didn't think about telling me any of this?'

'I haven't even thought about her for years. It was a long time ago. Then out of the blue, I saw her just before I left for this latest job and realised I had to tell you. I couldn't believe it.'

'Right.'

'There are loads of things that no one knows, too.'

'Like what?'

Robby was silent for a bit. 'She was a doom monger or whatever it is a person like that is called.'

'What?'

'She likes or liked doom and trauma. She was addicted to it.'

'Meaning?'

'She wanted to...' Robby paused and winced. 'Replay the accident, you know...'

'Oh my goodness!' Nina swore. 'What the actual?'

'That's when I gave her the money to get rid of her. She said she was in dire financial circumstances.'

'I can't believe it!'

'Afterwards, I realised that she wore the same clothes and stuff that were in the pictures of the accident.'

'That's disgusting. Then what?'

'Then, years later I got contacted by a solicitor who was acting on behalf of a group of men, mostly, who she'd done similar things to. Much worse things, actually. She would pretend she was pregnant and get them to pay to, well, you know… They wanted to know if I would give evidence.'

'And did you?'

'Yes.'

'It went to court and she was convicted of loads of different things. She couldn't come near any of us for five years, but that was ages ago. I haven't even thought about it until now.'

'Right. Okay, well, let me come clean. I already know about her. Nancy told me.'

'What? Why?'

Nina sighed. 'She's been hanging around me.'

Robby swore repeatedly. 'Ahh! What? This is a nightmare.'

Nina wasn't entirely sure what to say for the best. 'How does she know about me, do you think? It can't be a coincidence.'

'I can only assume she has fake profiles all over the internet and has somehow found out about us or I don't know.' Robby turned the palms of his hands up and shrugged.

'Right.'

'Then there's the Andrew thing.'

Nina frowned. 'What's that got to do with it?'

'I have *no* idea, but if Lindsay found out about him and you being a young widow… I don't know. I might be completely barking up the wrong tree, but I would lay money on it that it's that. She'd like that…'

'This is awful.' Nina swore.

'I know.'

'I don't think she will last long, though. Everyone in Lovely knows about it. Or at least they did. It was a long time ago now, though, I suppose.'

'I hope not.'

'Hang on. So why haven't you told me about her? What do you mean she's been hanging around?'

Nina shook her head. 'I didn't think anything about it at first other than that she was odd and I got the wrong vibes. Then I bumped into her with Birdie, then she asked me for a quote and got my number. Yeah, it's been sort of nothing and something at the same time. I've been so busy that I just didn't mention it. I just kept thinking it was odd and then forgetting to bring it up. Then I said something to Nancy and that's when I found out.'

'Right. I can't believe she's back.'

'What are we going to do?' Nina asked.

'I'll have to speak to her.'

Nina made a strange squealing sound. 'No! I tell you what we're going to do: absolutely nothing.'

'I'm not having her here. What if she tries something?'

'Like what? She can try. She can't actually *do* anything to us.'

Robby swore. 'Nope, sorry, Neens, I need to get rid of her.'

'How?'

'No idea!'

'She's probably *hoping* you'll threaten her or something. I bet she's trying to orchestrate that somehow through me. Bitch.'

Robby nodded slowly. 'It probably *is* that. It was how she operated last time, looking for a reaction all the time and then twisting things to get money. She did that to the other guys.'

'We're doing nothing but sitting tight.' Nina stated resolutely.

'No, no. I'm going to go to the police and see what they advise.'

'Pah! Fat chance of that doing anything. You can murder someone these days and get away with it. No, we're doing nothing.' Nina was adamant. 'She is not ruining anything for me in Lovely Bay. We sit tight and wait and see.'

43

It was a few days or so later, Nina was in one of the upstairs bedrooms of The Summer Hotel doing a few checks for Jill when, as she passed the window on the first floor landing, someone outside in the street caught her eye. She stopped, positioned herself so she could see but not be seen, and narrowed her eyes as she watched Lindsay peering at the For Sale sign. She looked down as Lindsay took her phone out of her pocket, pointed it up at the sign, and obviously scanned the QR code.

Nina shook her head and heard a strange, aggressive sigh come out of the back of her throat. She continued to watch as Lindsay tapped on her screen, looked up at the hotel again, took a few steps to her right, gazed up at the side of the building, and back down at her phone.

Nina shuddered as she watched Lindsay, wearing jeans a size too small and a cheap-looking electric green blazer with the sleeves rolled up, take a couple of pictures of the hotel. As far as Nina was concerned, there was no way it was a coincidence that Lindsay was looking at The Summer Hotel. From what Nina had ascertained from the internet and Nancy, Lindsay was not standing outside the hotel by accident. Nina had learned in her sleuthing that Lindsay obviously followed a strategy where she made herself known in someone's life and tried to wheedle her way in from there. What she'd failed to realise since she'd been convicted was that her game was up in somewhere like Lovely Bay.

It was now clear to Nina that Lindsay was somehow following her movements. It didn't make her feel good at all. The woman was creepy, evil, and a criminal to boot. Nina's heart raced as she watched Lindsay from a distance. The eerie feeling that Lindsay was tracking her every move sent chills down her spine. Nina had never experienced anything like it before. It felt so very personal and invasive.

Nina slipped her phone out of her pocket, swiped up, and tapped on her messages. She slowly read through one by one the text exchanges she'd had with Lindsay since Lindsay had asked her for a quote. Lindsay had sent *loads* of messages with various excuses to get in touch. Nina had shut every one of them down, but it hadn't seemed to put Lindsay off in the slightest. In fact, if anything, it was almost as if Nina's short-to-the-point replies fuelled her more. Nina shook her head. Perhaps that's what Lindsay liked: sending messages to people to try to get them to react. Maybe it was the thrill of the chase she got off on. Perhaps Lindsay had a plan that somehow involved Robby. Who knew how the woman's mind worked? Nina rolled her eyes to herself. She was having none of it.

Lindsay was creepy and obviously highly unhappy with her own lot in life. Nina didn't intend to let Lindsay say or do anything that was going to jeopardise Nina's well-being in *any* way. Nina was in a great place; happy, settled, in a fabulous relationship, and secure. Clearly, Lindsay was none of the above.

Nina watched Lindsay walk past the drive and front of the hotel, try the gate to the side, push it open, and step into the side garden. Not really sure what she was doing or if it was the right thing to do or not, Nina decided to confront the situation head-on. She marched down the stairs like a woman possessed, stomped through the living quarters, slammed out the tradesmen's entrance, and along the side path, her resolve firming with each step. Her heart pounded, and she could feel her breath quickening.

'Sorry, hello! What are you doing? You can't just walk onto private property!'

Lindsay turned, her expression unreadable at first as she took Nina in. Nina couldn't quite ascertain whether Lindsay was shocked at the forthright tone or spurred on by it. Whatever it was, Lindsay was unperturbed. 'Nina.' Lindsay beamed with a nod as if standing by the gate on the side path to The Summer Hotel was the most natural occurrence in the world.

'Why are you here? *What* do you want?' Nina asked as she scanned Lindsay's face.

'I was just over this side of Lovely and thought I'd come and have a look, seeing as it's up for sale,' Lindsay said, her tone nonchalant. The look in Lindsay's eyes was a mix of defiance and something Nina couldn't quite place. It was as if her words were saying one thing, but her face and body language were very much telling a different story altogether. A wolf in sheep's clothing. Evil personified by a regular-looking woman who apart from her overly bright clothing was nondescript and bland in every way.

'You were just over this side of Lovely, were you?' Nina repeated.

Lindsay pushed one of the sleeves of her cheap green blazer up further. 'I was.' She looked up at the building. 'Such a nice spot by the river here. It must be great to live somewhere near the water. I've always wondered what it might be like. You started off here when you first arrived in Lovely Bay, didn't you?'

'I did.'

Nina wasn't sure how to continue. It was clear Lindsay was

enjoying herself. It was as if Lindsay *wanted* to make Nina feel awkward. As if Lindsay relished it somehow. She knew that Lindsay's presence was more than happenstance. Lindsay thought she was leading the way, in charge, oh-so-clever; it was written all over her face, but Nina was one step ahead. Keep your enemies close. Then start on winning the game. She changed tack in an instant. 'Yes, well, that's what people *think* anyway.' She made a funny little conspiratory-type face.

Lindsay was surprised and thrown. She coughed. 'Sorry. What?'

Nina studied Lindsay quickly and pretended as if there was something Lindsay didn't know. She flicked her hand. 'Ahh, well, the story goes that I was house-sitting, yes, but, well, people believe what they want to believe sometimes, right? You'd know that.'

Lindsay's eyes narrowed and she shuffled her feet a little bit. 'Like what?'

Nina completely made stuff up on the spot. She surprised herself as she heard words come tumbling out of her mouth. 'Put it this way, I had a *motive* to be in Lovely Bay and it all worked out *just* as I'd planned. Of course, don't tell anyone that.' She flicked her hand again. 'It's a *very* good place to hide...'

Lindsay tried and failed to hide the shock written all over her face. 'What sort of motive are we talking?'

Nina did a weird witch-like cackle. She felt as if she was playing a game of chess swiftly taking over the board as she went. 'Ahh, now that would be telling, wouldn't it?'

Lindsay was quick. 'Would it?'

'Yep.'

'What, you came here for a reason, did you?'

'I might have done. Or as a reason to get away with something. Yes, that sounds a bit more like it.'

'Like what?'

Nina heard herself cackle again. 'That would be telling.'

Lindsay attempted to keep up. 'You see, when you have ulterior motives, you have to be careful, Nina. Not everything is as it seems.'

'Precisely!' Nina agreed. The cackle was having a whale of a time. 'Oh, no. No, no, no. Nothing is as it seems in this world, not even somewhere here like Lovely Bay.' She turned up the dial on being over-friendly and over-cheesy but added a bit of a sinister tone to her voice. Two could play at Lindsay's game. 'We all have dirty little secrets, don't we? Some of them nobody knows…'

Lindsay cleared her throat and took a step backwards. 'Err. What do you mean?'

'I don't mean anything at all. Just, you know.' Nina wrinkled her nose up, pursed her lips, and wiggled her head a little bit. 'What is it they say? Don't trust anyone or anything and certainly not what you see on social media. Know what I mean?'

Lindsay was rendered speechless. Nina beamed and blinked her eyelashes furiously. She then again swiftly changed the whole course of the conversation as quick as a flash. 'Anyway, what have you been up to? Did you manage to start running at all? All those texts you sent me must mean you're keen.'

It appeared as if Lindsay's brain was whirring, trying to decipher how quickly Nina was playing the game and changing the direction of the interaction. She'd been left for dead by Nina. The air crackled with tension. Nina held Lindsay's gaze as inside her heart felt as if it was banging against the side of her ribs and she moved another piece on the chessboard. She wasn't giving anything away, and the fabricated story about her motive in Lovely Bay hung in the air. Lindsay, thrown off balance for a moment, recovered quickly. 'Nothing much, really.'

'I've been swamped. Sorry, I couldn't fit you in with the decluttering either. Did you have a go yourself in the end?' Nina raised her eyebrows as if she was interested. They both knew she wasn't.

Lindsay fiddled with her cheap choker necklace. 'I, err, no, not yet.'

'Shame. Sometimes, it only takes a bit of effort, too. Yours didn't look too bad.' Nina's voice dripped with mock sweetness. 'Anyway, I must get on. Perhaps we'll bump into each other again soon. Funny, really, we seem to keep being in the same place. Strange how the world works like that. Coincidences, eh?'

'Ha, yes.'

Nina was quite enjoying herself. She turned back to the hotel. 'So are you looking at buying the hotel? I thought you said you were going to see the cottage or did I mix you up with someone else?'

Lindsay scrambled for words. 'I, umm, I didn't get it.'

'Shame.'

Lindsay's smile faltered for a second, and she looked at her watch. 'Actually, sorry, I have to go.'

'Oh, okay, well, nice chatting. See you around.'

Lindsay nodded as she turned. 'Maybe, yes.'

Nina watched her go. Her heart pounded in her chest, but something told her that the way she had just played the game had thrown Lindsay no end. As Lindsay reached the end of the street, she stopped and turned back briefly and then disappeared around the corner hurrying away.

Nina stood motionless for a bit. She replayed the encounter in her mind. Lindsay's presence was unsettling, and the cryptic remark about ulterior motives sent chills down her spine. She felt, though, as if she'd just been in a major chess tournament, one that had been going on for a long time. She'd just performed the move of her career. Check and mate.

44

Nina drove along behind a grey Mitsubishi as she steered Robby's car up and over a speed bump and inched along in traffic. As she came to a stop at a set of lights, her mind went over the situation that had occurred with Lindsay. Since the day in The Summer Hotel, she'd seen hide nor hair of Lindsay. It was as if Lindsay had vanished. One minute it had seemed as if she was around every corner, the next minute she was gone. Perhaps it was the way people like Lindsay went about their business.

She pursed her lips together and went over what had happened as she waited for the light to change. Nina shook her head as she recalled her words from The Summer Hotel's side garden. She had surprised herself with what had come out of her mouth. She hadn't known she had it in her. She sniggered as the words she'd heard herself say went through her head. She'd insinuated that Lindsay wasn't the only person whose motives weren't always nice and somehow injected a sinister tone into, not just her voice but, her body language, too.

Nina had no idea where any of it had come from, but by the looks of Lindsay's vanishing act from Lovely Bay, whatever it was that she'd said had worked. As far as Nina was concerned, she was glad that her actions had done the trick.

After the lights finally changed and as she was indicating to turn left to a client's house to finish off a job, Robby's dashboard lit up showing her that Nancy was calling. She pressed the phone button on the steering wheel and answered. 'Hey, Nancy, how are you?'

'Good, thanks. All okay with you?'

'Getting there.'

'What are you up to?'

'Just finishing off the last job and then I'm done and dusted until after the wedding.'

'Excellent. I've been meaning to say to you. Has anything else happened with Lindsay? Have you still not seen her around?' Nancy asked, her voice lilting into a question at the end.

Nina hadn't told anyone what had happened at The Summer Hotel, not even Robby. She'd decided, once she'd realised a few days or so later that Lindsay had vanished, that no one needed to know what had gone on. She'd keep her cards close to her chest. 'I haven't seen her, have you?'

'No, not at all, and I've asked around. It seems like nobody has seen her anywhere. I wonder what happened.'

Nina wasn't sure what had happened, nor did she care. 'No idea.'

Wherever Lindsay was, Nina was fairly sure her vanishing wasn't just to do with what Nina had said. Lindsay was an experienced criminal who had a serious track record with tried and tested results. One slightly tense exchange wouldn't have put her off as far as Nina could see, but then again, maybe Lindsay had always worked on the notion that people had no idea what she was doing. Now, with the internet, it was a different ballgame altogether.

Perhaps Lindsay had realised that she'd been rumbled and had given up the ghost. Nina wasn't sure what the reason was, but as long as Lindsay was gone, she was happy. She just hoped that they'd seen the last of her. She tuned back into Nancy, who was still discussing the fact that nobody had seen Lindsay anywhere in Lovely Bay.

'I was talking to the bloke who works with me here at the station, and he said that he hadn't seen her. I also chatted with Clive this morning when I was on my way to work. Nobody has laid eyes on her. It's like she's just completely scarpered. One minute she was here, nearly every day, and the next minute she's gone.'

'Well, all I need to know is that she's stopped turning up by coincidence in the same places as me.'

'Yeah, hope so. That must've been horrible. What an absolute creep.'

'Yes, I know, and an evil one at that.' Nina contemplated launching into the fact that she'd had the ding-dong with Lindsay at The Summer Hotel, but she changed her mind. Better that no one knew.

Nancy continued, 'Actually, I found myself googling her the other day. I had forgotten how bad it was before. She really is not a very nice character. When I told you to google her that night, I hadn't thought about it for years. Then, the other day, I was sitting with my feet up having a coffee, and she popped into my head, and I looked her up. It was not one of my better moves.'

'I told you how bad it was. There are so many articles about her.'

'I know. The worst thing about it all was that she worked in a hospital! In children's nursing! Can you imagine? Someone like that being around children. I bet she was so smug, too.'

'Oh, for sure! Always the way. Probably Miss Sweetness and Light on the outside to the parents.'

'What makes someone do that?'

'I don't know. I suppose she's not really right in the head.'

'Why would you enjoy somebody else's trauma and drama?' Nancy asked.

'Who knows? Just think, if it wasn't for the internet and the fact that we can access this information, no one would really have known. I mean, it might have been in some paper somewhere, but chances are she could have done it again and again.'

'Yeah, the internet has changed a lot of things. We can see exactly what she was convicted of and what she got up to. Thank goodness.'

'Makes you think that you *always* have to watch your back,' Nina said.

'Yep, you do. Even in somewhere like Lovely Bay, where our crime rate is almost nil, sometimes people come along and like to disturb the peace.'

'They certainly do. They drop in somewhere and spoil it for everybody else.'

'Yes, exactly. Well, let's hope she doesn't darken our door again.'

'No, hopefully not. Hopefully, we've seen the last of the likes of Lindsay, her dark ways and her dreadful garish clothes.'

45

Nina was in the back room of the deli, laying the tables for a speakeasy event that night. It was her very last job before the wedding. She had just finished putting glasses on the tables and was chuckling to herself at the sound of the Shipping Forecast that was accompanying her work when Birdie came in with two cups of tea in her hands.

Birdie lifted her chin to indicate to Nina to come into the kitchen. Nina followed her in. 'Thanks, I needed a nice cup of tea. I didn't have one earlier.'

Once Nina had sat down, Birdie tapped her hand on Nina's knee and sighed. 'I've got to tell you something. I wanted to let you know before the big day.' Birdie had a *very* serious look on her face. 'I'd like to call it gossip, but it's too significant to call it that. It's not tittle-tattle.'

'That sounds ominous. What do you mean?'

Birdie nodded and pressed her lips together. 'I have some information about Lindsay.'

'Oh, that's so weird. I was just thinking about her the day before yesterday. I spoke to Nancy about it, too. I haven't seen her around. It's like she's vanished.'

'No, you wouldn't have seen her. She's obviously steering well clear of us.'

'What do you mean? How do you know?'

'Someone in my family, one of the Lings, who owns a string of chemists along the coast here phoned me about her. So, long story short, it turns out they've had some dealings with Lindsay.'

Nina felt herself shiver. 'What sort of *dealings?*'

'Not nice ones! She was going out with one of the pharmacists and it turned nasty. By all accounts, she was blackmailing him somehow. Anyway, apparently it's been going on for months. She was caught stealing drugs... all sorts.'

'Right. Wow. She strikes again.'

Birdie put her tea down. 'She's been cautioned.'

'What was she cautioned about?'

'Well, theft, I assume.'

'I'm not surprised, considering what I read about her and the vibes she gave me.'

'I know. I realised when my cousin was telling me the story that I recognised her name. I'm not meant to know this, but I saw some of the CCTV pics. It's definitely her.'

'So, it's not on the internet yet?'

'As far as I know, no. They didn't have enough evidence for anything else either.'

'It's just unbelievable. You can't make this up. Who lives their life like that?' Nina shook her head and picked up her tea.

'I'm not sure, but it's not nice. That's all I know.'

'So it explains why she's not been around here,' Nina said as she thought about her interaction with Lindsay outside The Summer Hotel.

'Yes, it does. I'm glad to see the back of her,' Birdie added.

'Ditto. Do you think that's it?'

'Who knows, but I hope so.'

'Robby is going to be relieved. I'm going to meet him in the pub in a bit. Is it okay for me to tell him what you know?'

'Yep. Just tell him to keep it between the two of you.'

'Thanks. Will do.'

'All I can say is, hopefully, it's the last we see of her.'

∽

Nina watched as Robby came back from the bar at The Drunken Sailor. She smiled as he got closer, and it went through her head that she couldn't believe she was marrying him. She wasn't going to argue with it, though, that was for sure.

She remembered how she had been captivated by him literally as soon as she'd laid eyes on him when he'd stormed into the same pub. She'd only been in Lovely Bay for a day or so, and she'd wondered what on earth had just stepped into her life. Oh how she now knew.

It hadn't been long before Nina had fallen in love with him and everything about him. The straps had helped. They talked about everything; he just seemed to *get* her. Most of all, possibly above the straps was the companionship; it was like having a new best friend, only a little bit better – not that she would ever tell Sophie that. It wasn't very often that she and Sophie got onto a spaceship and took little trips up and down to the moon.

Robby put his drink down and placed Nina's on the table before taking a seat. Nina picked up her drink, took a sip, and then leaned forward on the table. 'I need to tell you something.

'Oh yeah? What? You've changed your mind; you don't want to get married now?' Robby joked. 'Is this the part where you go back to London and we never see you again?'

'Ha. Nope.'

'I know, you've decided that you want to sell the house and buy The Summer Hotel.'

Nina laughed. 'No, nothing like that. It's about Lindsay.'

Robby stopped halfway through putting his drink to his mouth and slowly placed his glass back on the beer mat. 'What about her? I thought you said you hadn't seen her. I certainly haven't.'

Nina sighed. 'It's nothing bad, or at least not to us, it isn't.'

'Spit it out then. I'm not sure if I want to know.'

'Well, when I was at the deli, Birdie told me she'd heard something on the grapevine about Lindsay. It's not nice.'

'I might have known it would be bad news,' Robby interjected.

'Yes, exactly what I thought, too. Apparently, she's been cautioned.'

'Hang on. How does Birdie know?' Robby asked.

'Someone she knows at one of her family's chemists phoned her and told her. She did the same thing she did to the other people but she got caught on the camera stealing drugs and whatnot.'

'Which explains why she's not been around.'

'I guess so. She's been rumbled maybe…'

'Is she really that stupid to do it again?'

'A leopard never changes its spot, as they say.' Nina said with wide eyes.

'They do say that. Wow. So, what does that mean really?'

'I don't know.'

'She's been caught again so maybe she's re-thinking her whole existence. As long as she's far away from you and me, I don't care.' Robby noted.

'I hope so.'

'So, we're rid of her by the looks of it. At least for now.' Robby said as he slowly nodded his head and took another sip of his drink.

'I hope so. I really do.'

46

Nina woke up in her new bed in the attic room at the top of the property overlooking the harbour. She could hear the fishing boats down on the water and church bells pealing in the far distance. She turned over and picked up her phone, smiling at the date. The day had finally arrived. The day she was getting married for the second time. Stranger things had happened at sea.

She couldn't quite believe it. Here she was getting married to Robby when not really more than a year before, she'd been in a completely different situation altogether. To be quite honest, she couldn't really wait for the official, legal marriage part to be over and done with. She was really looking forward to the party at The Summer Hotel. It was where the journey to her healed self had begun, and it held an exceptional little corner of her heart. The one right next to the space where Robby had made himself at home.

She pressed on the weather app and scrolled through with a sigh of relief to see a little line of bright orange suns all in a row. Just as the weather forecast had predicted, the sun was shining, and the temperature was warm. Nina couldn't believe her lucky stars that Lovely had pulled out the stops on the weather. She'd steeled herself for the fact that it might pour with rain, hailstone, or do all manner of things at any given time. Now the day itself had dawned, all the concerns they'd had about having to put up the marquees had come to nothing. Hoo-blooming-ray.

Pushing back the duvet, she put on her slippers and dressing gown and padded over towards the steep stairs down to the second floor. Shuffling over to the kitchen, she made herself a cup of tea and popped a croissant in the oven to warm. Ten minutes later, she was sitting by the window, looking out over the harbour, feeling *very* peaceful and *very* happy.

As she finished her tea, she gazed at her dress hanging on a hook near the sofa. Without its large train, the dress really was beautiful. It was much better than anything Nina had tried on in the wedding dress shop or seen online, and now, with Faye's help, it fitted like a glove. After a few wobbles here and there about whether or not she was doing the right thing regarding the dress, now the day had come, she couldn't wait to get it on and get herself married for the second time. Cost per wear was going up by the year.

About half an hour or so later and with her hair in a predetermined selection of Velcro rollers, as instructed by the girl at Beauty by Bianca, Nina poured Tom Ford body oil into water gushing into the bath and got in. Half an hour after that, she was back out of the bath in a new, soft, very expensive tracksuit she'd bought especially for the morning of the wedding. Apparently, what one wore on the morning of the wedding was a thing. She'd come across a multitude of articles on it when she'd been looking for shoes. Not that she'd cared less what the articles had said, but it had made her think that she didn't want to be turning up on the morning of her wedding in her ratty old tracksuit that had a hole in the knee.

Gathering her phone and bag and laughing to herself at the thought of walking along the street with her head full of pink

Velcro rollers, she'd just locked the door behind her when her phone buzzed as she was walking by the harbour wall.

'Hiya, how are you? Everything good this morning?' Sophie trilled down the phone. 'Just checking in with you!'

'Yes, it couldn't be better. I've had a lovely morning of peace and quiet.'

'You are funny, wanting to spend the morning on your own.'

Nina nodded. 'Yes, I just wanted to have a bit of time to myself to think about everything that's happened and make the most of it, you know. As my mum likes to constantly tell me; I'm a bit odd.'

Sophie agreed, 'Nah. I do know what you mean about peace because I never have any these days. It's a big day. I'm so excited; I'm beside myself. I've had to calm myself down.'

Nina laughed. 'I haven't been like that at all. I've been calm and serene. It's been lovely.'

'Have you heard from Robby?'

'Yes, he texted me while I was in the bath. He said his mum is driving him round the twist.'

'I bet. She did seem a bit full-on when I met her at the hen do.'

'Yeah, anyway, all good. I'm just going to get my hair and make-up done and then I'll be good to go. Colin is picking me up and dropping me at the registry office, and then we'll be on the boat to arrive at The Summer Hotel on the jetty.'

'How fab this has turned out to be. It's the loveliest wedding ever. We are all so excited, even Nick!'

'How appropriate, the loveliest wedding in Lovely Bay. Too funny.'

'The weather is performing for us. Fancy waking up to this, eh?'

'I know, right? I just had a double-check earlier this morning when I got up, and it's going to be a beautiful day.'

'Yeah.'

'How are the children? Everything alright there?'

'Yes, everything is done and dusted. All the outfits are sorted, and Nick is in charge for the *whole* day so that I can have a bit of time off and enjoy your wedding.'

'Right, well, see you there then.'

'Yep, so excited! See you soon.'

∽

Nina stopped outside the chocolate shop and smiled as Millie came to the door. She remembered the first time she'd been inside, at the back, and even though she was used to seeing clutter and junk from that end, from the front, it was immaculate, with nothing out of place; she still couldn't quite compute the two. Millie opened the door, leant on the architrave, and smiled a broad beam.

'Morning, how are you? Nice rollers.'

'I'm good, thanks,' Nina smiled back.

'Ready for the big day?'

'I am.'

'How's our Robby? Is he good?'

'He *is* good, yep. Just hope he turns up,' Nina joked.

Millie batted her hand. 'Don't be ridiculous, of course he will. How is everything with you? Have you had a busy morning already?'

'No, I haven't, not anything like it. I've had a lovely peaceful morning on my own.'

Millie chuckled. 'I see. I thought maybe you'd be with someone. You've got a best friend who lives nearby, haven't you? Or I thought you might be with Nancy or something.'

'I made an executive decision that I wanted the night on my own, and it was a good one. I've just had a nice bath, and now I'm on my way to see Bianca. I'm so chilled and happy.'

'Bianca will do well with you. Sounds like you don't have to worry about anything.'

Nina flicked her watch over and looked at the time. She pointed to her hair. 'I just need to get this done, go home, and get ready for our Colin to arrive.'

'Well, good luck for today and congratulations. I'll see you later.'

'Yep, thanks, Millie.'

'Where the party is concerned, everything is ready,' Millie said. 'Our Nancy is in charge and has assigned us all roles.'

'Good to hear I've been told not to worry about a thing.'

'Nope, you don't worry about anything at all. Just worry about marrying our Robby and having a wonderful day.'

'Thanks, right, I'll get on and get myself there.'

A few minutes later, after stopping and talking to somebody else and being congratulated by someone she knew who often came into the deli, Nina pushed open the door to Beauty by Bianca and was immediately surrounded by a tranquil feeling. Essential oils pumped around the room, New Age yoga music came from behind the desk, and everything seemed to calm via its neutral palette of white and cream. As every time Nina had been to the place, she felt as if she was a little bit grubby and doing something wrong. The difference to her first visit when Birdie had treated her to a few treatments, however, was that she'd learned to love everything that went on in Beauty by Bianca. The place was a dream.

Not long after she'd stepped in, Nina was lying on the bed in Bianca's consultation room, more or less in the dark, under a thick layer of crisp sheets and fluffy blankets. The whole room was lit by flickering candles and scented with essential oils. Bianca quietly padded around the room and whispered, 'Okay, just a treat for you this morning. Nothing that might set anything off with your skin, and I'm going to do a massage that will make you feel amazing.'

Nina nodded and whispered back, 'Thank you. You know how much I love it.'

'I do, and I know how different your face feels now.' Bianca laughed quietly.

'You've literally unlocked my face.' Nina whispered back. She smiled as she remembered when Birdie had first persuaded her to go to Beauty by Bianca. Then, she'd been completely apprehensive and concerned about how it was going to go. But after she'd undressed and laid down, about ten minutes in she'd floated off to another place. She'd realised at the time, as stress had seemed to pour out of her jaw, that since Andrew had died, she hadn't looked after herself and never really had anyone touch her at all. As Bianca has massaged, pushed, pulled, and pummelled her face, years of grief and tenseness had been released. It had been a long time coming.

Since that first visit via the kindness of Birdie, Beauty by Bianca was part of Nina's regular self-care, not that she liked those words at all, but she intended never to let herself get in the same state she had been in before ever again. Five minutes in, and Bianca's magical hands worked on the sides of Nina's face. Half an hour in, Bianca and another beauty therapist were massaging her neck and shoulders. *Best pre-wedding treatment ever,* Nina thought to herself as she revelled in the bliss of it all.

Later on, with her hair done and make-up in situ, Nina walked out of Beauty by Bianca as if she was floating just above the top of the pavement. She had been in two minds about whether or not to have a facial on the morning of her wedding, having read all sorts about it not being a good idea. Bianca had said it was poppycock and had assured her she knew her skin and everything would be fine. As she walked away from the salon, she knew she'd made the right decision. She felt relaxed, happy, stress-free, her hair was done, make-up on, and she was good to go. Bianca had worked her magic, as she always did, and Nina nodded to herself at a good decision executed well.

As she strolled through the streets of Lovely Bay in the direction of the harbour, she went over one of the smaller greens, crossed to the other side of the road, and made a detour to go over another green lined with beautiful trees. She smiled as she looked up at the weather. It really had turned out to be a gorgeous day. About ten minutes later, she was just getting to the harbour when her phone rang with a call from her mum.

'Hi, Mum,' she said with a bright tone in her voice.

'Hello, darling, how are you? I'm just coming back from the hairdresser. How was your time at the beauty therapist, darling?'

'It was good. I feel great. And how does your hair look?'

'Yes, it looks nice.'

'How are you, Mum? Are you okay? Is everything good with you?'

'Yes, everything is fine with me. We're excited. We are ready to go at this end. I've just put my outfit on. I was just checking in to see that you're okay.'

'Yes, I'm good. I have had a lovely peaceful morning.'

'Darling, it *is* funny that you wanted to spend the morning on your own, but then again, you are a bit odd. You always were.'

Nina rolled her eyes. She'd heard that so many times; in fact, her mum possibly said it to her every time she spoke to her. She was used to it now. She *liked* being a bit odd. 'Yeah, Mum, I just wanted to have a nice quiet morning on my own and think about things. You know?'

'Not really, darling, but there we are. You do you, as they say. I hope you're going to have a beautiful day.'

'Thanks, Mum. I appreciate that.'

'I'm so happy for you, darling. You've been through so much, and it's all worked out well.'

'Thanks.'

'So, you're sure you're okay to be on your own while you get ready? Will you be okay getting into the dress on your own?'

'Yes, I'm fine.'

'And the man from the boat, was it Colin or Callum or something? Christian? I can't remember. He's picking you up in the car and taking you to the registry office, correct?'

Nina sighed; she had told her mum the arrangements at least four times. 'Yeah, that's the plan. It won't be long, but I factored in plenty of time for any problems, just in case. So all being well, I'll see you there.'

'Yes, darling, okay, see you there. Love you.'

47

A few minutes or so later, Nina let herself into the back of the property by the harbour, walked over to the office area, and then made her way up towards the top floor. Checking the time, she went into the bathroom and analysed her make-up and hair. Bianca had outdone herself and both looked amazing. She had nothing to do apart from getting dressed.

She checked her watch to see how long it was before Colin arrived and went back into the bedroom, unzipped the heavy-duty cover over her dress, took the bodice off the hanger, pulled it up over her body, and struggled a little bit to get the zip done up. She then pulled on the skirt and attached the little poppers to the bodice. Looking in the mirror, she smiled at her reflection. A tiny little hint of happy sadness, if there was such a thing, about Andrew, flitted through her brain.

It didn't last long and Nina hugged herself and found herself humming as she popped on the beautiful wedding shoes she'd treated herself to from a handmade shoe boutique in Chelsea. She'd walked past the boutique many times on her way to work and never in a million years had she ever thought she'd be making an appointment to buy a pair of shoes, but here she was, popping her feet into a pair. Not only that; she was happy, settled, and ready for life with Robby. Things were good.

With plenty of time to spare, she slotted her phone, lipstick, and various bits and bobs into her bag and stood at the top of the steep stairs for a second, wondering whether or not it had been a good idea to get ready on the third floor. Deciding that there was no way she was going to traverse the stairs in the shoes, she slipped the heels off, put her bag on her arm, held onto the bannister with her left hand, gathered the dress up with her right, and balanced the shoes in the crook of her arm. By the time she got to the second floor, she realised she definitely should have got dressed downstairs. Doing the same thing on the stairs going down to the ground floor, she finally made it safely to the bottom, slipped on the shoes, and stood for a minute on the ground floor looking out towards the harbour, wondering if Colin had arrived yet.

A few minutes later, she was outside the back door, scooping her dress up with both arms and wondering whether or not, at this point, it would have been a good idea to have Sophie or Nancy with her. She looked at the back gate with the dress ruffled up in both arms, pondering how she was going to get it undone without letting the dress fall to the ground. Paying attention to the gate and keeping the dress off the ground, she didn't take any notice of the two little steps down from the patio. Just as she placed her foot onto the second step, its mossy top forced the sole of her new shoes to slip.

Before she knew it, in a split second, her feet came right out from underneath her. In a flash, she was trying to break her fall, putting her arms out as if in slow motion as she waited to hit the ground. It was her chin that took most of the impact first, cracking into the side of a patio brick. It was swiftly followed by her palms grazing the grass and patio edge. For a second, she just lay completely still on the ground, pain in her left elbow, and as she turned her palms over, she could see that little bits of grit were lodged into the heels of both hands.

Nina's heart pounded, and for a second, she wasn't quite sure what had just happened or what she was going to do. She tapped her chin nervously and, as she did so, felt warm liquid on her chin. Standing up, she stared down at the dress. Considering she'd had a mighty fall, there wasn't too much dirt on it. Cupping her chin, she didn't really know what to do next. Just as she was standing there in a daze, not sure what to think about her throbbing elbow or her chin, she heard a car pull up outside and then someone called out, 'Hello, anyone there?'

Nina called out, her voice sounding panicked. 'I'm in here. I have a problem!'

'What problem?' Colin asked.

'Let yourself in over the gate. I've fallen over!'

'What? Oh my God!' Colin yelled as he let himself in, and two seconds later, he was standing in front of Nina. 'Are you okay? What the heck have you done with yourself?'

'I think so,' Nina said, still cupping her chin.

Colin swore. 'There's blood all over your chin. What are we going to do?'

Nina shook her head, still in a bit of a daze.

'Do you think you need to go somewhere and get looked at? Hospital?'

'No, no, I'm fine. It's too late anyway,' Nina said. She looked down at her dress. 'I just need to get you to brush the dress off.'

Colin shook his head and interrupted her, 'You can't go like that. You've got blood running down your chin. Right, where will I find flannels and stuff like that? Or towels?'

'Top floor in the airing cupboard, or there's a bunch of towels in the kitchen area. I think I have antiseptic wipes in the bathroom.'

A few minutes later, Colin was back with a small bowl full of warm water, a pile of flannels, and a couple of cloths. Nina took her hand away from her chin and gasped at the blood on her palm. Colin started to dab her chin with one of the warm, wet flannels.

Nina winced as Colin dabbed. 'Oh gosh, that's really sore.'

Colin put his glasses on and squinted at Nina's chin. 'Yeah, it's not looking good. I think you're going need to get a stitch.'

'I can't get a stitch! I'm about to get married!'

Colin held another cloth to Nina's face. 'I think it's stopped bleeding now. It looked worse than it was with the gravel in there. It's a graze and a bit of a cut. Thing is, I think it might keep opening. I'm no doctor, obviously, but my kids have done this enough times.'

'What am I going do?'

Colin squinted again and got even closer. 'I think there's a bruise coming already, too.'

With her dress bunched up around her, about ten minutes later, Nina was sitting on a garden chair with a clean flannel cupped on her chin and a glass of water Colin had fetched beside her. 'How are you feeling now?' Colin asked.

'Yeah, I feel okay. It was a bit of a tumble. I think I was just shocked when you first got here.'

Colin nodded. 'It happened literally just before I got here?'

'Yep. I can't believe I did it. I was so focused on the gate and how I was going to get it open without ruining the dress that I completely forgot about the moss on those steps. I should've got it off ages ago. It's been on my to-do list since I moved in. You know how it is.'

Colin nodded and looked at the bodice of the dress that he'd already wiped with about four clean towels. 'Well, it looks like the dress is okay. I'm not so sure about your chin, though. It's a miracle you're not worse off.'

Nina held out her palms and shook her head at the sight of them. They were red and angry, and she could see that there were still little bits of grit in them despite what Colin had done.

'Well, we've got two choices, really,' Colin said, looking at his watch. 'You either put up with it and we go now, or you call ahead and tell them that we're delayed and that you're not going to make it.'

Nina shook her head. 'The thing is, there were no more slots at the registry office. Especially not today, but also not for weeks, maybe even more. It was so booked up. You know what it's like. Everyone and his dog wants to get married at this time of year.'

Colin nodded. He pointed to the flannel on Nina's chin. 'How is it under there now?'

Nina pulled the flannel away and Colin nodded. 'There is one thing. I've got some Steri-Strips in the first aid kit in the boot of my car, I think. I could try and put one of those on.'

Nina winced. 'I'm going turn up at my wedding with a Steri-Strip on my chin?'

'Don't really know what else to suggest,' Colin replied, throwing his hands up as if to say he wasn't sure. 'Stay there for a minute. I'll go in and get the first aid kit out of the car and see what I can find in there.'

Nina chuckled. 'I'm not going anywhere, that's for sure.'

A couple of minutes later, Colin was back with a small black plastic first aid kit. 'Look at you being all organised,' Nina laughed.

'I can't believe you're laughing.'

'I know, me either. You've got to look at the funny side of it. My mum is going to say, "I told you so". She said I shouldn't have got ready on my own. She was probably right. I didn't think it through properly. Best laid plans and all that.'

'No, she probably is right,' Colin replied. He started to rifle through the first aid box and then held up packets of white bandages. 'Plenty of plasters and bandages in here. I don't think this thing has ever even been opened.' He pulled out a syringe in plastic wrapping. 'Can sort you out with a syringe, too,' he chuckled.

'Luckily, I don't need any of those. Not yet, at least.'

'We'll save that for later.' Colin pulled out a packet of Steri-Strips. 'This is what I was talking about. I used similar on my son's forehead many moons ago. If I just put a tiny bit on, it might hold it together.'

'I guess it's about the only choice I've got,' Nina said with a sigh.

Colin went and washed his hands, came back, opened the Steri-Strips, and very carefully picked them up. Nina was surprised to see how carefully he handled them.

'You know what you're doing,' Nina noted.

'Not just a pretty face, you know,' Colin laughed. 'I've done this a few times with my children. That was a few years ago now, though.'

'I'm in your capable hands.'

Colin laughed. 'Right, what are we going to do? Are we going to text ahead and tell everyone what's happened or what?'

Nina shook her head. 'No, we've got plenty of time. I've factored in a good forty-five minutes for anything to go wrong, so we'll still be more than on time. And if I text ahead, my mum will panic,' Nina explained.

'So you're just going to turn up like this?'

'All I've got are some grazes on my palms, a throbbing elbow, and a Steri-Strip on my chin.'

'True, good point,' Colin noted as he put the remainder of the Steri-Strips into their case, put that back into the first aid box, and closed the lid. 'Right, well, as long as you're good to go, let's get on with it.'

48

After fussing with her dress for a bit and realising that the fact it wasn't showing any marks from her fall was because the weather had been dry and the yard had recently been swept, Nina thanked her lucky stars that the fall hadn't ended up a lot worse. It wasn't great, for sure, plus she had a Steri-strip on her chin, searing pain in her elbow, and her palms stung from the antiseptic cream Colin had so carefully administered. She was, however, overall fine and realised that it could have been a lot worse.

About ten minutes after Colin had finished with the strips, she was sitting in the backseat of his fancy black car, gripping her bag like a vice, not quite believing one, that she'd fallen over in her dress on her wedding day and two, that she was on her way to a registry office to get married for the second time in her life. All of it felt unreal, as if she was on a show on Netflix.

Twenty minutes later, they were sitting at a red traffic light. Colin flicked his eyes to the rear-view mirror and raised his eyebrows. 'Everything alright in the back there? You've gone very quiet.'

'Have I?' Nina realised she had been thinking about how her life had changed. 'I didn't realise I'd gone quiet. Sorry.'

'Are you okay?'

'I am. I'm fine.'

'Just checking you're not concussed. You have to be careful with that.'

Nina's eyes widened. 'I didn't even think about a concussion. I think I'll be okay. I only just hit my head, it was mostly my chin that took the whack. That shouldn't give me a concussion, should it?'

Colin shook his head. 'I don't really know, but I know that they do normally check for that, don't they?'

'Do they?' Nina asked. 'Oh gosh, imagine getting a concussion on your wedding day.'

Colin also laughed. 'Let's hope not. I'll be keeping an eye on you.'

As Colin's car pulled up to the front of the registry office, Nina could see her mum, her sister, Robby, and his mum standing, chatting. She felt her heart jump out of her ribs and take a seat beside her. What was she doing here? Who even was she? How in the name of goodness had she bagged Mr Straps? Robby, in his suit and tie, took her breath away.

Nina's mum made her way towards the car as Colin pulled up, got out, and opened Nina's door. Nina's mum took one look at Nina and gasped. Then she shrieked, 'What on earth has happened, darling? What have you done to your chin? You look terrible! Awful!'

'It's nothing, Mum,' Nina hurried to reassure her, trying to downplay the drama as she stepped out of the car. 'I just had a little tumble, but I'm fine, honestly. Nothing to worry about at all.'

Her mum, however, was not easily placated. 'A tumble? And you've ended up with that on your chin? Nina, you should have been more careful! I did tell you it was a ridiculous idea to be on your own this morning. Did you listen?'

'I know, I know. It was just a bit of bad luck. Colin's been a star, though; he patched me up.' Nina smiled.

'Well, I'm just glad you're alright,' her mum finally said, though her eyes showed concern. 'Make sure you're more careful, especially today of all days!'

'I will, Mum. Let's not let this spoil the day, okay?'

Robby approached, his eyes immediately zoning in on Nina's chin. He swore. 'What's happened here then?' Robby's tone and the look on his face were laced with concern.

Nina rolled her eyes. 'I took a bit of a dive on that mossy step out the back. It's just a scratch.'

'A dive? On today of all days?'

'Colin's fixed me up. Good as new, almost.'

Robby leaned in and squinted. 'Well, I've got to hand it to Colin. He's done a pretty good job. But are you sure you're alright?'

'My elbow is throbbing a bit, but I'm fine. We'll call it a battle scar. Adds to the wedding day drama, doesn't it?' Nina giggled.

Robby laughed. 'Right, hold onto me. I'd like you in one piece if possible.'

'I'll do my best.'

Robby nodded, pulling back to look Nina in the eyes. 'You're right. Today is about us. And nothing's going to spoil it, not even a tumble.'

As they walked up the steps to the registry office Nina looked up at the old building and thanked her lucky stars that it fitted quite nicely into the vision in her head of where she'd wanted to get married. Rather than like many towns where the council buildings showed off fine examples of brutalism and sixties architecture, instead, it was a beautiful old Victorian building towering above them. She laughed as they stood by the steps and her sister gave her a small bunch of flowers. 'Well, here we go, then. This is it. Don't forget to take loads of photos.'

Her mum shook her head and tutted, 'Darling, I did tell you that you needed to get a photographer. I can't be doing with fussing with my phone and all that. I want to enjoy myself.'

Nina kept her mouth shut and didn't say anything. She hadn't wanted to have a professional photographer. Just like everything else in the wedding, she'd wanted it to be simple and casual; there were no buttonholes, no photographers, no cars, and no formal reception. The only thing that was like a traditional wedding was the dress itself.

Robby squeezed her hand and whispered in her ear, 'You look absolutely beautiful. I'm so happy about today. Who would have thought, eh?'

Nina nodded. 'Me, too.'

'And it all started with paprika.'

Nina giggled. 'What?'

'When you had paprika all over your face. Remember that day?'

'Surprised I didn't frighten you away.'

'Then, when you told me to shove off.'

'You were being rude.'

'You told me to jog right on. Too funny.'

'Too right, more like.'

'Now we're getting married and it's not paprika on your face but a gash on your chin. You sure keep me guessing, Neens.'

Nina laughed and subconsciously touched the strip on her chin. 'I don't really care. I just want to get married and enjoy the rest of the afternoon and have the party. I think there might be a few cocktails going down later.'

Robby nodded. 'Half measures or full?'

Nina smiled. 'Full measures for sure.'

49

The ceremony was over in a flash, and as Nina stood on the steps of the registry office laughing as Robby kissed her, she felt herself slipping into a dream and taking a little trip to the moon. It was nice on the moon – warm, safe, happy, no grief there. She'd found the place where her heart was full and her mind was happy. She never wanted to leave.

Before she knew it, she was back in Colin's car, this time with a small posy of flowers in her right hand, a gold band on her left, and Robby's hand on her leg.

'Happy?' Robby asked.

'More than,' Nina replied. She'd never really be able to compute how much.

'Same. Now we get to party.' He looked out of the window. 'What a beautiful day for it. Luck is with us from day one if the weather is anything to go by.'

Nina agreed. 'We don't need luck.'

'I hope not.'

'That was really nice, wasn't it? I'm so pleased we kept it small and short and sweet like that.'

'Yeah, worked for me,' Robby said, his voice catching slightly.

Nina squeezed his hand. 'The best.'

About twenty or so minutes later, they arrived at the River Lovely. Nina squinted towards the water and jetty to see if she could spot the boat but couldn't see it in its usual spot. After Colin opened the door, she stepped out of the car, gathered up her dress to walk, and began to walk towards the small jetty. She gasped and her right hand flew to her mouth.

'Oh my God! I didn't know you were going to do that!' she exclaimed as she spied the old vintage boat on the other side of the jetty adjacent to where the main riverboats were usually moored. The beautiful timber boat was festooned with white tulle, gigantic bunches of wildflowers were attached to the front, and garlands of wildflowers were tied in swathes to the cabin and down the sides. Nina couldn't believe it. She hadn't even thought about decorating the boat and had assumed it would just be a short little trip along the river and a nice way to arrive at the party. Not at any point had she thought that the boat would be decorated. It was so pretty it would have been good enough to get married in, let alone arrive at a party in.

She clasped her hands together and let her dress fall to the ground. 'Thank you so much, Colin. I can't believe it! It looks amazing! I really wasn't expecting that in the slightest.'

Colin shook his head. 'Ahh, I just did what I was told. Birdie and Nancy were in charge and woe betide me if I didn't follow orders. It scrubbed up well, though. Not a bad job, even if I say so myself.'

A few seconds later, Clive peered out from the cabin. 'Bonjour! Congratulations!'

'Thank you,' Nina said, hardly able to believe how lovely the boat looked or that it would be taking her to her wedding party.

After gingerly walking across the jetty with her skirt lifted and rather concerned that in her dress, she might wobble and fall again, Nina giggled as she stepped onto the boat, holding onto both Clive and Colin's hands. A few minutes later, she was sitting next to Robby at the back of the boat, surrounded by a cloud of tulle and froth of wildflowers. It wasn't just the boat that was floating; Nina was too. Taking her phone out of her bag, she handed it to Colin. 'Take lots of photos, please. I love this! Thank you again. Talk about icing on the cake.'

She couldn't wipe the smile off her face, even though she could feel the strip pinching into the skin on her chin. She sighed and felt as if she needed to pinch herself to make sure that everything was true. 'What a gorgeous day,' she said to Robby as she looked up at the blue sky and the reflection of the sun in the water.

Everything was perfect. A perfect day and a perfect journey to start married life for the second time around. Nina Lavendar couldn't quite believe her luck. It had arrived on her doorstep out of the blue in spades.

As the boat carrying Nina and Robby pulled up to The Summer Hotel jetty, Nina felt as if she was in a dream, or a cloud, or a movie, or anything of a similar ilk. She'd only just gone and married a man she'd never, ever in her wildest dreams thought would be in her life. Not only that, she was arriving at her wedding party to celebrate the second and hopefully final time she would be getting married on a beautiful riverboat decorated especially for her.

If someone had told her that not that long after she'd arrived in Lovely Bay to house sit, she would end up living there permanently and marrying someone who wasn't Andrew, she would have laughed her head off or cried, one of the two or probably both. But it had happened indeed. Nina had just married a man who was not only very easy on the eye but felt like her best friend. She couldn't quite believe her luck that their paths had crossed.

Colin held up a camera phone and joked. 'Say cheese and big smiles to the loveliest couple of Lovelies in Lovely.'

Nina beamed and then laughed. 'I hope you won't be able to see what's going on on my chin in the pictures.'

Colin chuckled. 'Don't worry, there are loads of apps these days to make things like that vanish. You're all good, Nina, and you look amazing.'

Robby nodded. 'You *do* look amazing. I love you.'

Nina waved at the people standing on The Summer Hotel's little stretch of sandy beach. Birdie, a couple of Nina's cousins, Nancy, Robby's family, Sophie and Nick, her mum and sister, and Millie from the chocolate shop.

As she and Robby stepped from the jetty to the beach, they were showered with confetti and as they walked up through the garden, Nina took in a sharp inhale of breath at the set-up. Nancy had outdone herself. The whole of the garden area of The Summer Hotel, the space that Nina had brought back from the dead the year before, was beautiful. A long line of trestle tables was doused in layers of pretty vintage tablecloths. All through the centre huge posies of wildflowers took pride of place, and overhead from the canvas market umbrellas, tiny little paper lanterns swung back and forth in the breeze. At each seat, vintage plates and cutlery were ready to go and pitchers of iced water filled with lemon fitted the warm afternoon.

'It looks so beautiful,' Nina gushed to Robby. 'I didn't expect everything to be so amazing!'

Sophie walked up beside them. 'Wow, Nancy has really outdone herself.'

'Yes, she really has,' Nina agreed. 'I'll never be able to thank her enough and you, Soph. If you hadn't nigh-on forced me to come here, none of this would have happened.'

'You're worth it.' Sophie smiled.

Robby kissed Nina. 'She's not wrong. You most definitely are.'

Nina Lavendar swooned. How fabulously good it felt to be loved.

Nina and Robby headed over to where a couple of Lovelies who worked for Birdie in the chemist were standing serving drinks. 'What would you like?' Robby asked.

'What do you reckon? Champagne to start?'

'Sounds good to me,' Robby nodded, picking up two glasses and handing one to Nina.

As they clinked glasses, Nina took a sip and looked around at everyone mingling in the garden. 'This is really nice, isn't it? We made such a call with this place. What a great day. It's so good seeing everyone here together.'

Robby smiled. 'Yeah, it's perfect. Just what we wanted.'

They wandered a bit, chatted with a few of the guests, and meandered through the gathering of family and friends, drinks in hand. 'It's a bit surreal, isn't it?' Nina mused, her gaze drifting across the garden. 'All these people, here for us.'

Robby squeezed her closer. 'It's nice to have something so positive to come together for.'

'Yeah, exactly.'

Birdie bustled towards them and Nina found herself caught in a hug. Birdie whispered in her ear, 'You've done so well. Proud of you both.'

'Thank you. You've been such a part of it. I'm grateful.'

'Ahh, don't be silly.'

About an hour or so later, Nina and Robby had ambled through the guests to the bottom of the garden in a quieter corner. Nina started taking a slow sip of her champagne as they both stared at the River Lovely and then turned and gazed up at The Summer Hotel. 'This is more than I ever could have imagined. It's not just the wedding, but being here, with you, in Lovely Bay. I love you, Robby.'

'It's like we've been given a second chance at happiness. And I'm grateful every day for it, and for you. Love you, too.'

'I can't believe we pulled this off,' Nina laughed.

'We make a good team,' Robby said, wrapping an arm around Nina's waist. 'Maybe we need to make a few more like us.'

Nina giggled. 'Not sure about that.' She leaned into him. 'Here's to us then,' she raised her glass again.

'To us. Can't wait to see what comes next.'

'Same, our Robby, same.'

Nina Lavendar sat back and settled in, ready for lots more trips to the moon.

BUY THE NEXT PART
SEASHELLS AT THE SUMMER HOTEL LOVELY BAY.

SEASHELLS AT THE SUMMER HOTEL LOVELY BAY

Sweet, small town, romantic women's fiction you'll adore. Discover this uplifting, heartwarming, small town story of second chances, new starts and life in a little beach town where everybody knows your name.

Nina Lavendar has settled into rural coastal life in Lovely Bay and is living the dream baby. Working for herself, living by the sea and surrounded not just by new love but new friends, too. She hardly remembers the person she was before she arrived in the third smallest town in the country.

After a little bit of luck, she is having a whale of a time in just about all areas of her life. Things are going swimmingly until she finds herself somewhere she thought she wouldn't, has a few wobbles or six, and life decides it might like to throw a little problem her way.

Get ready to immerse yourself in Lovely Bay, where the sea sparkles, the lighthouse towers over the town and the small coastal community smiles as you as you go about your day.

If you're a Babbette (IYKYK), you're going to love, love, love it.

READ MORE BY POLLY BABBINGTON

(Reading Order available at pollybabbington.com)

The Summer Hotel Lovely Bay
    Wildflowers at The Summer Hotel Lovely Bay
    Seashells at The Summer Hotel Lovely Bay

The Old Ticket Office Darling Island
    Secrets at The Old Ticket Office Darling Island
    Surprises at The Old Ticket Office Darling Island

Spring in the Pretty Beach Hills
    Summer in the Pretty Beach Hills

The Pretty Beach Thing
    The Pretty Beach Way
    The Pretty Beach Life

Something About Darling Island
    Just About Darling Island
    All About Christmas on Darling Island

READ MORE BY POLLY BABBINGTON

The Coastguard's House Darling Island
    Summer on Darling Island
    Bliss on Darling Island

The Boat House Pretty Beach
    Summer Weddings at Pretty Beach
    Winter at Pretty Beach

A Pretty Beach Christmas
    A Pretty Beach Dream
    A Pretty Beach Wish

Secret Evenings in Pretty Beach
    Secret Places in Pretty Beach
    Secret Days in Pretty Beach

Lovely Little Things in Pretty Beach
    Beautiful Little Things in Pretty Beach
    Darling Little Things

The Old Sugar Wharf Pretty Beach
    Love at the Old Sugar Wharf Pretty Beach
    Snow Days at the Old Sugar Wharf Pretty Beach

Pretty Beach Posies
    Pretty Beach Blooms
    Pretty Beach Petals

OH SO POLLY

Words, quilts, tea and old houses...

My words began many moons ago in a corner of England, in a tiny bedroom in an even tinier little house. There was a very distinct lack of scribbling, but rather beautifully formed writing and many, many lists recorded in pretty fabric-covered notebooks stacked up under a bed.

A few years went by, babies were born, university joined, white dresses worn, a lovely fluffy little dog, tears rolled down cheeks, house moves were made, big fat smiles up to ears, a trillion cups of tea, a decanter or six full of pink gin, many a long walk. All those little things called life neatly logged in those beautiful little books tucked up neatly under the bed.

And then, as the babies toddled off to school, as if by magic, along came an opportunity and the little stories flew out of the books, found themselves a home online, where they've been growing sweetly ever since.

I write all my books from start to finish tucked up in our lovely old Edwardian house by the sea. Surrounded by pretty bits and bobs, whimsical fabrics, umpteen stacks of books, a plethora of lovely old things, gingham linen, great big fat white sofas, and a big old helping of nostalgia. There I spend my days spinning stories and drinking rather a lot of tea.

From the days of the floral notebooks, and an old cottage locked away from my small children in a minuscule study logging onto the world wide web, I've now moved house and those stories have evolved and also found a new home.

There is now an itty-bitty team of gorgeous gals who help me with my graphics and editing. They scheme and plan from their laptops, in far-flung corners of the land, to get those words from those notebooks onto the page, creating the magic of a Polly Bee book.

I really hope you enjoy getting lost in my world.

Love

Polly x

AUTHOR

Polly Babbington

In a little white Summer House at the back of the garden, under the shade of a huge old tree, Polly Babbington creates romantic feel-good stories, including The PRETTY BEACH series.

Polly went to college in the Garden of England and her writing career began by creating articles for magazines and publishing books online.

Polly loves to read in the cool of lazing in a hammock under an old fruit tree on a summertime morning or cosying up in the winter under a quilt by the fire.

She lives in delightful countryside near the sea, in a sweet little village complete with a gorgeous old cricket pitch, village green with a few lovely old pubs and writes cosy romance books about women whose life you sometimes wished was yours.

Follow Polly on Instagram, Facebook and TikTok
@PollyBabbingtonWrites

AUTHOR

PollyBabbington.com

Want more on Polly's world? Subscribe to Babbington Letters

Printed in Great Britain
by Amazon